Distracters

A Novel

Maulik Sompura

www.mauliksompura.com
www.distracters.net

ISBN: 0-9853-8200-7
ISBN-13: 9780985382001
LCCN: 2012906138
Maulik\Sompura, Rancho Cordova, California.

Dedication

To my late grandmother, *Mrs. **Tara Sompura***,

Without whom I would not have been able to write any of this.

Had she not instilled the imagination, the creativity, the thought process, or even the passion for telling amazing tales that teach moral values with such fervor—which she did so well even at her ripe old age—when I was a young boy, I would not have been attracted to stories as I have been throughout my life. Be it a short story, a novel, an article, or a movie, good stories excite me, and they have always been a part of my life. I just feel empty without them. Without the hope of a new dawn; without the victory of good over evil; without fantasy, life wouldn't be as exciting. For me, that accolade of inspiration goes to my favorite person, who was not only an amazing storyteller but also an incredible human being.

I will always miss you, *Ba*.

Acknowledgments

My profound thanks to my dad, Mr. Jayantilal Sompura, whose writing genes definitely have helped here, and his inputs have been always invaluable. My mom, Mrs. Heena Sompura, has been a great pillar of strength, and her creativity also shows in my writing. Their unconditional love and encouragement has transpired this novel. My lovely little sister, Mrs. Niyati Joshi, whose inputs were indispensable. These folks improved the novel. My brother-in-law, Mr. Keyur Joshi, always inspires me to do high-quality work. My uncle, Mr. Mahesh Trivedi, with all my aunts have been a great inspiration as well.

My wife, Mrs. Krutee Sompura, and my daughter, Ms. Arshia Sompura, have been supportive and very understanding throughout. My sincere thanks to my mother-in-law, Mrs. Bharati Trivedi, and Mr. Jayendrakumar Trivedi, without their unreserved help it would have been really hard to write. I would also like to thank my sister-in-law, Mrs. Maitreyee Dwivedi, and my brother-in-law, Mr. Siddharth Dwivedi, who gave precious tips and appreciated the effort greatly. Love to my second lucky mascot, Ms. Vedika Dwivedi.

Further, my deepest gratitude toward friends and colleagues who one way or another helped this novel fall into place. Thanks to Komal—an avid reader and a dear friend who doubled my enthusiasm to get the work published. I'm also thankful to Tom, Shelley, Robbie, and Brian. I am really thankful to Mittal and Chintan for keeping it real, and for some good suggestions. I am also really grateful to my uncles, Mr.

Rashmin Sompura, Bhardvaj Sompura, and Tushar Sompura, without whom I would have not been exposed to international stories at a young age and probably would have lacked the panache. I would also like to extend my thanks to my close friends who know who they are and would help promote and buy more than one copy just to support my endeavor.

Finally, thanks to the editor for comprehensive assistance in whipping this book into great shape!

PROLOGUE

Present Day
New York

In an abandoned and dilapidated manufacturing plant, near the coast, it was eerily quiet. One could hear a few pigeons cooing and fluttering their wings as the Sunday evening drew near. On the second floor, in the east corner in a vast room that overhung long pipes that were once used for this chemical factory, a table was propped against an opaque-glass wall covered with pigeon poo. The musty smell of the ramshackle space flared the nostrils of Shawn who had been cleaning his AK-47 with a cigarette in the side of his mouth. Shawn had cropped-cut hair, short stubble, and deep- brown eyes that gazed through the cylinder of the assault rifle. The checkered tank shirt showed his dragon tattoo on the right bicep and a skull holding a rose in its mouth on the other. He wore a pair of tattered jeans and steel-toed shoes. His tall and muscular build, buzz-cut hair, and expressionless face almost gave an appearance of a soldier. He looked more southern American than a British lad.

He somehow couldn't keep his mind on just cleaning the gun. His mind was drawing close similarities between this job and the Dubai job they'd done in the past. He thought of the entire plan and where they had made mistakes. Mistakes that were mostly due to Mike, who was to be absolutely avoided in the next venture. Strangely, his mind kept drawing vivid pictures of last year's Dubai job, maybe because the next one sounded like that job. He thought, overall, that it was a job well done. He thought of everyone's position and what an important part everyone had played, except Mike. As a leader, he had annoyed him like an old sore.

November 2009
Dubai

Dubai, all in its nightly glory, was awe-inspiring. It was a feat of engineering in the twenty-first century. As the picture frames of one skyscraper after another formed by the zipping glass windows of the Dubai metro, Mike, in his police uniform, stood there reminiscing about the briefing they had yesterday. He knew there was no margin for error and his team had to deliver. This was their entry into the big leagues. He knew if he scored this one, there wasn't going to be any looking back. Soaring twenty-five feet above the ground, sandwiched between two huge roads, the Dubai metro spanned about seventy-five kilometers of area, making it the world's longest fully automated metro network. Mike briefly wondered if the Dubai ruler was hell-bent on making the biggest, tallest, longest everything in Dubai. Suddenly, his thoughts were broken off by what he heard on his radio. "Mike, I'm ready. It's three minutes to eleven."

"Yes, sync up with Shawn and do it exactly in two minutes," Mike replied.

Tina looked like a Saudi model rather than a taxi driver in her Lady Taxi pink uniform with lighted pink triangular sign on the top of her pink taxi van. Underneath her light pink *burkha*, there was a lot of necessary padding. She looked at the watch and gunned the engine. A few miles away, on the other end of the road, Shawn, in his blue jump suit, throttled his garbage truck, adjusted the side and rear-view mirrors, and right away started racing through the four-lane road, weaving through cars with the monster. He might have covered only a mile or two when suddenly a police car took a sharp left from roadside parking. The cop car started following him with its wailing turret and emergency flashing light. Shawn smugly looked at him in the rear-view mirror and floored the accelerator. The Dubai police car chasing the truck at night wasn't so difficult, but the cop was just unlucky. At one of the intersections where the truck had swiftly passed, the traffic jammed at the light and it took a few seconds for the cop to get out of that mess.

On the next cross section, a thunderous noise echoed when the pink taxi van met the garbage truck head on. As soon as they collided, the van rolled like a piece of dice a few meters away and the truck was toppled to a side and slid across, making an ear-piercing sound, and gas started leaking beneath it leaving a huge streak on the road. Since the traffic was sparse this late, it seemed to the neighboring cars that the truck had its right of way but the taxi van never stopped. To the scattered onlookers, both drivers flung out of their vehicles, were badly hurt, and remained lying on the road. The cop following the truck called for a backup and saw the disaster happening in front of his eyes. He was aghast.

"What?" the officer on the other end asked.

"Yes, it's on Three-Thirty-First Road and the second cross. Traffic will jam soon. Send an ambulance quickly," the cop replied in panic.

"Oh, man! This means I need to inform Sheikh Omar's party to change their direction and take the Sheikh Zayed Road." The guy sighed with fear.

"Yes, I need to go now." The entire conversation happened in Arabic.

He turned off his radio and started walking toward the truck driver who lay on the ground. From where he stood, the cop couldn't see his face.

Mike had already gone through the whole length of the rapid transit's four modern bogeys and found a few scattered passengers that were still there. There wasn't much time. Without any further delay, he flashed his police badge and asked everyone, in Arabic, to gather in one of the front chambers and take the next station because of a bomb threat. With a few screams and panic, everyone lined up at the doors to get out. As the automated caution message voiced in two languages, and once the automatic doors slid open, everyone hurriedly rushed out. They jostled one another, stomping on others' feet. Mike didn't wait for the train to move ahead. He went directly to the second compartment of the metro and quickly took out his geometric compass-like instrument and cut the glass of a window. He slowly cut a big circle of about two feet by two feet as the train slowly picked up the pace and headed to meet its fate. Opposite to him but next to the exit door, he placed a green box and quickly plugged in the detonators to the green box and turned it on.

Prince Sheikh Omar, the only son of Dubai's ruler, Sheikh Abdullah, was riding in his Bugatti Veyron, but the cavalcade covering him was enormous. He was protected by a couple of Humvees and a few Lincoln Navigators in the back and front. The Prince had just inaugurated a mall and partied there for some time. He was about to inaugurate another tall but the thinnest building in the world at twelve a.m. Obviously the weird timing was to accommodate Prince's busy schedule plus it was becoming a trend for late night inauguration and follow up parties that lasted till the wee hours of morning. Since both inaugurations were very close, he had decided to ride in his one of the many prized possessions and his grand security was to take care of the rest. Most of the intersections were halted because of his cavalry but the last minute change due to an accident on Three-Thirty-First made them take a rather busy road—the Sheikh Zayed Road. The cavalry was going swiftly to keep up with Prince's Bugatti. Two police cars in the front of the cavalcade with sirens and flashing lights made the way so the Prince didn't have to wait.

At the intersection of Three-Thirty-First Road, an ambulance arrived at the scene. The driver jumped out and said in Arabic, "Help me take these guys to the hospital." The police officer who looked at his watch was rather amazed at the speed with his the ambulance came by. He asked, "Are you alone? Why didn't you bring someone with you?"

The driver replied, "Uh…uh…call…orders….urgent… couldn't find anyone at this time." The driver seemed to have some difficulty in his speech and a weird accent in Arabic. The cop thought maybe he was new or in a hurry to save lives.

The police officer nodded and helped the driver carry both bodies into the ambulance. The officer noticed blood dripping from the truck driver's forehead. He could now see the face covered with beard. He asked loudly in Arabic, "Are you okay?"

The truck driver moaned and shook his head as the ambulance door was closed. The officer stared at the name of the hospital that was scrolled across the ambulance. He walked toward his car and just as he opened the car door and was about to start his radio for the towing trucks, another ambulance arrived.

Mike looked at his watch and from the glass window of the metro and stared at the cavalcade of cars beneath him riding along. He quickly moved to the opposite wall of the compartment and looked down from the glass window. He wasn't sure, but without wasting any time, he went back to the opposite side, triggered the box, and spoke into his radio.

"Where the hell are you?" he exclaimed.

"I'm just beneath you," the voice came.

"But I only see a white Navigator; I thought we had black v—"

He was interrupted. "I had to switch cars last minute. Come on now, we don't have much time," the voice hastily replied.

"Okay, as you know, I'm on the second compartment, third window. Here's some light." Mike turned on a small LED flashlight and flickered it by putting his hand out from the opening he made in the glass window.

His watch showed him ten seconds. He saw that the Navigator was running nicely parallel to the metro route on one side and the cavalcade on the other but the road was taking a three hundred degree change ahead for Mike's ride. The metro was moving at forty miles per hour in a straight direction and the Navigator matched it, but he had to be very precise for a twenty-five-foot jump. He swiftly kicked the rest of the glass to make room for himself. He took his head out and was about to jump but suddenly a waft of air passed by his nose due to a pole which missed him by six inches as he caved in just in time. He carefully looked in both directions again this time and took a leap of faith. He landed awkwardly on the Navigator roof with his legs dangling on one side with a big thud. As a natural reaction, Catherine ducked inadvertently as if something had fallen on her. He quickly clutched the roof bar, slid to the front, and swung open the front passenger door and heaved himself as the car took a full circle turn.

There it happened. The cavalcade was driving along on the other side of the road and suddenly the middle compartment of the metro exploded in to flames with mind-numbing reverberation. The ground shook. The jolt moved the rest of the compartments while the train was moving twenty-five feet above the cavalcade. With an ear-deafening roar, the monstrous metallic snake flung, with all its windows shattered; and like a broken chain of fiery beads, landed on the cavalcade. But only two sweltering compartments landed on the cavalry like giant meteors. While to the other side of the road that just wound in an opposite direction, Mike said, "That was just awesome. Did you see that?" Mike's blue eyes reflected the explosion.

One compartment dangled in midair, partially pierced through the curled-up, torn tracks. The last scorching section just landed on the circular turn and bounced, first on the ramp and secondly on the road vertically following Mike's van on the downward slope as if to take revenge. Mike and Catherine looked back and Catherine furiously throttled the Navigator. They saw the enormous, burning, vertical bogey right behind them ready to smash the van. Just in time the Navigator escaped the giant hammer as it hit the road, narrowly missing its target; but now it slid on the slope on its belly and again followed them wrathfully.

Catherine exclaimed, "Shit!" She saw a couple of cars ahead, she bobbed and weaved but the bogey was coming with full momentum on the downward slope and hit the first car that she had just left behind and that car in turn slid across all lanes moving forward and hit the Navigator. Catherine and Mike both rocked with the force and the van skidded a couple of lanes to their left but Catherine managed to keep control and steered it straight. She again slammed the gas pedal on the straight road ahead. At last, the still burning compartment now skidded on the road, horizontally covering four lanes, and stopped when it was stuck between a car and the ramp. The two burning windows looked at the Navigator as it cruised far ahead. Mike sat back and blew air through his mouth and blurted, "Wow!" Catherine shook her head and took a sigh of relief. The Navigator safely was cruising to their next destination—Dubai port, their escape route back to the United States.

On the other side of the road, panic ruled the cavalry. Both of the smoldering compartments landed awkwardly on the four to five cars that were covering Prince's Bugatti from behind. The front protection was just a little apart from Prince's Bugatti. Suddenly, Prince slammed the brakes to look at the devastation but the security radio blasted in his car and asked him to leave as soon as possible.

"Well, good job, Catherine. That was some bad-ass driving." Mike winked at her.

"Did I pass Dubai's driving test?" Catherine winked and laughed.

Mike's earpiece barked, "Hey, this is John. I heard the explosion. Seems like everything went well."

"Yup, it was awesome. Do you have Shawn and Tina in one piece?" Mike asked looking at Catherine.

"Yeah, Shawn's bruised but other than that, we are fine."

"Cool, Tina did a pretty good job there for her third job," Mike commented.

John then said in Arabic, "They are fine but I'm taking them to the hospital to get them checked." John smiled and looked at Shawn and Tina in the ambulance." Everyone laughed.

Suddenly, Shawn's train of thought was interrupted when he heard of a car coming from a distance. He took a long drag on his cigarette and placed the gun parts on the table before running toward the north of the building where there was another opaque glass wall. He peeked outside from a couple of broken glasses out of the wall. Beneath him, a silver sedan car slammed its brakes and parked outside at one of the smaller north entrances on the gravel. Just behind it, a red van screeched to a halt. Shawn stubbed out his cigarette on the parapet, smirked, and returned to his cleaning. There was a sudden excitement on his face, as if now was his time of action. Now his skills were again going to help someone and he felt like a crust of rust had just fallen off of him. Nothing would stop him to take on the challenge and he will once again come out as a winner as he did for the last two years. One thing that had not changed for many years, even after staying in the United States, was his accent and his love for British cuss words.

Big thumping sound came from the below iron ladders as if an army of soldiers were marching upwards and were planning to shatter the ladder. Mike walked across the vast emptiness toward Shawn with a big black duffel bag in his right hand. Behind him were Tina, Catherine, and John.

Mike was tall, lean, with chiseled face, hazel blue eyes that were protected by black Armani glasses, and short hair that were spiked up. His sideburns meticulously matched between left and right. A day's worth of stubble enhanced his handsome face. He was clad in black overall. The black over-coat billowed as he walked close to Shawn taking off his shades. He had an air of confidence in him. He shook Shawn's hand and hurled the bag on the big table that laid the AK-47 parts.

"Shawn, I see you are early. That's a change," taunted Mike.

"I am looking forward to this job because after your last goof up we hardly did any serious work since last six months. Hopefully we'll see a change in our arrogant hard arse now, Mike," Shawn ridiculed, and looked at the others.

Mike's voice was now high-pitched. "You have this job because I fucking created this genre. And we completed the job successfully. Don't you remember the Dubai job and the Egypt job? There is always some risk involved. What about the Montana job? I am the fucking crea…"

"Ugh…already started. Enough of your stupid male ego, let's get to work," Catherine snapped. "Let bygones be bygones. It is a dangerous field; we've all signed up knowing the risks.

Death is certain anyways," she chuckled. Catherine was suave yet the outspoken and the most daring one in the group. Her martial arts training and long legs were unmatched, as was her long brunette hair.

"Yes, let's start our day with a good note, Mike. Let's not kill the mood guys. We haven't even started," Tina said with disgust on her face.

Tina was ravishing and alluring and an obvious bait for "the mark." Her beautiful long, blonde hair, which was straightened out, lay on her brown leather jacket. Her bodacious, curvaceous body was simply envious. Catherine wasn't sure if it was Tina's thrill-seeking and adventurous side that brought her in or if it was the crush she felt toward Mike that pulled her in the group. Mike obviously hadn't noticed the signs so far, or so Tina thought. Hence it was just another chance to be with him with every other task; and of course, who didn't love the great money the jobs brought.

John listened to his group's arguments patiently, standing last clad in blue pair of denims and a collared white tee. Short in stature, black spectacles, and curly hair made him look like a geek, and indeed was he. Not only was he well versed with computer hacking and breaking firewalls and codes, but he was the total package. He was the tools guy. He was almost like an encyclopedia with the working knowledge of most of the stuff you could use in this venture. He knew a lot about weapons since he worked in the weapons industry as a consultant for a long time; an asset to Mike's organization!

"What's the plan, Mike?" Tina playfully put a hand on Mike's shoulder and looked into Mike's blue eyes. Mike could simply dive and swim into those beautiful grey eyes, but he would rather keep things professional.

He grabbed one end of the tables in front of them and looked at Shawn, signaling to pull it in front. Shawn took the other side and they yanked the table in the middle of the room. Mike opened the zipper of the big, black bag and pulled out a roll of map. He spread the map across the table and used the cylinder and the magazine of an AK-47 on opposite corners to hold down the map from folding over. All five gathered, encircling the table. The dim-lit light hanging above the table didn't help much but was enough to see where Mike was pointing. Everyone was engrossed; that was their next mission.

Once Mike finished explaining the directions, the spots, the vehicles, and the overall plan, he took out a bundle from the bag and broke it. He threw wads of cash to each of the members. "This is the advance for the job. This is a big job and at completion, we'll each get about five times this. As I explained to you, I've done enough research so no stone remains unturned since this is definitely going to be the riskiest one we've done so far."

"I thought Dubai one was more risky?" Tina had to ask.

Mike turned to her and looked at her with a lopsided grin, "That was just a trailer my dear for the industry and believe me it was less risky than this one. We did that because that was our entry into big boys' circle. I'd rather do local jobs."

John interjected, "Dubai mention begs one question. I heard on the radio that the Dubai attacks were zeroed in on an American gang by Dubai secret service and politically it's getting discussed all the way up to Mr. President. Don't you think it's a concern?"

"Short answer is that I'm not worried. Long answer: We haven't left any trails. Don't know where they came up with this American gang phenomenon. I am pretty sure it can't come to us. Maybe when the prince was rescued his security may have observed Americans. I'm not sure but not worried. Let's focus on things at hand. If I have to I will worry about it and if there is something will inform you folks."

After a pause he continued, "Don't improvise without notifying other members especially me. I don't want to dwell on the past but without blaming anyone, let's make this one a success." I may have another job ready for us, I heard the rumors. Let's focus on this and let's not get hurt. So we meet tomorrow at the dockyards at 9:00 a.m. John, please be ready with the weapons and the mannequin. Mannequin should look perfect. Shawn, we need your agility and sniper skills. We are the best in this business. So let's do it people. Any questions?" Mike was almost short of breath from his emphatic pep talk.

"What happens to the guy we rescue? I mean, what's he gonna do next? Is this a good one? What if he bombs the city in a few days?" Tina's instincts took the better of her and she blurted out the question which she kind of knew the answer to already.

"Tina, we are not in a non-profit organization doing social work. This is the same kind of job with which we started. We don't ask. We don't tell. I can't know the identity of the person calling. We get the deal, we take advance for our preparation, we do the job, and we walk away. We are 'The Distracters.' We have nothing to do with the ultimate motive of our contact. We create a distraction and let them do what they want to do. And you should assume that they are going to be big jobs because only then would they need another team helping them out."

"Anyways, we will mostly read the real motive in a few days in the papers or watch it on TV, which is generally not very good. But it should be none of our concern." Catherine's stoic reply succeeded somehow in closing the argument.

"Seems like your job will be easy this time, Mike," Shawn smirked.

"It depends on the timing, Shawn. If they don't come on time, my job will be much harder than to just shoot and flee..."

Tina interrupted Mike. "Let's go everyone. It is already midnight and we need to wake up early tomorrow." Tina barely completed the sentence with a big yawn.

"Nine in the morning is not early, Queen Elizabeth," Shawn teased, shrugging his shoulders.

Tina rolled her eyes.

Mike grabbed the bag. Shawn reassembled the AK-47 and took it with him. The pigeons fluttered and flew away as the engines roared and exited the abandoned premises with a ricocheting sound as they passed through between the empty factory buildings, leaving dirt clouds behind.

chapter

ONE

Mike couldn't help thinking about the last job he'd botched up. He wallowed in his bed for several minutes but couldn't catch any sleep. He wanted to focus on tomorrow's task, but his mind kept pulling him to the past failure. He couldn't take it anymore. He got out of the bed, reached for a Guinness in the refrigerator, and stood against the window bare-chested, thinking. It was about six months ago, but he had its vivid memory; he touched his right thigh where a big scar had bumped out after healing.

❧

Six Months Ago
New York

It had been a similar night except strangely the clouds had not been as heavy as they were today over New York's skyline. The job had been simple. The team needed to kidnap a seventeen-year-old boy who was a business tycoon's son and release him the next day to any location. They weren't asked to make a call for ransom or anything of that sort.

This was the first kidnapping for the team. Although he told his teammates that they weren't concerned of the ultimate motive, his mind also always showed the inquisitiveness of what the party is going to do with this. He couldn't wrap around his brain that what this meant. But as always, he trusted himself in what he did. 'No questions asked' was his motto and it had served him well for all these years now. Mike was not going to change that. The job was small but the money was good.

Mike, in his research, discovered that the boy went for a swimming practice in the evening every Mondays and Wednesdays. "He generally comes out of the swimming practice at 8:00 p.m. The parking lot is dark and not many people are around during that time plus the place is secluded. He drives a silver Mercedes 350 CLK special edition. Should be easy to identify. He is a thin built guy, should be about five feet nine inches. Here's the photo that was sent. " Mike positively engaged other team members to get the discussion started.

"So, mate, we capture him there, put a mask, and get him into the van and drive back here. Is that it?" Shawn asked curiously.

"Yes, next day at night we release the boy to a random location. But we need to be watchful as police will be on lookout for this guy and us," Mike cautiously reminded.

"So you think they are going to ask for the ransom and we may be the fuckin' scapegoats?" Shawn's pessimism crept in.

"If I thought so, why would I even take this job, Shawn? There must be something else they might want from this fucking brat because they've asked us to release him next day."

"But how did you get the snap, Mr. Johnny English?" again Shawn showed his nosiness.

"The contact told me on the phone to look in a specific trash can at the convention center. It was stuck beneath the lid. So I grabbed it from there," Mike explained.

"Hmmm…smart," Tina asserted.

On the next Wednesday night, the sky was clear. The Moon floated barely one quarter and the parking lot of the Aquatic Center was almost forsaken. It was indeed not very well lit. It was dark in some spots, even with the parking lot lights, due to the shadows of nearby trees that hovered over a few cars. There was a mild breeze, but it was extremely quiet in the lot near Queens.

Both Mike and Shawn came out of the van, which they parked near the Mercedes, and stood stealthily behind the van, waiting for the boy to come out. In about ten minutes, they saw a beam of light near the exit; someone had opened the door. They saw the boy who came out talking on the cell phone and his sports bag on his shoulder. They had to quickly improvise due to the cell phone communication. They couldn't allow the boy to look at them.

Shawn whispered, "Hi, ya, now what? What are we going to do with his fuckin' phone?"

Mike signaled Shawn to put his stocking on his face. Mike put his on. Tina slumped down in the front seat as she saw the boy coming out so as not to be seen. When the boy was close enough, Mike jumped out of the shadows and grabbed the boy's neck from behind and snatched the phone away from him and threw it hard on the ground. The boy could only scream, "Uh, oh!" before the phone was shattered. Shawn followed Mike and grabbed the legs of the boy. Tina revved the engine, but as soon as they carried the boy, the boy jostled and quickly took out a Swiss Gear knife from the sports bag that swung on his elbow and jammed it right into Mike's thigh. Mike groaned and let go of his neck. The boy punched Shawn in the face, gave a swift high back kick in the face of Mike, and flung into his car from the open left window. His Mercedes had a keyless starter with finger print detector so he just revved the engine and drove off. Luckily, he didn't have the cell phone, but it was a complete disaster for the distracter team.

Tina throttled the engine. Mike and Shawn reached the van from the side door, their legs still hanging outside. The van's tires screeched and the smell of burnt rubber filled the inside of the van as it careened from left to right and finally got to a straight trail. Mike and Shawn gathered themselves up from the floor of the van.

There were two paths coming out of the private Aquatic Center. One headed further into the countryside and the other toward a freeway going to New York. It was obvious that the boy would have to take the latter for his chance of survival.

"Fuck you, Mike. The boy seemed to have some sleek mixed martial arts moves. Didn't you know that? And he keeps a bloody hell knife with him. Don't you think it was a big miss on your part?" Shawn screamed angrily. Tina focused on driving. "Shut up, you asshole. It never came up in his research. Do you think I am God, you punk-ass? For all we know, he may have bought it today, you dumba..." Mike was lying on the floor and groaning in pain. He wrapped up his wound with a rag.

"Tina, let's catch the fucker before he catches onto the freeway. How many miles to get to the freeway?" Mike demanded.

"About ten, but his fucking car is ten times faster than this piece of shit," Tina grunted from behind the wheel. Her right leg was completely stretched out to the gas pedal. She could see the white Mercedes rocketing ahead.

Mike winced, got his cell phone out, and called Catherine. Mike quickly explained the situation and shut off his phone. He pressed the puncture wound hard and cursed. Shawn looked away, he was still so mad at Mike that it didn't matter. He definitely was not going to help Mike, at least not right now.

Troy was very fast but didn't expect a double turn from his capturers. He was now almost a mile and a half ahead of them. He was happy to lose them. He probably thought of getting to the freeway, taking an exit, and getting onto the other direction before making a phone call from somewhere. But to his surprise, from a distance, a car was coming directly toward him on the right side of the road. As it came a little closer, it appeared to be a van-like vehicle; the road was one lane, sandwiched between the fields on both sides. Sinuous roads made it harder to guess whether it was coming on his side or the opposite and whether it was a van or a smaller car. After a moment, it was ominously close and he realized that it was rushing directly toward him. He slammed his brakes, trying to make a quick move to get past the van from the other side, but the van actually hit its brakes too. The van took a 180-degree turn and blocked both ways of the road right in front of his sports car, which also was facing the wrong side of the road now. He'd already noticed in the rear-view mirror that the black van continuously followed him from the Aquatic Center. He had to make a quick decision. From behind the black van's tires, strong skid marks were left on the road as Tina decelerated and stopped sharply.

The boy instinctively thought he was in grave danger and jumped out of the car toward the field. He didn't have time to think. It was dark and he couldn't see any faces from the other van. He just dashed into the field, gasping for air, and kept running with all his energy.

The black van had stopped within inches of the Mercedes, jamming it between itself and the white van. John already had the head start as he jumped off from the white van before it fully stopped to catch the brat. Mike and Shawn slid open the doors before the van stopped and ran toward the field. Mike was a sprinter but struggled with his injured leg. Shawn had this uncanny passion about winning and right now, he was so mad that he would do anything to win. Before John could reach the boy, Shawn hustled up and caught up with the boy and tripped him. Both appeared as a tiny speck in the middle of a large field to Catherine, who sat in the white van. Finally, John came next to Shawn and the rich kid. He put a mask on the boy's face and tied up his hands at the back. John and Shawn took a breather. The boy grunted with a muffled voice, "You don't know who I am. You are making a big mistake. My dad will kill you."

"Shhh, you fucktard, or I'll give you a knuckle sandwich; that's the reason you are being taken hostage…" Shawn stopped short, controlling his emotions after looking at John.

Shawn wanted to respond further but John put a finger on his own lips, gesturing Shawn not to talk anymore. Shawn shook his head and they hurriedly walked toward the van and hurled him in the back of the black van. Everyone took off their stocking masks once seated and both vans drove toward the factory. The roadside was fortunately still empty. Not even a creature could be seen to the end of both sides of the road. Tina drove the van that carried the boy. Much to her chagrin, Shawn voted to stay with her. The other three grabbed burgers to eat and all met at the usual place.

chapter

TWO

Everyone looked at Mike at the factory while Tina bandaged his wound. "You could've killed us out there."

"It could've been me or Tina for Christ's sake," Shawn snapped again.

"You asshole, nobody's dead and there are no guarantees in this business, do you understand that?" Mike's furious voice echoed in the decrepit place.

"That's not the point. You missed a very fucking big point in the research. That's inexcusable." Shawn pointed a finger toward Mike.

"God, you're a retard. I did the best research based on the information provided on this guy and with the security around him at his home. I don't think you guys could've found out either. There is no way you can find out everything. John hacked a lot of things on him but he also missed this one. Why don't you yell at him, you fuck?"

Pissed, Shawn walked away from the group and into the darkness of the hollow space.

"Shawn's mad right now. I think we all make mistakes. Let's not talk about this anymore and concentrate on tomorrow," Catherine intervened.

Shawn, still angry, yelled from the back, "What if we'd decided not to take another van? The other van was just for a cover in case someone saw us. What then? Huh? We'd have completely botched the assignment and that would have been because of you. Bloody stupid."

Mike, groaning from the flesh wound, started to speak but Tina put a finger on his lips to stop the arguing. Mike stood up with the help of Tina's shoulder and ordered, "If you have finished eating in this madhouse, I'll stay here and the rest of you can go."

Tina couldn't resist the temptation of staying together with Mike and asked, "I think you need help. I can stay over tonight with you."

Shawn took a couple of rounds in the nearby, dimly lit open area and gathered his senses back.

"Hmm...lad is a trouble. I don't trust him at all. I am staying as well." Or he simply just didn't trust that either of them could carry the task of keeping the boy from escaping.

Surprisingly, Catherine and John also agreed to stay for the heck of it.

Tina sighed with disappointment for once she had an opportunity to be alone with Mike and share her feelings but now wouldn't have any romantic chance tonight with rest of the three musketeers in the house. She finished bandaging the wound, supported and elevated Mike's foot, and brought him some pain-killers.

The crumbling location had a couple of beds on the first floor. The ladies slept there and the guys stayed close by to the kid. Because of their frequent adventures like this one, they had kept a few temporary beddings.

Mike was lying on his back with his hands folded beneath his head as he thought about tomorrow's location to drop off the boy. The boy was covered in a mask, but he would know how far he had travelled to reach the plant if he was smart enough and had calculated starting from the field where they nabbed him.

He wanted to think more but the pain in his thigh was killing him. The obnoxious smell of the old chemicals emanating from the pipes and an occasional pigeon fluttering in the surrounding wasn't bothering Mike now. He should have been almost asleep because of the high painkiller dosage and stressful evening. He wasn't prepared for the boy's retaliation like this. Although he argued hard with Shawn, he knew that he'd messed up and was slightly feeling blameworthy; but he definitely couldn't show, after all he was the leader. Orthogonally, his brain diverted his thoughts toward Tina on how she cared for him and wanted to stay with him. He started having those feelings. He knew he was getting hints time and again from the beauty. He chuckled and closed his eyes.

Shawn felt like apologizing for his rash behavior when he finally came to his senses after a bout of barbarism. "Sorry, man. I snapped. I couldn't stop myself. How is your bloody leg now?"

Mike didn't answer, as if he was going into a deep slumber. He tried hard not to think about the boy whose hands and legs were securely tied with a muzzle in his mouth and a mask on his face. He was in a small chamber that had possibly been used for clerical work during the factory's heydays.

"That's okay. Getting better. Good night, guys." He eventually thought of replying and burying the hatchet. Shawn gave a glance and rolled to the side.

The next evening, around five o'clock, the time had come.

"Are you sure, Mike? You want to do this by yourself? I mean, we are all here. Catherine, John, or I, or anyone, can do this. I think you can trust us." Tina expressed her anxiety about Mike's injury.

"It's not about trust; it's about commitment. If I don't do this, I don't set a good example. Don't worry, I'll be fine."

Mike was big on talking straight and keeping commitments. He was no softy when it came to responsible behavior and keeping the commitments. Shawn wasn't surprised because his neck was under the guillotine more often than not, given that he was regularly late for the meetings and even some times during the "job," which peeved Mike a great deal.

Mike signaled to take the silver Ford Fusion just in case someone saw their vans plus police might have started inquiring by now. Shawn and John carried the boy, who still had the muzzle in his mouth; hands tied to his back and his body slouched. Shawn dumped the boy in the trunk of the car. They hadn't provided anything to drink or eat to the rich kid. It would have meant opening his mask, which they couldn't.

Shawn hopped in the driver seat. Mike trudged and floppily heaved himself in the front passenger seat by holding his one leg and carefully placing both legs inside the passenger seat. He moaned in pain. He shut his door and ordered, "Let's go, Shawn!"

"Rock and roll, fasten your seat belts," Shawn replied.

Although Shawn masked his hatred right now, which he wasn't good at, deep down he wasn't sure of Mike's ability to run this team. His mind meandered as to what could be the intention to kidnap the kid and not ask for the ransom or anything.

Mike's being duped this time. These guys must have made a shit load of money off this kid's ransom whereas we get a puny share of money when we took all the risk. His leadership is questionable. I don't know, man!

He sighed, shook his head, and tried to concentrate on driving. As previously directed, he took highway 495 W first, drove about a hundred miles, and then took 678 S and drove about forty-two miles. Then he took an exit and drove another thirty-three miles on 678 N before taking another exit. He then drove in the city for twenty-three miles before they were near a large field area.

After giving the boy some spin on location, there was an old, rundown barn to the right side of the road which was fenced with barbed wire. It was dark with no one around. The tires screeched as Shawn pulled the car over near to the barn. Both guys had seldom spoken in the sedan throughout the three-and-a-half-hour journey.

Mike limped coming out of the car, as his leg was very stiff by keeping it in one position. Just before closing the trunk, after shoving in the heir, Shawn had taken out the blindfold. Both Shawn and Mike put their masks on and got the young lad, who was now almost unconscious, out of the trunk.

As the trunk opened, Troy meekly tried to protect his eyes from the streetlight coming through the slit. Shawn quickly took out the blindfold from his jacket's front pocket and fit it snugly on his eyes. Mike propped himself to the backside of the car and pulled out a folding chair from the back seat that they had taken from the factory. He sat the boy next to the barn wall and tied him loosely to the chair. Mike said, "Here, you have a blade wedged at the center of the chair so you can cut your ropes. Careful, don't move or try to stand up or slide sideways because the blade will cut you bad."

The teenager whimpered. He could hardly focus on what Mike was saying. His senses couldn't keep up with his brain; they just wanted to shut down. His stomach was growling now and his face was all red. His mouth hurt so bad from the muzzle, as it had cut into the sides of his lip and was bleeding badly. As he heard the car leaving, his brain could slowly register now what Mike had just said. He felt the edge of the blade near his hands at the backside of the chair. He started rubbing his rope that tied his hands against it. The youngster clearly could hear now that the car had swerved and left.

The millionaire's heir finally cut his hand ropes. The first thing he did was take off his blindfold. Squinting and squeezing and rubbing his eyes, he quickly removed the muzzle, untied his legs, and freed himself completely. He felt a relief but was tired and hungry. He looked around and found total darkness and an old barn, which he kind of recognized before his eyes were even open because of the peculiar smell it gave off. He started walking toward what seemed like an endless country road. He wearily walked about ten miles in whatever direction felt right and then he could see the lights. He plodded hurriedly to a nearby bar and called his family.

A couple of days later, Mike received his full payment. He gathered everyone at the den and doled out the money.

"Did you see the article in the newspaper that came out this evening?" Catherine asked.

"No, does it describe anything about our distraction?" Shawn's voice was anxious.

"How stupid can you be, Shawn?" John shook his head and looked intently in disgust.

Shawn stood up with a clenched fist but Tina just took his arm and sat him down next to Catherine.

"I brought the copy here. It says, 'Mr. Peter Sellers, the software and shipping industry mogul has launched a complaint against its rival company for malpractice in licensing and patent fraud. It is to be noted that Mr. Sellers had complained to the police about his son Troy Sellers missing couple of days ago. Troy was later found the next day near Meadow Lake. Information on his captivity or ransom was unavailable. Police are still investigating the whole issue and were unavailable to comment. They seem to have some clues from where Mr. Sellers's son was found. Mr. Sellers, in his litigation, informs the court that in between the chaos of his son getting kidnapped, he was fraudulently trapped into signing some papers that he didn't get a chance to read. He further says that he would have never signed the papers had he known the content of the material. The VP of the company is also under investigation who claims that he had checked the papers before sending it to the CEO for signature. Mr. Sellers has launched a complaint against United Web, its biggest rival, who seems to have benefitted from the inadvertent relinquishment of the patents and licenses. It is interesting to note that Mr. Sellers's son, Troy, who is a young whiz in the biz, handles investment capital and has some stocks in the company's portfolio.

Mr. Sellers's Universal Inc., along with other tech stocks, recently purchased a large number of United Web's stocks. Mr. Sellers or his spokesperson was not available for any comment at this moment.'" Catherine read it like a parrot reading the news who probably had to compete with a fast teleprompter.

"So the whole drama was to get a fraudulent signature, huh?" Shawn sneered.

"They paid well. Who knows what games people play?" Mike shrugged his shoulder and grabbed a Guinness from an old refrigerator that squeaked every time its door opened.

"Mr. Sellers is a big tycoon himself, why would he do such a thing? Before even going there, I find the software and shipping industry combination rather bizarre," Catherine questioned.

"What if they really successfully replaced the papers that would give an undue advantage to United Web?" Tina raised her brows.

John was quiet till now. "It's not highly uncommon to have other companies' stocks which are a lot of times competing against you. It is a strict business. If you knew that the 'tech segment' is going up, then the capital goes toward that segment with a lot of other analysis done in selecting the appropriate stocks."

"Guys, guys, guys, we are not going to solve the riddle and it is not our job to solve this puzzle. I respect your intellectual minds but we can just guess. We can speculate who was behind all this, but I don't think it's gonna help us. It is better we take our share and not meddle in someone else's business. I will notify you once I have a new assignment." Mike held his hands up as he spoke and guzzled his beer.

Catherine was a little disappointed as to how Mike was so cool and completely unperturbed by the events that were part of the aftermath of their ventures.

How could he be so unconcerned? Does he know something which we all don't know? How can you be not at all curious as to what's going on? What people are really doing? What their ulterior motives are?

Mike shook his head as to uncover the shroud that was veiling the present from the past. He unwound his brain from the past incidents and brought it back to reality. Mike didn't realize that it was already half past midnight and he had chugged two beers by now. By thinking about the whole incident, he somehow felt relieved. He conjured up the courage to think that he didn't mess up the mission. He successfully completed it. The satisfaction was enough for his fatigued body.

Tomorrow was the day he had been waiting such a long time for. The crimson-red tower was being splashed with yellow paint on which Tina swayed in a fluffy, violet, short, satin gown with a French-braided hairdo. She looked exquisite. She was calling him; fingers in black velvet gloves called him. She blew him a flying kiss. Suddenly, he saw through the target lens, a sniper aiming at Tina and immediately he jumped to push her away from the line of sight as the bullet brushed past his thigh, causing him to sit up in panic in his bed. He gasped for air and groggily looked around and touched his thigh only to find himself in the bed and the digital clock flickering '4:23 a.m.' in green light. He pulled the comforter closer to his chest and again went to catch some sleep.

chapter

THREE

The next morning, The Distracters met at the dockyards sharply at 9:00 a.m. It was drizzling and clouds were scattered but not showing signs of going away. Catherine had already checked the weather and it was going to shower throughout the day. At the dockyard, from the top, the containers looked like different colored rectangular Lego pieces that were stacked and scattered to form a sprawling mansion made up of iron boxes. They were smack in the middle of one of the goods container's cargo with no company around.

Mike was in a much better mood today. "Ready, gents and ladies? You all look fabulous in black attire. John, can I see the mannequin?" he asked with gusto.

John slid down the van door, which was now brown colored, and pulled out the mannequin. It was a full-body mannequin clad in black leather pants and a matching jacket. The right hand was almost ninety degrees from the elbow and molded in such a fashion that the forefinger curved slightly and the rest of the fingers folded inside the palm, like it was pointing to whoever was in front. The left hand however was held up straight in the air making a fist. It looked bizarre but for the team it was just perfect.

"Great work, John. Now let me see the sniper rifle. Shawn, come and check it out." Shawn lifted the rifle and marveled at its unique design to give the sniper a comfort grip. He shook it feeling it slightly heavier than he'd expected. The telescopic sight was large with a zoom of forty times normal sight. It had a big silencer loaded on top near the front side of the nozzle. Shawn adjusted the eyepiece by looking in to it with his left eye closed and put his finger on the trigger.

"There is a safety lock down below near the magazine…" Before John could finish his sentence, Shawn held his hand showing the palm gesturing to stop. "I've used one of these before. What is the range?"

"Definitely more than sufficient for our task," John responded with a tone.

"I'd still like to know the range," Shawn demanded.

"Well, if you have used one, you should know it. However, it's an after market close to M110 SASS; range is about 0.8 kilometers with 0.308 caliber with a seven inch scope. Take into account the wind and the rain, it won't be that easy."

There it was, Shawn asked for it. He awoke John's inner geek.

"I know my job, you arsehat," Shawn smugly replied, without looking into John's eyes, and sat the rifle down.

"Chop, chop, ladies! Let's hit the road, we can't afford to be stuck in New York traffic," Mike arbitrated. He looked at Catherine and said, "Catherine, you'll drive the brown van. Take John and drop off Shawn at the Bell Towers near the Twenty-First Precinct. Shawn, the fifth floor room keys are given to you. Please be normal and mix well with the crowd while walking from the entrance. Tina and I are going in my car and will keep in touch. Wait for my signal and keep your earpieces tucked. We need to be ready at least one hour before they arrive with Shahab Al-Hasan," Mike demanded.

"What? Why didn't you tell us that it was going to be that fucktard?" Shawn queried.

"Was it going to make any difference? Well, we'll know that it was going to be some prisoner that we are helping to escape." A slight rise of anxiety from the group was palpable to Mike after he revealed the name.

Taking a puff on his cigarette and putting in the side of his mouth, Shawn blurted out, "He is a bloody terrorist who was once accused of the bombings of Chicago's Sky Mall building. He could bomb the whole United States for I know. I know that it is just a business for us, but I still do care about my family and the United States of America. Shame on you all; I'm English and I don't see patriotism in the United States." He smirked and winked as he loaded his bag in the van.

Catherine looked at John and shook their head. Both smirked but Mike, as usual, took it seriously. "And you think I don't? If we don't help them, they will get it done by themselves or get someone else's help. If they are going to bomb some city, they aren't going to inform us first. No matter what you do, we are very small players to be anyways affecting these Mafias or terrorists. Do you get that? Do you want to make money or not?" Mike said, at the top of his lungs now. "Do you all get it? Now, who is in?"

No one answered. All nodded their heads. They all felt that Mike over-reacted but nobody bothered to explain. Shawn finally said, "Chill, you kooky!"

Shawn slammed the door and sat quietly in the front passenger seat of the van. Catherine revved the engine and John sat in the back seat. The van snaked past through a narrow winding passageway between a series of tankers and disappeared. Mike and Tina hurried to the sedan and first grabbed the costume that John had brought for them and wore it. Mike fired up the engine and hasted toward the city.

Everyone was a little disgruntled, but they all knew Mike had a point. But no one had the guts to say it and although they felt guilty in some ways, money trumped for each of them. Catherine was focused on the road and suddenly the earpiece crackled. "Don't go speeding, we don't want a ticket or attract any attention." Catherine slightly raised her right leg to ease on the accelerator. "Got it." She switched off her mic.

Catherine asked casually, "Shawn, slightly off topic, did you hear about that United Web's gig?"

"Blimey, yeah, I heard that they identified an unknown employee who switched the documents for signing the papers and they might have visual evidence from one of their security cameras."

"Yeah, damn it! I read that as well. What if they reach to us via the original goons? I'm a little concerned."

"Don't panic, Cat. They have just identified the person but not found him or her and although I don't like Mike as much but he is one hell of a son of a gun. As we don't know the entity and information about the original mission or the contacts, he also keeps it a secret so the assignee doesn't know who they are working with. So far he's been successful or at least that's what I've heard my darling. So far better than a poke in the eye with a blunt stick."

"Hmmm...I've heard on couple of occasions in the past they've tried to identify him but he's come out clean so far. Or at least he tells me that." Catherine smiled as she reverberated.

"I'm not worried aye. They definitely not know us," chuckled Shawn.

Shortly thereafter, they crossed the Long Island Expressway Bridge and were now heading toward the downtown Manhattan area. All lanes were packed with taxis, other cars, and tourist buses. Mike and Tina took a different route and reached on the other side of the block from the police station on Twenty-First Street.

chapter

FOUR

Catherine stopped the van on the side about a hundred meters before the Bell Towers entrance. She stopped the vipers because they were making an annoying shrieking sound while coming up. The tower was not fully visible from the side window because of its extreme height. Today, the skyscraper couldn't cast its monstrous shadow due to the overcast weather. At one point, it was strictly a business/office building. But with the recent downturn in the economy, they converted their fifth to fiftieth floor in to a four star hotel. It stood tall, right at the crossroads of Third Avenue and E Twenty-First Street. John slid open the door and handed over Shawn his guitar case. John and Catherine gave thumbs up to Shawn. Shawn entered the tower with his faux musical instrument. The van was steered further down to take a left on Twentieth Street.

Shawn wore dark green goggles and donned a hat which couldn't hide his ponytail. His French beard and silver earrings, along with the leather jacket and pants, made him look like a rock star. It wasn't uncommon for a rock star to be in Bell Towers. A lot of the rooms were rented out to corporate consultants or celebrities. Shawn located the elevator and hurried his steps toward it. One of the clerks at the booth actually noticed him and came swiftly to him and asked smilingly, "Sir, are you checking in?" Shawn, now flustered, mustered the courage and thought of an appropriate response. "I am with White Soup Group, I already have my keys. Thank you." The clerk was a newly landed Indian who wasn't well aware of obscure music groups that existed, so he just obliged and got out of the way. Shawn patted himself for his quick response. Before wasting any further time, he went to the elevator and pressed number five. In that corridor, before the four elevator doors, there was a young couple hugging and kissing. The couple smiled at Shawn and said "Hi. Looks like you're in some band. Can we get two tickets to your show?" They looked at each other and giggled. Two doors opened and Shawn quickly took the one that the couple was not taking. Just as he stepped in he said, "Ah! Good that you mentioned it. Come tonight to the Rockefeller Center. It is free." Shawn smiled and waved good-bye. The couple waved and entered the other doors. Elevator zoomed to the fifth floor. Luckily, the couple didn't step out on fifth floor.

Catherine and John waited for the traffic signal when her earpiece crackled again.

"Catherine, are you guys there?" Mark's voice seemed hoarse.

"Just reached there. We've dropped off Shawn and reaching our destination in two minutes."

"Good, we have reached ours." Mike now somewhat appeased, looked at his watch.

Catherine looked from the corner of her eye at car's digital clock which showed 10:30 a.m. She knew that the show wasn't beginning until 12:00 p.m. She turned left on Twentieth Street and immediate right on the Second Avenue and again right on Nineteenth Street. Then she took Third Avenue again to make a right on Twentieth Street. Eventually, she parked in front of a four-storied building toward the left of the street and at the crossroads of Twentieth Street and Third Avenue. It was a small motel, nothing compared to the Bell Towers, but they had converted the top floor to an open restaurant adorned with flower vines surrounding the top edge; however, the restaurant business didn't flourish and was shut down. The motel was in business but the restaurant had been closed for more than three months now.

Catherine stepped out of the van and gave John the wheels. She dragged out a big guitar case which looked like cello case and hauled it right to the front door of the office. She wore a blonde wig and big pair of goggles, and wore a big mole on the right cheek. She was wrinkly on her face and her hands. Everything else was covered by her grey pajama pants and sweatshirt.

"Hi, can I get a room on the third floor? I don't want rumbling on my head from the upstairs guests." She had the quiver in the voice of an old lady.

The clerk filled out the information from her fake ID and handed out her the card key. "Here you go, lady!" She paid cash.

She came out of the office shaking almost as if she had Parkinson's disease and headed for the outside iron stairs and gave thumbs up to John in the van. John smiled, and said in his mouthpiece, "Over acting." She chortled and lugged her big cello case with one hand and purse on the other side to look authentic. The instrument case bumped with each step and made a loud thumping noise. She reached her room, slid her card key, and carefully got the case inside and sat down on the bed with a sigh. Avoiding any procrastination, she came out and noticed the motel's iron stairs leading up to the restaurant, but was blocked by a locked door. There were no other rooms toward that alley.

She was cocking her head, looking a way to go to the top and suddenly someone yelled, "Hey, are you looking for something?" Looked like one of the junkie tenants.

Catherine swallowed the saliva and with it her panic and stuttered, "I...I was looking for the ice machine. Do you know where it is?"

The guy looked sideways and pointed in the opposite direction. "Take a left from there and at the end of the passageway in the corner it is sitting there. I wouldn't count on it working though. I get mine from the gas station from across the street. Looks like you are new."

Catherine, now in no mood of frittering, gave him the money and asked him, "You look like a good man. Can you please get me some ice and cigarettes? Here's a fifty. It will be a great help to this old lady." She coughed and slouched with one hand on the wall for support.

"Are you okay, lady?" Junkie asked.

"Yes, keep the change." The coughing got louder and Catherine looked down. *Now go, you nut job. Let me do my job.* Catherine, of course, didn't say it aloud.

The junkie got more money to get his week's worth of cigarette supply. He happily descended.

Without dawdling a moment, Catherine climbed a few stairs and grabbed on the ledge on the right, cleared some flowery vine, and climbed up on the rooftop where the restaurant was laid out. Old tables and chairs gathered moss and dust and were now stacked in different corners. She observed the rooftop for some time and then quickly descended down to her room dragged her musical instrument case up and with great effort lifted it up and slid it on the rooftop's side. She swiftly then climbed up on the top and she could view Third Avenue clearly in front of her and Twentieth Street on the side. She could view the fifth floor of Bell Towers to her right. She switched on her microphone and said, "John, there is a junkie in green shirt and jeans pants heading from the motel to the gas station near you. Make sure he doesn't reach the motel before I finish here. Over."

"Don't worry. I'll take care of him. Over." John looked at Catherine's direction from the van and sighed.

Catherine quickly opened the giant coffin-like cello container and took out the mannequin and its helmet that laid in the case as well. She quickly mounted the helmet on the dummy and took out the zip-line gun. She crouched down, her entire body parallel to the floor, and looked at the building in front of her by peeking from behind the flowery vines which were located on Third Avenue. The board in front read *Elite Bank of Manhattan*. Located on the second floor, it was one of the oldest and most rare banks in the city. The entrance was right in front of her at a downward angle, because she was on fourth floor. She noticed two guards; both guards walked the entire length of the balcony to the left and right of the entrance. She could see there was an overhang on top of the third floor balcony. Catherine's hands were shaking but she knew that this was the most critical part to their success. She waited for both the guards to be on each corner of the balcony. She whispered in the microphone, "John, ready? Now."

Mike snapped in between, "Why is it taking so long, Catherine?" Catherine didn't answer. She needed all her focus on doing the job at hand to accomplish it successfully.

John, who actually parked behind a small car on the road, immediately pushed the car via his big van into the crossroad, which in turn rammed into an oncoming tour bus and produced a big thud. Right then, Catherine aimed and fired at the overhang above the bank balcony and small iron arrow went directly in the wall. The string for the zip line was almost invisible plus the overcast made it impossible to see. Both guards were also busy looking below at the accident at the cross roads of Third Avenue and Twentieth Street.

Catherine got the other end of the string and slowly returned toward the middle of the roof slouching. She looked at right and left which was covered by tall stacks of tables and chairs on both sides.   HK MP5K into its right hand and the finger that was slightly curled directly touched the trigger of the machine gun. She hooked its left hand on to the zip-line. Now the dummy was ready to zip through the line clad in all black leather and face covered with black helmet but still standing on the rooftop of the motel. She tucked it and tied on to one of the top table legs to give height leverage. The zip-line was slanted enough and the dummy's left hand finger where the zip-line was tucked had a motorized pulley which sat on the string.

The bus driver noticed the van that pushed the car but before he could come out. John's van swiftly took a right on Third Avenue heading back toward Twenty-First Street and then disappeared after turning on to Twenty-Second Street. There was a big chaos with everyone honking as the car that blocked the center didn't budge so four police members from the nearby twenty-first division came to intervene.

Catherine whispered, "Mike, I am done here. Over."

Mike replied, "Great. Get the hell out of there as soon as the test's done. Wait for my signal. Shawn, are you there?"

"Yes, I am here. I am done with my setup here as well," Shawn replied.

"Can you attempt to use your remote and see if it is working on the actual range?" Mike asked.

"Catherine, this is a test. Be ready." Shawn, looking down from the fifth floor window of Bell Towers in front of him, turned his remote control toward the mannequin and pressed the "Go" button. The mannequin began its descent but was immediately caught and held by Catherine.

"Yes, Mike, it looks good. John, you da man." Catherine was enthralled.

"Phew...okay. Okay, cool. Setup's done and it is five after eleven a.m. According to the information, he's going to be here any time between eleven thirty a.m. and twelve p.m. Everyone wait for my signal and act instantly once signaled, so be ready," Mike ordered.

chapter

FIVE

Shawn set up the M110 rifle from the fifth floor window and watched Catherine's move through his telescope. Catherine's motel was one street over, right in front of him. The building in between the Bell Towers and the motel was a one-storied large grocery store. He could see people coming in and out of the store. To his slight right, down on the second floor of the bank balcony, he observed the two guards taking strolls. He could slightly see the Twenty-First Street going in from Third Avenue. He also noticed the New York Police Department's Twenty-First Precinct to his extreme right from the window and caught sight of three police cars parked in front of the precinct. According to the research Mike had done, there were at least twenty police officers in and out from the precinct. The place was secure as hell so the plan was to try and allow as much time before they took him in the station.

Catherine unlocked the MP5K and put the mannequin back into the position that was not directly visible and from where it could be easily glided through the zip-line. She quickly ran toward the stairs, but to her misfortune, she met the junkie again. In an old lady's shaky voice she said, "Please, put it to the side at my door. I need to go to the office downstairs to complain about the bathroom." The junkie looked puzzled and rolled his eyes but nodded. "Whatever, okay." He shrugged his shoulders and climbed up the stairs.

Catherine then swiftly crossed Twentieth Street, entered the store, and through the big grocery store, directly came out on Twenty-First Street. Then she went onto Bell Towers's west entrance and crossed the building to come out onto Twenty-Second Street, where John's van was waiting on the side with flashing lights. The old lady immediately hurled herself inside the car and banged the door closed and the van took off. "You didn't take care of that junkie. I told you to."

"Sorry, I kept an eye on him but before I could do anything you cued me for the accident drama. I couldn't do it all," John defended. Catherine angrily got out of her costume and dashed the wig and the artificial wrinkly skin and goggles to the back of the van. John glanced at her while driving when she was removing the makeup and her sweatshirt and pajama bottoms.

Mike and Tina were dressed in Amish disguises and sat waiting in a sedan on the third floor of a Twenty-First Street parking structure, slightly away but exactly opposite to Twenty-

First Division—the police station where the extradite was going to be brought. Mike had put on a long, salty beard and a black hat with a green shirt, black coat, and black pants. Tina was dressed in a flowery gown and her head was covered with an old lady's fluffy cloth hat that was tied with a knot below the chin. Mike could see a couple of miles straight on to the Twenty-First Street to his right, not toward the Third Avenue but the opposite side—the Park Avenue side. Tina had requested to go to the restroom a couple of times by now that he had already rejected.

Mike took out his binoculars and waited. After about ten minutes, he saw a police van coming from the east of twenty-first street and coming toward the station. Making sure what he saw was right, he screamed in his mouthpiece, "Shawn, now!"

Shawn immediately pressed the *Go* button on his remote and a remote trigger for the sub-machine gun. The mannequin flew down the string with open fire toward the bank. The two guards quickly reacted, looked up, and started firing back but the guy didn't seem to be hurt. He kept on coming in their direction, firing a deafening barrage of rounds. While the guards were trying to combat the immortal enemy in front of them, Shawn aimed and fired two quick shots from his sniper rifle and both guards hit the floor on the spot. The shooting above was noticed from the crowd below, where the accident had jammed the traffic and inside the bank as well. The bank manager pressed the emergency button and automatic rolling shutters closed down both exits.

Shawn had trouble seeing the string but he could see the mannequin hanging right at the ledge of the balcony near the entrance of the bank still firing. He looked intently into the eyepiece and triggered a third shot right at the mannequin's hand. The string got cut and the mannequin came down, flying toward the ground, but landed on a taxicab's bonnet and the machine gun flew away in another direction. The very slow-moving traffic again halted completely and the cops quickly blocked the cross-roads and fired up the sirens on two cars that were strategically parked. Red and blue lights quickly appeared at both ends of the road. They barricaded Third Avenue and Twenty-First Street's access. Things were happening in a quick succession and cops couldn't comprehend what was really happening. Shawn could see about ten policemen rushed out of the precinct toward the firing. Three to four were already managing traffic. Now he calculated there must be another six to seven in the station, which should be manageable by Mike.

But what his eyes saw in the eyepiece, he couldn't believe. He saw that the police van that was coming toward the precinct had stopped couple of blocks away from the venue on the side as they might have been alerted by the chaos and the firing. Mike saw the change as well. "Mike, do you think we need to improvise? The van might take a different direction to another police station. They are in between Park Avenue and Lexington Avenue."

"Yes, I see that. Give me a minute to think, Shawn. Catherine, John, start driving toward Park Avenue where the van has stopped. We need that van to come to Twenty-First and take Shahab out. If it doesn't happen, you follow that van we'll join you immediately."

"I still don't understand how the assignees are going to know all about this and once we free him how are they going to take him. They must be hiding like us as well somewhere," Tina said, finally breaking her silence; it wasn't hard to keep mum with a bloated bladder.

"I'm not worried about that. I need to get him free. These guys have paid a huge amount and they precisely know the location where he is going to be taken before the ultimate location—California and then, after a possible hearing, to Guantanamo Bay. So, yes, they are here somewhere but wouldn't interfere in our work. They are waiting for our job to be done," Mike said disinterestedly.

After a brief pause, he continued, "John, can you scramble the frequency to listen what they are saying?"

John, who was already headed toward Park Avenue, abruptly hit the brakes, pulled over to the side, and jumped to the back of the van. Catherine took the steering wheel. John hastily put on his microphone, which was connected to what looked like an old radio with big knobs and buttons on it. He adjusted some knobs and flipped a few switches and then smiled. "Got it. Hold on for a second. I can't hold it; it gets scrambled so the frequency keeps changing. I can do it for one piece and then I have to try for another, but let's see what we got here," John said with partial excitement with his head leaning close to the speakers.

"Looks like they are saying that some bozo tried to loot the bank and they are entering the bank premises cautiously, they are still prudent of going close to the dummy as it is covered from head to toe and are fearful of a suicide bomber. They gave a green signal to the van."

"Phew...there it is; it's moving, mates," Shawn said with a cheerful sigh.

"Cool. We are going down to the police station. Shawn, once you see the cops' van opening the door to the division, get the hell out of there. Catherine, John, hold your position. Once Shawn confirms it, pick up Shawn first and then drive toward Twenty-Third Street and Second Avenue. We'll meet you down there. From there, we can take First Avenue and leave."

chapter

SIX

Officer Charles Mann was in charge of the twenty-first station. His wide shoulders, tall frame, clean-shaven face with wrinkles, and almost baldhead showed he'd weathered numerous criminal activities. During his service he'd seen it all—from robberies, rapes, murders, and gang violence to riots to celebrity protection mishaps. His still eyes were observing the pandemonium. He was still very calm, dressed in an immaculate ironed officer's uniform. The personality and honor of this man was such that all the nearby precinct officers came to salute and meet this man.

He came back to his office after watching his officers rushing to the scene. His office was decorated with myriads of awards he had gathered during his spotless tenure. He dialed an extension to the thirty-third station. "Hello, Officer Anderson. This is Charles Mann from twenty-first. Can I borrow Officer Sweeney and some of your boys to help out here? You might have already heard about the situation near the Third Avenue. We have had a bank robbery attempt and on top of that, a traffic jam madness going on at Twenty-First Street and Third Avenue. On top of that, we've an extradite coming for temporary overlay before going to his next location. Hence, I need some more men."

"Very well, sir. I can definitely send them but to reach there in rush hour traffic along with a deadlock on twenty-first seems difficult even with sirens on. But I will try to get them to you as soon as possible. Do you need a bird's eye? It will be faster as well. I can call Officer Wayne to bring it in."

"Nah, I don't think we need a bird as of yet. We'll have the situation under control soon. My men are already working on it. Just that extra security never hurt anyone especially since our new guest is well-known, and I was ordered from up that his security is of paramount importance and the highest priority." Charles calmly replied.

"I presume that he hasn't reached the precinct. In that case, if you want I can host the overlay due to unforeseen circumstances at your division. It will take may be an extra forty-five minutes to an hour for him to reach here but once you have settled the chaos, we can bring him in at twenty-first and will let you handle the paperwork," the officer candidly offered a solution.

"I appreciate the gesture, Officer Anderson. I pondered it myself about that and have decided that since they are very close and I still have about five officers here, we shouldn't have any reason for concern. Just send me the men and that'll be it. Good day officer." Charles sighed, put down the telephone, and stretched in his chair.

"As you please, sir. Will send you the men ASAP. Good day to you, sir." The officer completed his greetings anyways or never heard Officer Mann putting down the phone.

As Charles Mann stretched, sector's junior Officer Gable knocked on the door. "Sir, the prisoner's here. What do you suggest?"

"Send Peter in," ordered Mr. Mann.

"Okay, sir."

"Sir, Peter Schares reporting, sir," standing in salute, a very tall and fit Peter said.

"Peter, as I discussed with you before, you'll be escorting Shahab Al-Hasan," Charles said with the least butchering of the name he could. "You'll remain with him once he steps out of the van along with two officers that brought him in. He'll be handcuffed and his legs are also to be cuffed. Any questions?"

"No. Thank you, sir," Peter replied with high intensity and loud vocals as if he'd drank five Red Bulls at the same time.

"Shouldn't be hard. Let me know if you need anything. You can leave now. Thank you," winked Charles, with a fake, lopsided beam on his face.

Peter saluted and made an about turn to focus on his immediate duty.

Charles, shaking his head, couldn't believe that his day started with a traffic jam, a bank robbery attempt, and now had to house the terrorist's stopover for two days. Not to mention several calls of misconducts and couple of small fire eruption event from different locations that had been registered that day. Peter stood up, stepped outside Mann's plush office, and got himself a glass of water from the *Alhambra* water dispenser that sat just outside his door. From there, he looked toward the aisles and noticed tables that were cluttered with papers and phones, which occupied most of the middle of the vast space going all the way to the opposite wall. To the right of that wall was the division's entrance. On both sides of the big room, were small booths, which they used for private conversations or a quick huddle, and a couple of the closed, glass rooms were used for interrogations. The cells were way in the back left from Charles's office.

Charles had to see the terrorist himself, although he fully trusted Peter to do his job, given his pristine record. He walked toward the entrance passing down aisles of tables, most of them empty. He noticed couple of phones buzzing on the empty chairs but he knew he had to focus on the current issue first. He observed that two of the officers sitting in the front were engaged in customer complaints face-to-face. One was handling the calls to the right corner and Peter had just stepped outside toward the van.

"Mike, what's going on? Why aren't you near the police station? I can see they are just about to take out Shahab," Shawn questioned.

"Shhhh…Shawn, you can't see us but we are just crossing the road; jaywalking in front of the cops. But, hey, we are just a couple of Amish folks; we aren't well acquainted with the city life. And anyways, there are a lot of other things they need to worry about right now," Mike replied.

"Okay, okay. Got it, bloke. Do you know what they have planned?"

"Don't you think it is too late in the game to ask?" rebuked Mike.

"I knew you would hide something from us. What are they are going to do? How are they going to rescue this gangster?"

"Hmmmm...I don't think now is the time. We are almost there, beside the van. But the short answer is I don't know. I am supposed to keep a couple of cops busy with my problems. That's the only thing I know. Over and out."

A menacing tall figure emerged from the van. His legs were locked with ankle chains and prevented him from making a sudden step down from the van. The black facemask wasn't helping either. He was in long white kurta-paijamas and traditional shoes. Two watchdogs pointed their guns throughout his exit from the van. His height had made the two officers standing next to him look like hobbits. Peter was just making the entrance with the terrorist when, suddenly, an Amish couple tried to hurl into the station, cutting them from the right where they were stopped by the two officers. Charles almost dropped the cup of water that was in his hand. "What is this?"

One of the officers asked them, "What's the rush? Let us take him inside and then you can enter." Both officers were right in front of them blocking their entry into the station. Peter took Shahab inside and the officers then let them in.

The Amish guy replied in a somber voice, "We are from the Amish community. We are in deep trouble" and started crying incessantly. Looking at the man, the woman now started crying boisterously. Charles and the other two police officers in the precinct came to the couple to calm them down. Before they could think, there was a Beretta 92 FS brandished in front of them. Shots were fired. The two escorting officers near Shahab were dead on the spot. One officer on the phone in the corner tried to get his firearm out but he was too late. Charles was in shock but he ducked down behind one of the tables and started aiming. He was in complete disbelief that Peter could be a traitor. The two officers didn't have weapons so Peter just pointed his DSC pistol at them and whisked it in the air gesturing to move sideways into the division. He came close and gripped Shahab's elbow. In the ruckus, Mike and Tina also ducked under one of the tables. Charles fired a couple of shots, but Peter swiftly moved Shahab out of the station and a taxi was waiting near the venue. Charles rushed to the door with his pistol firing shots, but the taxi already took a U-turn and went toward Lexington Avenue. Weaving through lanes, he overtook other taxis and disappeared in the sea of yellow cabs. Charles rushed back to his office and spoke in the radio.

"Security breach, this is Officer Charles Mann. Code-red, we need men and the Sikorsky S-76 immediately. Several men down in Twenty-First Precinct. The subject has escaped with an accomplice. Officer Peter Schares is a mole; don't trust him. I repeat; Officer Peter Schares is an accomplice. They are in a cab and its number is 5–A–8–1–0–2." His breath was extremely heavy, as if someone had put a stone on his chest.

He turned around to go toward the entrance and saw the Amish couple take off in trepidation. He followed them and screamed, "Hey!" His head was spinning. His mind couldn't wrap around the fact that an Amish couple had come to the police station here in the city and were crying, but that was a lot of thinking in a split second. The Amish couple took off without listening. When Charles reached the entrance, a couple of cops came rushing to the station from the traffic jam area after hearing loud shots and after listening to the radio commentary. Charles saw the Amish couple going into the building on the other side of the road. He screamed, "Follow the cab. Stop it!" The two officers aimed and one even took a shot, but there were so many civilian cars and other taxis that they had to refrain after firing a couple of rounds. The overcast and rain was making it even more difficult to judge.

Followed by his previous order, Charles again demanded, "Follow the Amish couple. Rest of you, follow the cab 5–A–8–1–0–2." His age belied his accuracy and reflexes in times of turmoil, for which he was trained in the police academy and passed with highest honors. "They took Shahab. I haven't radioed the number yet. I need the S-76 for better traction, now. Go! Radio Timmy to join me here. I need to brief him about the perimeters we need to set up. ASAP." Charles's face was red and he had sweat beads covering his entire forehead on a cool afternoon. His frustration was through the roof. He screamed, "Peterrr…" and slapped his hand hard on the table for the unacceptable carelessness he thought he'd showed and his unconditional trust in Peter. He thought for a second that the couple might have gotten genuinely scared and ran away, but he wasn't going to trust anyone now. There weren't going to be any lose ends this time around.

Mike and Tina covered a good bit of ground but Mike knew deep down that Charles would send cops behind them. They ran quickly to the rear exit door of the grocery store. Catherine, sitting in the driver's seat, was anxiously looking at her watch once she heard shots on her earpiece. She sat up attentively when the doors of the building in front opened ajar and out came two frantically running Amish folks. She started the engine and both Mike and Tina leaped into the back. Tina and John helped pull them in as the van sped up, made an immediate left at the next light, and disappeared. The cops came out of the rear exit, but didn't see anything obvious.

chapter

SEVEN

During the ruckus on Twenty-First Street, one officer took off with his wailing siren to chase the cab. Shawn had seen the whole drama unfold from his sniper rifle telescope, but he wasn't sure what happened inside the police station. He had seen, however, that the same officer who took Shahab inside brought him outside and then rushed in a cab along with him. By now, cops on the terrace of the bank were looking with binoculars at surrounding buildings. Shawn stealthily glanced and quickly hid behind the glass window. Four officers were investigating on the rooftop of the shady motel as well. The clerk was already out of the office looking at the chaos. One officer inquired him about a few recent guests who looked different and they found out about the old lady and her musical instrument case.

In the action, Shawn thought that the cop following Shahab might be successful, especially with a bird support. Without even a blink, he shot the police car that was about to follow the cab. The police officer right away stopped the car and went outside and looked at the big dent the shot had made on the left side of the rear bulletproof glass. He instantly radioed a couple of police on the terrace of the motel.

"This is Dan Fisher, number 2–0–3–2. I was about to chase the cab with Shahab but I was shot from rear. Looks like it came from Bell Towers, the motel, or from the store. I am leaving now. Over."

One of the officer on the roof replied, "Roger that. It can't be the motel; we are standing here on the rooftop right now. But we'll check. We are onto it. Thanks, Dan. Over and out."

"Catherine, where is Shawn? He was supposed to be here before us," Mike inquired anxiously.

"Umm...sorry, he said he'll come on his own. He thought he needed to be there if something happened in the police station to rescue you guys."

"What? For how many years are we doing this? Never mind..."

Before Mike could yell at Shawn, Tina intervened. "What are we doing with the silver sedan in the parking lot that we left?"

"Too close to the location, we'll draw too much attraction. Can't risk it and hence I asked Catherine to take Shawn first and then us. We'll take it later."

"Shawn, where are you? Why the hell you aren't here? I told you not to change the plan last minute," Mike barked in his earpiece.

"I saved your arse, Mike. One of the officers could have caught on to that cab if I hadn't shot at him," Shawn replied tersely.

"What? You shot at a police car? Are you out of your mind? We can't give away your position. Are you on the move?"

"Relax, mate, I am already downstairs, walking toward the exit of Bell Towers. I will take a cab."

"You moron, hurry now. Do you think just one shot will stop the cops from chasing?" Mike shook his head to the rhetorical question.

"Crikey Moses, Mike, two cops are coming toward me." He pressed and held the 'On' button on his earpiece.

"Hello." Mike could hear Shawn's polite but trepid greetings to the police. Shawn and everyone in the van were on the edge of their seats. Anxiety reined the van.

Just when they thought Shawn was out of trouble, they could hear one of the policemen say, "Excuse me, sir."

Shawn turned around bewildered, "Me?"

"Yes, you may want to buckle your guitar case properly. It seems half open."

"Oh...oh, yeah...yeah, thanks officer." Shawn's face was red and his hands shaky while closing the buckle.

Then they all just heard Shawn calling a cab with his whistle and the taxi door slamming. As if a mountain was moved, the relief hit all of them and they moved back to their seats to the support.

Mike, shaking his head, bellowed, "That fool will kill us all someday."

No one said a word. Everyone was still in the panic mode as relief had come, but the danger still lingered. They all could hear the helicopter that was droning above them in the city.

"The cops chasing you guys didn't see the van that I know for sure. But we aren't gonna take chances. Catherine, in about a mile, please turn into Sim's underground parking." John convinced everyone out of some sort of fear.

Mike was thinking aloud. "I'm impressed. Their hands are so deep...a police officer helping in an escape. Who would have thought of that?"

Everyone nodded and heaved a collective sigh.

"Shawn, are you out of trouble?" Mike's voice was now solemn.

"I think so. The two guys directly went to the concierge's desk, also my rock star image helped." Shawn said with a faint hint of smile, let alone solemn. He grinned at yet another victory of his. He also could hear the S-76 droning in the background of the afternoon New York traffic clamor.

"Okay, I think we are also safe. But from now own, would you care to brief everyone about your improvisation? I don't want to argue right now. They can come to our tails. We'll change the brown van with our blue one in Sim's underground parking lot. Let's meet at Betty's Diner. They may check the surveillance camera from where we passed by and might put out our pictures if they are quick enough. I still think our avatars should have covered us well," still a slightly concerned Mike opined.

"Okay, sounds good."

Shawn was really pleased with himself that he saved the back of everyone. He knew that he's emergence like a hero would not go well with Mike. He never liked him, but he gave him credit that he was innovative, intelligent, and gutsy; but "bossy" was the word Shawn hated about Mike. After about fifteen minutes, he asked the cab to be stopped near Thirty-Third Street when he saw a public restroom. He tipped the driver and vanished into the restroom. He quickly came out with his signature grey tank top, a pair of blue jeans, steel-toed boots, and a hat with a cigarette in his mouth. He shed the guitar case in the restroom. He took the rifle parts and put them in a black garbage bag that he had rolled up in his pocket. He looked more like a street fighter than a musician, but with rock stars, you can't tell a difference anyways. *Probably a musician buying groceries*, he thought. Promptly, he made a call for another taxi and gave direction to go all the way out of the city toward the docking yards toward Queens.

chapter

EIGHT

According to Charles's direction, perimeter was set and police was stopping each car and looking for two Amish guys and whoever looked suspicious. The search was more for Officer Peter and Shahab, but Charles specially had warned every petty officer at the perimeter that they would stop all who looked suspicious and interrogate without affecting traffic too much. Shawn wore his jacket but removed his cigarette, took his hat off, and started reading a magazine from the back of the cab.

As Shawn's cab approached the Long Island Expressway toll booth, the police asked to roll down the window to the driver and looked at them. They showed a blurry picture of Officer Peter, Shahab, and an Amish-looking couple and asked, "Have you seen any of these guys?" Both shook their heads. Shawn had hid his bag close to his legs. Looking at his tough appearance, one of the officers asked Shawn, "What brought you to this side of the town?"

"Howdy officer, today was my turn. I was visiting my daughter. We went to Central Park and I played with her till her mom picked her up. I try to do this at least twice a month," Shawn replied calmly. The officer nodded and motioned his head to go forward.

"Mike, this is Shawn. There is a perimeter set. I was questioned about an Amish couple, an officer, and my own whereabouts. Pretty serious business going on, mate. Take care." He shut off his cell phone.

"Wow, I think we just got lucky that we all passed the perimeter before they can establish a check point. I saw them putting a barricade just after we crossed through the bridge. We took about five minutes to change the vans in the underground parking lot. We were about fifteen minutes ahead of you and you were slowed down by the perimeter traffic...." Before Mike could finish his sentence, his van stopped and he could see a big line of cars in front of them. Mike just realized that he'd forgotten that there was one more possibility of a perimeter even after crossing the bridge. They actually halted highway traffic where Brooklyn Queens Expressway met the Long Island Expressway.

"Fuck, I'll be damned," Mike swore. "John, all of us look good? This van's clean?

"Yes, of course." John sounded confident but had a quiver in his voice.

"Let's act as couples. And you brought what I'd asked for if the need arose?"

"Yes, I just placed them in the glove box. Here, you want to see." John leaned forward but stopped as he heard Mike.

"No, keep it with you in the front."

The van reached the barricade. There were four lanes. They allowed most of the cars to go in the first two lanes if they'd had been interrogated before at the bridge but they knew the timing of the post setup at the bridge and the time it took to reach to this juncture after crossing that bridge. This was a temporary spot until they covered the vehicles that passed the bridge point. The cop came close to the driver's seat and asked Catherine to roll down her window. He flashed his light into the van to see other faces and checked each corner of the van.

Convinced, the cop showed them a fuzzy photo of the Amish couple from the store surveillance that Mike and Tina passed through and asked if they'd seen someone like them. They all answered no with a straight face.

Then he showed Peter and Shahab's photo and asked the same question. All answered the same.

Then the police asked them, "Where are you guys coming from?"

"We went to watch the Giants game."

"Do you have the tickets by any chance?"

"Uh...yeah. Just a moment." A lightning went through John's body when he just realized that he hadn't torn the tickets that were in the glove box. "Let me sss...see, I...I...I just put it in the glove box." He fumbled through other papers and candies in the glove box when he already had the tickets. The policeman was standing at the driver's side when someone else called him. "Hey, James, you want to look at this?" The officer looked at the guy for a second and replied, "Yeah, coming in a minute."

He turned around and saw half-torn tickets that John passed to Catherine to give to him.

"It shouldn't have been done by the time you guys left to reach here," Officer James inquired.

"Yeah, it was 21-7 and we knew that there was no chance for them to come bbbb...bbbb...back with ten minutes of play remaining unless there was a god's miracle. Also had to avoid the city's crrr...crrr....crazy traffic this time around." John put it as nonchalantly as he could. Fortunately, during the whole hustle and bustle in the city while he and Catherine were waiting for Mike, Tina, and Shawn to join them, John had looked at the score on his iPhone.

"Okay." The cop shook his head sideways to gesture that they could go.

John sighed.

"Tell me about it," Catherine joined.

Just as she cleared the barricade Catherine heard, "Wait."

"What team were you rooting for? I mean I don't see a Giants jersey or a shirt, no big foam hand, nothing of that sort." The officer was just playing now.

"Sir, we had a couple but we just threw that in the garbage once they lost. Really, we are very disappointed," Mike interjected from behind. The officer gave him a stern look and then eased up.

"Hmmm...I think they'll come back against the Falcons next week. Don't lose hope yet." He smiled and tapped his hand on the van door and screamed, "Let them go."

"Wow, one after another close encounters," Tina whispered. Everyone was silent.

The sun didn't set yet but it was already feeling like night-time because of the dark clouds covering the entire city. Across town, near the docking yards, Betty's Diner was decorated with a neon sign that could be probably read from space. It hummed and flickered in red and yellow lights, at least attracting the insects. Mike, Tina, Catherine, and John all looked a little tired but jubilant. The place was busier than they thought it would be. They entered the busy American diner and saw Shawn had already booked a table in the corner which was away from other tables. They all sat down and ordered beers and food.

"Hey, Mike, what's up? How was it? Looks like people are right, cab's always faster." Shawn, as usual, goaded Mike and started tapping fingers like drum sticks on the table.

"I'm in no mood of arguing what happened and what could have gone awry? It was a very close call today. Let's eat some food." The other three felt a big relief of not having to referee the imminent fight between the two.

The mood in the group, after some food and beer, was much better and they were chatting about what everyone would get with the new money and about their online friends. Tina came down after her long-waiting restroom visit and sat in her seat next to Shawn and Catherine, opposite to Mike and John.

She announced, "Guys, when are we going to do something big, something our own?"

"What do you mean? This wasn't big for you? Baby, you're hard to please. How big do you need? Mike, your big is not enough for her." Shawn smirked and winked. Everyone had to laugh at that joke. Tina rolled her eyes and looked down and then up at Mike with a grin.

"This was the biggest in terms of logistics, risk, and money. What are you saying?" Mike joined, ignoring the grubby comment.

"I'm simply saying that we've now started killing people which we didn't agree upon at first, but the need of the tasks have gotten bigger and bigger. I am not saying that I don't like the money, but if we are going to take all these big risks and get a paltry sum, then there is no point in doing it. How long are we going to play sidekicks? Let's do something of our own."

"Hmmm...first of all, it is not our business. Secondly, we are not actual killers or kidnappers; we are the accomplices. This is the first time he had shot the security guards because they would have been a hurdle. Tina, we are the lineman so that the quarterback can throw the ball accurately to the receiver. If we start becoming the quarterback or the receiver, then who'll stop the opposition? The team can't succeed that way."

"I see your analogy, Mike, but what team are you talking about? Are we even on the same team? I don't think so. The glory and the fame goes to the quarterback and receiver. We lineman are not part of that same team. We are just bunch of morons who risk their lives for little amount of cash." Pointing to everyone, she continued with a pause, "This is your team."

Catherine put down her third bottle of beer. "So you are saying that now we should be terrorists? We should directly contact the terrorist group to get out these extradites in order to gain some more money? Tina, sometimes I think if you had some brains to go along with your beauty. Shhh...shhh..."

"No, I'm not saying that. I think we should generate ideas on how to get the full sum of the money without huge risks or with as much risk as we played a part in today. It will be our gig, not someone else running the show."

"Tina, the money is good. I think relative risk is less compared to the actual guys who probably are currently being chased by...," John stopped in between so that the waitress could clear the table, "the cops. Why take so much risk when we can have good amount of money with relative anonymity in the Mafia world? A lot of people know what we do in the underworld but only a handful of people might know who we really are, which further reduces our risks and that can be peaceful. Don't be greedy," added John.

"I actually like her point, no matter what. If we take pride in what we do, then it should be our gig; not someone else's, mate. Let's plan out something on our own." Shawn had pondered before taking sides.

"I think you guys are forgetting who we are. We can do things on our own but it is not about the pride. I take pride in what we do. It is about what you want. As John said, do you want to risk your lives with some more money? I concur with Catherine; do you want to be a terrorist? Do you want to blow up a hotel full of people? If your answer to all these questions is yes, then you can do that. Not me." After a long pause, he continued, "Anyways, why are we discussing this now? Enjoy the evening and the money." Although Mike made sage advice, he didn't seem to be fully convinced himself. Deep down somehow he thought Tina did have a point, but for now, he was happy.

"Mike, when do we get our rest of the installment? What if they are bloody unsuccessful?" Shawn asked.

"It doesn't matter. If they succeed or not, our payment has to come. That's how we do our business. Our work is guaranteed and we did our job successfully. They can't deny that. I should get the money in a week. I'll handover to you then." Mike looked uncomfortable not because of the topic but something else.

"But if they don't know who we are and we don't know who they are, how are we going to chase someone for payment if the ties are severed?" Catherine inquired.

Mike raised his eyebrows. "Looks like everyone wants to be the leader of this group. Guys, I have contacts. How do you think I get these jobs?" Mike made quotation marks in the air. "And the 'few people' that John talked about that know who we are, are powerful. Believe me, I know how to run this and we won't be screwed. I have tactics to get the money back by hook or crook if the deal goes sour."

Throughout the restaurant conversations, Tina lifted her leg and rubbed it on Mike's legs underneath the table. A couple of times, John, who sat next to Mike, said sorry to Tina as if he'd accidentally touched her when Tina's leg missed Mike. Mike didn't let his expressions give away the fondling.

Everyone left a hefty tip and left the restaurant.

Mike and Tina went to Mike's apartment and made long-awaited love. They both lay cuddling each other when Mike said, looking into Tina's eyes, "I knew you had the hots for me."

"You never reacted as if I had?" Tina asked with a grin, her hand on his bare chest.

"Can't lose focus on the job, baby," said Mike, as he ruffled Tina's beautiful hair.

"How about you, you never felt anything for me?" Tina asked casually, as she looked up into Mike's hazel-blue eyes.

"I always had. You know what, I can jump from a building, kidnap someone, help a prisoner escape, but I am scared of saying. I didn't have the courage to say anything to you." Mike revealed his weakness.

"You liar. If you had something, I would have known by now." Tina smirked and canoodled with his chest hair.

"How do you think in each task you always end up with me and not Catherine or John?"

"Hmmm...I didn't think about that. I can see now. You can mask it really well. Good actor, I like it." Tina kissed him passionately.

chapter

NINE

A week later, all gathered at the chemical factory since Mike had promised about the money. It was a bright Sunday morning. Light shafts entered the second floor of the forsaken place through broken glass, making abstract patterns on the floor. Those openings provided a pathway to a fresh drift of air as well. Pigeons made nests inside a couple of rooms, a perfect hideout to be away from the occasional showers. There was a big beehive on the east corner and growing.

Pointing to the beehive, Catherine said, "They say it brings good luck." Her beaming smile and big eyes reflected the fervor.

"Who says that?" John inquired.

"Some Asian cultures believe in that," Catherine, still looking at it with passion, replied.

"Hmm...interesting."

"Guys, did you hear about the investigation? I was watching TV the other night and they said that Shahab was recaptured within an hour of his escape and a police officer was killed in the encounter. They couldn't clear the perimeter. The cops didn't let the news of Shahab's escape leak until they had it all sorted out." Tina's voice quivered.

"I know. I don't understand after this much planning and risk taking, how can they not clear the perimeter or how can they fail? I mean you spend so much money, risk your resources, and at the end, nothing? " John looked puzzled and frustrated.

"It is hard to believe that they weren't successful," Mike chimed in. "What do you think, Shawn?"

"I am...just...don't know...what to say. It is just...arse over tip. I can't understand what was so difficult about it. You could have stayed in a fucking hotel, lay low for some time. I mean there were several ways to elude the police for some time. Sorry, I just can't...it is anti-climactic." Shawn raised his voice from one dark corner of the room.

"Maybe they're keeping it from the public before some reporter discovered that Shahab was captured. They might not have captured him because they don't show it on the TV yet, you know what I mean?" Catherine's wink had a hint of a big guess.

"So you think they are just faking it. What if the terrorist organization came out with Shahab's video? The image of the NYPD will be ruined then. I don't think they can be that stupid," Tina argued.

"She's got a point. I also don't think that it is some kind of bloody hoax," Shawn chimed in.

"Actually, because of the barricades, the reporters did get wind of the search. One of the reporters went through the checkpoint and was shown the photo of Shahab, who he recognized and later published an article on his website. The article went viral and was then announced in a huge number of websites and print media, but the police completely denied the story and now everyone's saying it was the reporter's fault. He just wanted to become rich and famous quickly. They must have caught him and shushed the reporter, " John explained.

"As always, let's not focus on the past. Well, here's all your money. Spend wisely. I will call you guys once I have a new *job*. Also, lay low for at least a month. Police haven't stopped investigating the bank robbery attempt and the Amish folks. They might even try to get Shahab to talk." Mike tossed bundles of dollars to each individual.

"Moreover, John, let's paint the vans again. I had gone to pick up the car and it needs pimping as well," winked Mike with a grin.

chapter

TEN

Six Months Later
Near Sacramento, California

Zach was driving a huge fifty-footer truck to get close to the Elk Grove Boulevard exit near Elk Grove, CA. Zach was in his late twenties, had long brown hair parted sideways, and a few curly facial hairs that looked like someone had yanked off a full-grown beard from his white skin. His green eyes were highly focused. His thin build and normal stature gave an appearance of a harmless, cheerful, young boy. The timeline given for this task was very specific. As a first-timer, Mike didn't want Zach to do this job. But with Catherine's relentless convincing and him being a racer in the illegal night derbies, Mike finally had agreed, but only on one condition, that he took full training of driving trucks and passed the Class A examination. Zach knew that he could win this. His concentration was one hundred percent. He knew that he had to be very precise. The day had finally come after all his training.

It was a nice summer day in California. There was a mild breeze blowing through the grove of trees that shadowed the massive expanse in front of the Sacramento Capitol building that stood proud and tall. The governor of California, on December 2011, had just briefed a team of paper pushers for promoting an increase in tax on the importers for the already debt-ridden state. Generally, it was always bad news after bad news for the state due to an economic crisis and his inability to do something about it due to the lobbies, laws, and unions. Today, he was happy that at least he could bring some jobs back to California. A small, independent, South American carmaker had promised a couple of months ago that they would open a hydrogen-based car plant near Stockton, California. It was green and was going to bring some greenery for Californians, although he had to cut a lot of slack in taxes over the course of the next ten years. The hope was that this deal might trigger a few more companies to sign the dotted line.

His Lincoln had arrived and was waiting at the capitol. The chauffeur jumped out and reached the rear door, swinging it open in front of Governor Joe Sinclair. In his late fifties, with nicely combed hair and a muscular body that would shy away any young athlete, he wore an immaculate dark blue suit. After all, he was no less than a celebrity. A leader of the world's sixth largest economy, Sinclair was no lesser than a president of a huge country. The governor ducked in the car, looked at his expensive watch, and signaled the driver to take off. There were two motorcyclists and a police car at the front and rear of his car for protection and security. The emergency siren, with ululating wail, and a turret light beaconed pedestrians and vehicles to give way to a dignitary.

Gov. Sinclair's mind was occupied by a myriad of thoughts. He only had three hours before he had to go to a Sacramento school where a shooting had recently happened. Luckily, no one was injured, but his presence was essential for the public to make them sure that California was still safe for them and their children to live in. He flashed his speech for a moment. He again thought he could have saved two hours if he could have gone in a government chopper. Unfortunately, the pilot and his backup pilot both had died in a car crash in downtown Sacramento earlier that day. The news wasn't welcomed news and the city had started an investigation. There was a couple of people at the capitol who could fly a helicopter, but he didn't trust them. Besides, Stockton was so close that it wasn't worth all that. He could simply drive back from his meeting with the CEO of this car company, as it was only about fifty minutes away from the state's capitol. He thought it would be great to see California by road as a governor anyways. This trip was supposed to give him something good to talk about in California. After all, he was bringing a thousand jobs back to the state.

Gov. Sinclair somehow didn't seem to be as excited though. He wasn't particularly happy because after his second term, he'd faced a lot of controversies from church authorities for his favoritism to gay rights, abortion, and other libertarian view. He had tried his best to juggle both his thoughts on American freedom and the religious mentality of the strict Christian clergy. It made it more difficult because the media had turned him into a disbe-liever—although born into a Catholic family, he remained athe-ist all his life. He believed more in science and knowledge than the myths, the secrets, and the religion. He also faced criticism when he proposed for a recent tax increase in imports. He knew that he needed the money and jobs to revive California from its massive deficit. However, his thoughts wandered back to those two pilots that were killed in a crash recently. It was one of his busiest days and he should have allowed others to fly the Bell 206 and be done with this meeting, he thought. He looked at the car in front and two motorbikes ahead of them and a car be-hind them all cruising at seventy miles per hour on I-5 south. A scheduled meeting with a book writer who was keen to publish a biography got cancelled last minute or else he would have saved the time and would have been occupied throughout the fifty or so minutes interviewing with the lady. He took out his reading glasses, followed by his smart phone, and looked at the agenda.

Zach was now ready with the trailer and the big iron pipes that were saddled on the back of the monster. He gunned the engine as Shawn had called him to be ready at around 12:30 p.m. He was parked on Elk Grove Boulevard, which was going from east to west right above the I-5 S freeway. He now saw a tiny speck of helmet-clad officers on bikes and three gubernatorial cars behind them at equidistant. Of course, the center one was the Lincoln in which Gov. Sinclair sat. He geared the truck and slowly began his march. The timing was very important. The distance between the two motorbikes and the car behind them was about a slightly less than four hundred meters and probably same for all other cars. Zach now hammered the throttle; he had to achieve about eighty miles per hour in a short distance. He slammed the accelerator down to the floor. Once the speedometer showed him close to eighty miles per hour, and when he reached the middle of the road, he steered the truck in an acute sharp left turn. The mammoth truck skid sideways and tipped over from the small railing. As it hit the cinderblock wall and the iron bar, the gargantuan truck made a monstrous, earsplitting noise, rolled over the iron bar, and was free falling directly onto I-5 S, the tires rotating in the air. With a boisterous thunder, it hit the road beneath it, and the pipes began to sprawl on both sides of the road, making a strident rattle. The timing was immaculate. The two motorbikes and the police car in front of the governor's carriage had passed through and the truck lay just before the governor's car which had screeched to a halt to avoid the pipes that were bouncing and rolling toward them. One last pipe rolled just over from the pile, rocked, rattled, bounced, and was about to land on the hood of the Lincoln when the driver made a swift move by reversing just in time to avoid it.

Governor Sinclair and the chauffeur were awe-struck. They couldn't believe what had just happened in front of their eyes. Before the driver could think, the radio on his car buzzed. "Hi, this is Officer Ray in the car behind you. Sir, are you okay?" He sounded anxious. The chauffeur looked at the governor as he nodded and replied. "Yes, we both are fine."

"First thing to do is to get the governor to a safe location. The pipes are scattered all over the freeway blocking the road on both sides and the center divider due to this huge truck. The other guys will figure out their way to come to this side, but I suggest that we immediately take a U-turn and take the next exit. I can help with the traffic behind me with siren and emergency light, but we'll drive over the shoulder in the wrong direction. Sir, does that sound okay?"

This time the governor picked up his phone and hurriedly spoke. "Yes, Ray, that sounds fine. What in God's name? Does it look planned?" Governor Sinclair had heard about a lot of incidents but never had witnessed something like this in front of him. He wiped off his sweat beads and tried to calm himself as the driver carefully started making a U-turn. He really started believing that he should have taken the bird instead.

"With all due respect, sir, it could be but I can't focus on it currently. First, I need to get you out of here."

Ray switched on his radio again and barked, "Code Red. Charlie, Greg, Sam. As you may have heard, we are taking the governor to the Laguna Boulevard exit which is about two miles from here and will drive from inner city and back to the capitol. You can take the next exit and drive from the inner road and meet at the previous exit where we're heading. Be alert. I've asked Elk Grove police for help. Sam, please contact the highway patrol if they are close by." His voice shuddered with fretfulness.

"Any sign of the truck driver?" Greg asked curiously.

"Couldn't see properly with the truck being upside down, scattered pipes all over, and Gov's car in front of mine. I will ask to get a dispatch here immediately. I couldn't go out to check the driver because I couldn't risk the governor's life if the truck had explosives in it."

Zach had made a huge accomplishment and he was very happy about how it turned out. John came as expected in the nick of time. Zach had jumped out of the truck on the road just as the mammoth truck was tipping. John came on a bike and both men wore helmets. They rode east from the ramp and after driving about four miles down the road, the bike climbed up on a steep ramp which went into a semi-truck that Tina was driving at about sixty-five miles per hour. The huge ramp door closed all the way up and the semi took 99-N toward Sacramento.

The police car was now spearheading the way for the governor's car. Both cars balanced on a tiny shoulder and avoided hitting the oncoming traffic.

"Gentlemen, we are now about to take the exit." As Officer Ray moved on the sinuous ramp, he was thinking about the whole incident, and he thought this time he would be of real help in this crisis. He cleared off the sharp ramp and could see the oncoming traffic light that was green at the exit. Suddenly, as he was approaching ahead, a gigantic telephone pole on the side of the road came crashing down on his car. A big thud smashed his car and Ray had no chance of doing anything. Governor Sinclair again witnessed another tragedy in front of his eyes and the slight glimmer of happiness he had of going to the car manufacturer suddenly turned into a nightmare. His mind was clobbered with panic. He didn't speak for a moment and neither did the chauffeur. The governor shook his head as if clearing his wavering thoughts and picked up the radio and screamed, "Officer Ray, are you there? Help. Officer Ray is down at the Laguna Boulevard exit on I-5 north. How far are you guys? We are blocked again on this ramp just before the light." His voice trembling now. A few scattered cars were going that route; however, the pole covering all three lanes horizontally on the exit ramp didn't allow others to cross the lights.

"Please hold your position sir; we are about two miles away now. We are coming ASAP. I've also called S-76 from the station. They should be there in no time," Officer Charlie replied, hurriedly.

Unexpectedly, two guys on a motorbike came from the other side and showed an Uzi to the chauffeur and signaled him to come out of the car. The chauffeur stood out with his hands up and started walking down the ramp where they'd signaled. Both wore a helmet that hid their face and dressed fully in black leather suit. One of the guys hopped in governor's car. Looking at a man with his hands up, a couple of cars that were coming on the ramp, stopped, and one of the drivers vehemently drove in the wrong direction of the exit on a narrow shoulder.

chapter

ELEVEN

"Awesome, Zach. My man, you've come a long ways just in six months. Catherine, your find is perfect. I am impressed. Zach, to tell you the truth, I was very reluctant of you joining this team. You're a young guy, driving crazy cars with no fucking criminal experience other than couple of petty thefts. You did have martial arts training like Catherine, but I thought you might have never used it. You know Tina now; even Tina had to stay on the bench, if you will, for a while. I made her do so much menial work that anyone would give up. And she was from one of the teams already working on this type of shit. So you were lucky because there was no way I was gonna give you this task that you just passed with flying colors. I must say that you've proven me wrong and shown you're worth man." Mike raised a toast with a big beam on his face.

"Great work, dude!" Tina echoed.

"I second that," John said.

Shawn nodded, smiled and raised a beer bottle in appreciation. Catherine gave a lop-sided grin and grabbed a beer from the refrigerator of the Sacramento Hotel where they had been staying. This was Mike's suite where they all had gathered at the night before leaving for New York next day.

Zach smiled back, lowered his head, and replied, "Thank you. It was a team work. You guys are great to work with. I look forward to our coming adventures. Cheers." The beer bottles clanked together. Mike patted Zach's back and chugged his beer. Then Mike stepped away and reached to the balcony to get some fresh air. Tina followed.

Catherine eyed Zach from head to toe from a corner. Their eyes met. There was an unusual chemistry between them. She kept staring at him while her thoughts wandered in the past. She had once dreamt of being with him when they both attended the martial arts class together. She was a simple girl with normal aspirations, nothing huge. One day she got a call. Her father was killed by a Mafia gang outside of a bank when he refused to hand over money he was depositing on behalf of a small business for which he worked. She was devastated. She screamed uncontrollably with incessant tears rolling out of her eyes, but no one was left to console her. She couldn't fathom why someone would kill this loveable guy.

But she had the guts like her father. She went to the location where he was killed. Her eyes were now still; no twinkling of a little girl was seen. She looked at the darkened area where the blood had clotted. And even when the city services had cleaned the area, she could smell and see the darkened spots. She could visualize her dad cocooned with agonizing pain and tears. She right away decided she would satiate her vendetta against whoever murdered her dad. She was still young to make life decisions, but she deliberated a lot on the issue. At the end, she decided to join the police academy. At the time, she was friends with John, who knew Mike.

When asked once, John, a family friend, told Catherine about the work he does with Mike, and John had even asked Catherine if she would like to join. John didn't know that she was already going to the police academy. She definitely had become tough after her dad's death. Catherine pondered on John's work and his unconditional trust on her. Joining John's team was lucrative, exciting, and a faster way to meet the Mafia. She often went on a guilt trip that she would help the guys who probably killed her father but she immediately jumped on the prospect and quit her police academy in the middle of the program to join Mike's team. It had been more than five years and there was no looking back now. In those five years, a small-time crook who murdered her father was gruesomely murdered and was found in a ditch near a highway close to New Jersey. Her conscience after joining the academy wouldn't have allowed it otherwise. John had helped a great deal.

Catherine came out of her flashback and noticed Zach was not standing where he had been. Tina, Shawn, and Zach were talking about today's task in a large couch in the corner and Mike was talking on his cell phone in the balcony. She didn't see John around.

"What are they going to do with the governor anyways? Are they going to kill him?" Zach's curiosity crawled.

"We don't ask and we don't tell. That's what bloody Mike would say," hooted Shawn with a frown.

"Zach, you will see soon in the newspaper or TV. Be patient," Catherine chimed in.

On the balcony…

"Mike, this is Mase. Listen, we got a problem, man," Mase blurted in his Jamaican accent.

"Hey, Mase! What's up, man? How are you? Long time no see." Mike was still in a jubilant mood.

"I am good, but listen, I am in trouble. Remember you guys did the rescue mission?" Mase's hushed tone sounded fearful.

"Before you say any names, yes, I remember. What about it?" Mike was now alert.

"The party thinks…well, can we meet somewhere, man? I need to talk to you as soon as possible." His voice was shaky.

"You know that I don't meet anyone, man. Besides, I am not in the city currently. I am flying back to New York tomorrow morning."

"You gotta listen to me." His voice was now almost screeching. "These guys are dangerous and I am under pressure."

"Hmmm…I take it that it's serious. You won't be bugging me if it wasn't significant. Let's meet at Zaplin's Bar at 8:00 p.m. tomorrow. Take care, Mase. I think it'll be all right."

"Thanks. See you tomorrow man and be careful." Mase sighed and put down the phone.

Mike flipped his phone closed. Mike somehow had a hunch now where this was going. He understood that only one thing could be happening and that's the reason Mase had asked him to meet. He started pacing the balcony from his leaning position. He declined the thought that any member could have done that. Mike now had an inception of doubt on his team members. He thought about that day. He started recalling all the details of what had happened in New York about six months ago, which were somewhat vague. Intertwining threads in his brain jostled his memory and what came to surface was not helping much either.

Tina noticed Mike's grave expressions as he stepped in the room. She placed the bangs of her beautiful hair at the back of her ear and asked, "What's the matter? You seem to be upset."

Everyone talking now was silent, looking at Mike and waiting for his response.

"Nothing. It is just that the payment of this job might get delayed. So I got pissed, and I've a headache." Mike sighed, scrunched up his nose, and put his left hand on his forehead.

"I think we should leave now. It is getting late and we have a plane to catch. I'm heading to my room. Take care, Mike." John reappeared and disappeared.

Everyone nodded their head and headed toward the door.

Shawn couldn't resist, "Is it our payment that got delayed or is it just yours, bloke?"

"Fuck, Shawn. Don't start it right now," Mike barked.

Shawn shook his head and swore as he left, throwing his bottle into a far corner trash can to show his anger and distrust for Mike.

Everyone left except Tina. She massaged Mike's head as he crashed on the bed.

"Mike, I know something's bothering you and it is not the time, but I'm thinking of us. When do you think we can stop all this and live a normal life?" She sat with Mike's head in her lap.

Mike looked up into Tina's eyes and raised his voice. "Tina, I told you there is no turning back from this life as such. Plus, you were the one who wanted something bigger, some big-ass task, isn't it? We haven't reached there yet." Mike closed his eyes. "Yeah, but...see, right now nobody knows us. Our identities are secret. There is still a chance, I think we have enough money together to start something legal and be happy rather than going through this...sorry, couldn't stop. I'll be quiet now." Tina gestured a finger on her beautiful lips and looked down at Mike's opposite face and started pressing gently on his forehead.

Mike looked at Tina's luscious lips, pulled her closer, and branded a kiss on her lips. Mike pulled her into his arms. Fatigue and a headache were no more an issue. The night was young and it danced frantically.

chapter

TWELVE

Next Day
New York, Downtown

Mike was worried sitting in his apartment as he waited for 8:00 p.m. to draw closer. The same thoughts filled his mind that he had thought about last night. *Could that be it? No, how can it be? It doesn't make sense. There is now way these guys can break my trust. If they wanted to, they would have long done it. Besides, what can they gain? They are sometimes buffoons and can make errors but that's it. That's it; I think it's those errors that might be causing doubts in the assignee's minds. This is simply a mistake. But then why had*

Mase seemed so anxious? What has he been going through? He called an urgent meeting which meant something really important.

He recalled that the only time he met Mase was the first time he had to establish the business. Mase had been a middleman for a long time. Mike knew that Mase hadn't been his original name. He had picked it up in this profession. He had been the ultimate negotiator between two Mafia gangs. He solved their area encroachment issues; he solved who gets what from Cuban drug lords, weapons division, the whole nine yards. Mike found about him through his friend and contacted Mase. It was significant to meet him for the first time since Mase, at the time, was a far more important figure than what he was now. He was going to bring the business. Mike knew that his idea would catch up fast and the Mafia's would need decoys and cover ups everywhere which would make their work a lot easier. He knew that Mase was the right person to bring upon the famous gang leaders. Soon it began to be true and Mike and his team started building their reputation with small and medium jobs. It was mostly small explosions to create diversion, act as someone, halting traffic so the cops can't get through at certain times, and even getting jailed for misdemeanor so that the big guys could escape and play their games and so forth. Mase was pivotal in their success. Although he had been telling his group that one of his contacts made the job possible, it was the only contact for a couple of years. He could depend on him to bring continuous jobs that would pay well and avoid any personal contacts. Today was different. After more than six years, Mase had requested to see him. Mike had gotten a lot bigger and his demand exceeded his ability to supply, only due to his pristine record. The gangs had tried to do it by themselves but invariably failed at the distraction itself and got caught. A few recent setbacks weren't going to tarnish his reputation.

Mike changed his getup. He put on a beard and a blonde wig. He put on an immaculate black Armani suit and whisked fragrant Armani perfume on it. Black Italian leather shoes and a blingy Coultier watch made him look like a perfect businessman or a finance guy. He headed downstairs and paced toward the rental car that he had rented from the airport to get back home today afternoon.

Zaplin's Bar, New York at 8:00 p.m.

Mike entered the trendy bar. It was dark with jarring, occasional light beams that sparked the room, and the place was filled with alcohol and smoke odor. Groovy loud music played in the background. He gazed at a lot of adult teenagers dancing to the music in the north of the hall. On the left, it had a huge, semi-circular-shaped stainless steel bar table with glass top which seated at least twenty people who were chatting and drinking. The place was extra crowded. Trendy pink and orange lighting hung above the steel bar. There were three bartenders constantly attending customers who had to yell to be able to be heard over the loud music. The place was buzzing with rich kids who were planning to get laid sooner rather than later. There were lots of black suits and middle-aged guys and gals who either wanted the same as the kids or were telling their sob stories about the financial market turmoil or their broken relationships to their friends, who inadvertently had to become the garbage bin so that their friends could trash them with their whining.

Mike remembered Mase as a tall, large-framed, crop-cut Jamaican guy who belied his age. He was like a big football player. Just the look on his face was enough to make weak-of-hearts shiver. His personality was menacing. It seemed that this guy alone could take easily up to four to five guys without any trouble. Mase also kept his identity very private. He kept a couple of trusted henchmen who worked for him and the majority of the deals were done on the phone in code words.

As Mike placed his hips on the stainless steel with dark brown, faux-leathered barstool, a hand came from the back on his shoulder. "How are you, man?" A thick Jamaican accented voice came from behind.

Mike immediately recognized the accent and the large hand that grabbed his shoulder. His getup had worked just like it had six years ago. He smiled and turned around to shake the big guy's hand. He seemed even bigger this time but his face looked the same. He had the same grainy beard, his hair had more grey now, and his dark and shiny skin didn't give away his age. Both ordered their drinks and Mase turned around to Mike.

"Mike, you may have guessed why I called you here." Mase's grave face now showed wrinkles.

"No, I am not sure. You said something but you stopped. I am sure it is important." Mike shouted to be heard over the loud music.

Mase inched closer to avoid screaming. "They think that one of your men did something to alert the cops and that's why Shahab got captured."

"What? That's bullshit, man. What's the proof? You know we have delivered every job successfully. If they can't execute, how is it our fault? Besides, why are they bringing it up after more than six months?" Mike spit out a barrage of questions.

"Listen, man, these guys are very serious. I am really in trouble. They found out my identity. Actually, this has been going on for some months now. You know Gabe?"

Mike nodded. He knew that Gabe was one of Mase's henchmen. He ran more than thirty percent of his businesses. Mase couldn't live without him. "Yeah, what about him?" Mike curiously asked.

Mase's mouth came even closer to his ears. "Man, they shot him last week," Mase whispered in a quivering voice.

"What? Are you fucking with me?" Mike now faced Mase in surprised anger.

"No. I saw one of my right-hand getting killed by these bastards. I'm not kidding, man. I kind of know who they are but can't do much about it. They are after me now. I am hiding and trying to stay low. It was important to tell you that they want to find out who's the mole. They think that I'm not the mole but the team that worked on has a mole. But they are after me to get your identity."

"First of all, I don't believe that. None of my men did anything that would raise a concern and all of us worked in pairs except…" Mike stopped short, thinking something.

"Secondly, I hope that you are not being followed or you'll jeopardize both of our lives Mase," Mike continued, but now being watchful. He gazed 180 degrees with his hazel-blue eyes.

"It is not important what *you* believe. It's what *they* believe." Mase stressed on the pronouns.

"So what's your point? What should I do?" Mike gulped his drink in one shot.

"I'd say just lay low for some time and don't take any assignments. The one in California was successful, I hear. Don't take any more from anyone else but me because if someone else gave you a job that is from those goons, you guys will be in trouble. You'll be the 'target' and the actual job will be a decoy, you know what I mean. Also, jar your brain and see if there is a traitor indeed in your team. You were thinking before when you said except..." He chugged his whisky.

"Okay, I'll look into it. Thanks for the heads up. I appreciate it." Mike shook Mase's hand, and in a blink of the eye, the big guy just lay collapsed on the steel and glass counter throwing off his glass, making a big thud and quivering the bottles and glasses that rattled over the counter. Everybody's gaze directed toward big Mase's corpse.

Immediately a few screams followed and everyone started running amuck near the bar. Due to the loud music and the bar being at the corner, a lot of people on the dance floor were dancing completely oblivious to the fact that a bullet had been launched in the bar. Mike's gaze instantaneously went toward the sight of fire but he couldn't capture a glance of the shooter who lodged a bullet on big Mase's back. Now the awareness of the death became prevalent with more screams and all of a sudden fear had spread like a wild fire across the dance floor and the entire club, accompanied by cacophonous music, had turned into a frenzied chaos.

Mike was in complete shock. He just watched his good business partner die in front of him. His hands were shaking as he tried to wake Mase up in vain. Mase's head rested on the bar on the side and his eyes squinted looking at Mike in shock with his mouth agape. Mike's brain was on overdrive now. He thought he should be next because he who was friends with Mase had to be their enemy and he didn't know if they weren't looking for him. With Mase's penultimate warning, it became all the more evident and reality hit him hard. Hairs on in his neck turned straight. With a reflex, he jumped from his barstool behind the giant bar area and ducked. Squatting, his eyes met two frightened but beautiful bartenders who were sharing the hiding space. Mike could hear the shriek and squeal of the patrons running. He stealthily signaled to one of the girls to his right asking where the back door led. She whispered to him that it went to the storage and folded to a narrow path, which led to a loading area at the back.

Mike hurriedly rushed to the door, pushed it open, and rolled into the tiny space that was filled with racks of liquor boxes on both sides of the wall. He then walked through a narrow path, which felt never-ending. Once he reached a wall in front of him, there was a small door on the right-hand side that led to a slightly wider, dark corridor. But as Mike approached at the mid-section, he heard a loud noise from the door slamming and footsteps. There was nowhere to hide except the dark chasm of silence and emptiness. It wasn't too dark to miss him. At least his silhouette would definitely draw an outline for the shooter. He madly dashed to the other end of the long corridor.

"Wait," a voice he heard so clear that he couldn't run. He froze. For a split second, he just closed his eyes and his entire life flashed at him. He thought he heard something different. He rubbed all that off from the mind's slate and focused on what he had just heard. He realized that it was a voice of a female and was more for help than a threat. He opened his eyes and turned his head slightly back and saw the bartender running toward him crying.

"Please, take us with you."

"Us?" Mike had already forgotten that there were two bartenders when he started on his escape route.

"Kayla is behind me."

"Hmm...hurry, did anyone see you walking this way? Did you close the door behind you?"

"No and yes," she replied, but her eyes were filled with fear.

"Okay, let's get the hell out of here, shall we?" Mike smiled to calm their fears down.

"How do I open this shutter?" Mike pointed to the rolling shutter at the back of the store which remained open only when a truck was there to unload the inventory.

"Press the red button to your left and that should do it," Kayla submissively answered.

Mike pressed the button and cold air brushed his cheeks and his wig's hair started blowing off, which he thwarted quickly by putting a hand on his hair and jumped off on the ramp. He helped the ladies climb down and dashed toward the parking where a white pickup was parked on a slightly worn down and dimly lit parking lot to their left. Mike tried to open the pickup's door, but it was locked. He broke the glass out of the driver's side door with his fist and opened the truck door, which sounded the alarm.

He climbed onto the driver seat quickly. He hadn't forgotten to hardwire cars. Both ladies followed and climbed into the truck. The engine grunted and the white truck took off madly on the street. A black Cadillac van hastily followed the truck onto the street. As soon as the truck went on the street, in the parking lot, Mike climbed down from the tree underneath where the truck was parked. He rapidly shed his wig, beard, the jacket, and the tie there. He sneakily went to the side of the road and captured the license plate number of the Cadillac on his cell phone's camera. He'd easily avoided the threat but he had to find out who these people were and what exactly they needed.

He looked around and quickly saw a Harley Davidson Fat Boy Lo lying on the side parking area with a bunch of folks talking a few feet away. It was unlocked and he swiftly jumped onto it and started to follow the van. The guy screamed and quickly other riders followed him. He followed the Cadillac through a couple of streets which was following the white truck. He had to be subtle without getting recognized. After a few lefts and rights, he saw that the goons had pinned the girls. He was still mounted on the bike but now halted and hid behind parked cars in the downtown area and watched from a distance about a block straight ahead. He had luckily avoided the Harley riders. He saw that the guys got the girls out of the truck and started searching the truck. He could see the frustration of the two men who were yelling and throwing their hands in the air. Now, Mike had to make his move. He turned his Harley directly toward the guys but suddenly, from the far end, he saw police car lights appearing in the horizon. He promptly changed the direction of the motorbike and took off. Before he took off, he saw that the goons also had noticed the cops and left those girls alone and moved on. He still had to avoid the other riders by getting rid of this bike, which he kind of liked. He took a few one-way streets but the thunderous sound of Harleys was hard to hide in a relatively quiet area of downtown at night. As soon as it was safe, he got an opportunity; he quickly got a taxi and left the bike in a downtown alley.

chapter

THIRTEEN

Mike couldn't sleep that night. He was in a complete shock. He was lying in the bed, thinking. *What just happened? Mase got killed. I could escape narrowly. And there is a mole in the team?* He had to wrap his head around all the different possibilities and the future of the team. *Who can it be? Why are they so desperate on finding it? They do have connections high up so it could be true? Or whether this is a mistake due to Shawn's stupid and careless act of firing at the cop last minute when the escape of Shahab had just occurred. The bigger question is how do I know the truth? Also, now who should I take our next assignment from? Who can I trust outside and inside? Fuck, if what Mase said was true, then we'll be in deep trouble. If the cops hadn't come, I did have a chance when I followed the guys from the bar.* He wallowed in the bed, weltering in confusion.

Somehow, the seemingly never-ending night ended but Mike was still groggy with a headache when he woke up to the bell that rang on his apartment. He rubbed his eyes and suddenly was wide-awake with some thought and quickly took out the revolver from his drawer. He stealthily stood up from the bed, stepped sneakily without making any noise and reached to the door and looked through the peephole with his magnum held in both hands to the side of his shoulder. He inched closer and looked. To his surprise, there stood a beautiful blonde with a kid that looked to be about seven years old. He couldn't recall properly, but it seemed like he'd seen the lady before. She was about 5'6" with carefully colored and layered hair, more lipstick than she really needed in a semi-casual black, wearing white corduroy capris and white-buttoned shirt. She looked smart with a heart-shaped face through her designed hair and had a well-maintained figure. He carefully hid the gun in his pajamas and opened the door halfway.

"Hi, how can I help you?"

"Hi, my name is Heather." She extended her arm to shake Mike's hand. "Sorry to bother you. Looks like you were still in the bed."

"Ummm...that's okay. I was up."

"I am your downstairs neighbor and...I was wondering if you could please babysit Jason, my son, for half an hour to forty-five minutes. I need to meet a client and the babysitter ditched me. You know how the teenagers are," she begged.

"Look, I'd like to help but—" Mike rubbed the back of his head and was interrupted.

"Please, it wouldn't take long. I'm in a hurry and I couldn't find anyone else so you're my last resort. I don't want to lose this client. I hope you don't have to go anywhere for about an hour. Sorry to impose on you like this but I'll always remember your help." Heather looked extremely beautiful, probably even more so while pleading.

"Okay, okay, but I've never done this type of stuff...so, he'll just wait for you for forty-five minutes or so, is that it? Do I need to feed him?" Mike asked.

"Great. No, I've fed him already. You just need to watch him while I am gone. Thank you very much. I really appreciate it." Heather carried a big smile now.

"You're welcome, but make it fast. By the way, my name is Mike." He extended his hand again.

"Thanks once again. I'll make it as quick as possible. Bye, Jason; Mamma will see you in a short time. Be good. Don't be trouble for this gentleman, okay?" She shook his hand, kissed the boy on the cheek, and left.

The boy didn't say anything and looked at Mike. Mike jerked his head to insinuate to the boy to come in and closed the door behind him.

"You wanna watch TV?" Mike asked politely.

The boy just nodded his head. Mike's loft was trendy and modern. He had a contemporary white microfiber sofa and love-seat and a circular smoked glass and steel coffee table sitting in the center of the room but adjacent to a wall and on the opposite wall hung a sixty-five-inch LED TV in his living room. Near the door was a giant fake tree in a decorative golden pot. The wall below the TV stomached a cool fireplace with pebbles and to the right of the sofa were huge sliding doors as an entry to a big semi-circular balcony. The boy walked on the plush, beige, abstractly designed carpet and sat on the sofa. Mike turned on the TV and let it run whatever was coming on. He went to the kitchen and picked out orange juice and offered it to the kid. The boy replied coyly, "My mamma said not to drink or eat anything from a stranger."

"Hmmm...that's a good advice but that is when you are with a stranger. Your mom wouldn't have put you here if she felt I was a stranger to you. Would she have now?"

The boy thought about it and timidly replied, "Okay, I'll have some juice."

"That's like a good boy," Mike cheered and poured the boy a glass of orange juice.

Suddenly his ears heard something that made him turn to the TV. He got the remote and turned the volume up.

'The crash of the giant trailer to kill Governor Sinclair in California was thwarted with cop's quick thinking. However, as we know, senior police officer Ray died at the scene. Soon the governor was securely taken to a safe location. This is one of the biggest direct attacks on any political figure other than the President of the United States so far. We'll cover more on this story as we've been giving perfect coverage of the incident for two days now. We have our expert Dr. Kraznichkov to shine some light on the incident.'

'Dr. Krazh, what do you think of these attacks and what does it mean to California?'

'I think the attackers are powerful since they knew exactly where to attack the governor. Someone will be soon coming out with a motive. To answer the second part of the question, I think Californians don't feel safe when they leave their homes anymore because if the head of the state is vulnerable everybody is. The government needs to take concrete steps to thwart and proactively search for this type of terrorist activities and nip them in the bud. The businesses and shareholders are suffering. If they as government set a few good examples only then people's faith can be restored.'

'You brought a good point—motive. We still don't have any ideas why the governor was under attack. Some say it could be anti-gay men, some say it could be military men just from the look of the attack, some say it could be some personal family members, or simply a terrorists' activity. What is your take on it?' the correspondent asked with a serious face.

'We can all speculate but I think the governor would know about it better. I am guessing that a huge team effort is going on to get to the bottom of the attack. Personally, I think it could be any of the above or someone else.'

"Can I watch cartoon channel? I don't like this channel," the boy said, interrupting Mike's thoughts.

"Shhh..." Mike paused the channel on his DVR. He looked at the kid without losing his patience. "Give me five minutes and I will change the channel. Okay, Jason?"

"Hmmm...okay." With a big sigh and raised eyebrows, the boy agreed.

Mike ignored him and played the channel.

'Thanks, Dr. Krazh. Now, what do you think about the terrorist Shahab who was brought here after he tried to escape once in New York. Does this have to do something with that?'

'As I said, we can guess all we want to but governor hasn't said anything. Or he might have which might have been kept under tight wraps from the public. It certainly could be but we won't know until something is disclosed to the general public.'

86

'Okay, thank you, Dr. Krazh. It is always a pleasure.'

'Thank you. Pleasure was mine.'

'That was our expert Dr. Kraznichkov in the fields of terrorism and gubernatorial activities and his book *Will Faith Decide Our Ultimate Fate?* is releasing this Friday, so buy your copies soon. You can order it on—'

Mike first changed the channels to see if some other agency was covering the stuff or if governor was saying anything but nothing else seemed interesting. Then Mike zipped through channels to get to Cartoon Network. The boy noticed that Mike's facial expression had turned grave but the kid was happy to concentrate on the cartoons.

Mike speedily went to his bedroom and started pacing in the room thinking, *That was the reason Mase got killed. So the whole drama was still to try and rescue this terrorist. They are still attempting to rescue Shahab, but if that was the case and if they didn't trust us why would they hire us again? That doesn't make any sense. Were they testing us? But it's an expensive test? I don't think so. What if Shahab still doesn't get out? Does that mean someone in my team is bribed? If he gets caught again then...*

If I call a meeting and ask them directly, none of them are going to tell the truth. If I test them separately by giving individual tasks, all will have to perform and will perform. The only way to test their honesty, especially this one person, without making them know, is to test it live in the field and keeping tabs on everyone myself. I still have the element of surprise factor working for me. He thought of a myriad of things to clear his mind out of this knot.

Could it be Shawn? Shawn did shoot at the cop that alerted other cops. He also thinks that I am incapable of running the team that I started. He probably doesn't have the ethics to stay honest and is disgrun-

tled. He doesn't look like he is on cops' side though. He may have gotten bribed by someone else to create a bad reputation for me and the group.

Mike's head was preoccupied with bazillion thoughts, commotion ruled the brain, and a loud doorbell brought him back to his tensed life. He hadn't realized that it was almost an hour and the lady was already back to pick up the kid. While walking toward the door it struck him and struck him hard. *Fuck, he also wasn't a part of the California job, and it went smooth.*

Clearing his expressions, Mike opened the door.

"Hi, I'm back. How was he? Did he give you any trouble?" Heather smiled and coyly asked.

"No, in fact, he is a great kid; behaved awesomely. I took the liberty and gave him some orange juice. Hope you don't mind." Mike talked as a benevolent neighbor.

"Great. Thank you very much for your help. I really appreciate it. Jason come on, we gonna leave." Her hand stretched out to grab Jason's.

Mike looked back on the sofa and smiled. "He seems to like it here."

"We should go out for coffee sometime, or you could come over to my place sometime." Heather looked into Mike's eyes and put it as casually as she could.

"Sure, thanks, it'll be fun. I'll let you know." Mike liked the idea but immediately he thought about Tina. She wouldn't like it a bit. He could have asked her for a coffee or breakfast but right now his mind was pulled in a different direction and now wasn't the time.

"Bye, Jason." Mike smiled, patted the boy, and rubbed his hands on the boy's hair.

He winked at the lady and shut the door behind them. The same thoughts came rushing back. *If I could only ask expert John to tap everyone's phone but then it clears John from the accusation. What should I do?*

chapter

FOURTEEN

Three Months later
Somewhere in the Atlantic Ocean

It was March's cold breeze that hindered Mike's cigarette from lighting. Moreover, it was the vastness of the open sea and the wind that followed which was making it difficult for Mike to light a cigarette when suddenly a hand appeared that covered his light. It was an elegant hand of sultry siren Tina who was dressed in a magnificent red gown that frilled on the side with a transparent large, red ribbon which hung from the waist down and laid couple of feet on the ground. She looked exquisite with matching red high heel Jimmy Choos. The breeze caressed her face. Mike was in a relaxing mood on the Imperial Bermudan cruise and was clad in a black tux leaning against the railing overlooking the Black Sea with a half-moon reflection and listening to the soothing lapping of the waves.

He took a long drag on his cigarette and looked into Tina's eyes, "You know I feel you were right. We should settle for something simpler. Look at the gorgeous moon and ocean's calming waters. We could probably live in Bermuda for that matter and be happy forever."

"Why so romantic and different all of a sudden?" Tina pursed her lips and smiled.

"The ambience itself makes you romantic. I looked at couple of old folks. You know they come to these cruises to forget everyday qualms and have a good time. Their lives are so simple. Here we are standing on this magnificent cruise ship's top deck looking at the ocean and I am thinking, 'Am I lucky or what to have you as my companion right now?' I mean, we still have to think of the job instead of enjoying all of this." Mike made a gesture with his hands apart and palms open.

A big wave splashed on the ship and Mike had to hold the bar of the perimeter to prevent himself from falling, and he grabbed Tina's hand so she didn't either.

"Hmmm…it is odd that you are not thinking about the job," Tina questioned.

"Job still isn't on till tomorrow and I am still worried that what will happen to these people, these folks. It's quite a big cruise ship." Mike's voice was shaky.

"Hmmm…I don't know. I am hoping they hijack this ship and ask for a ransom or whatever they want. Hope they don't do anything else." She shook her head and continued, "Ah, let's go to the party again. Let's dance some more and forget about it till tomorrow. As you said, romance is in the air and let's make the most out of it tonight." Tina tucked her hand into Mike's and pulled him away. Tina felt like a role-reversal. She was the one in the group who cared more about people and the damage that followed their acts usually and Mike was the one who seemed wisecrack at the time.

"As you say, sweetie." Mike and Tina climbed down to the lower deck and just before entering the elevator, Mike extinguished his bud on the side on an ashtray that was made on top of a small trash can. The doors closed and Mike turned to Tina and looked into her big entrenched eyes. Tina turned her head toward Mike, adjusted her lock of hair by placing it carefully behind her right ear, and blushingly asked, "What?" He suddenly pulled Tina closer from the waist and kissed her passionately on her luscious lips. She had to hold the bars from being off-balance for it to go long enough. Then she quickly pushed him straight when the door chime sounded. It opened to the grand foyer where the ballroom dance was going on. She rubbed off the smudging of her lipstick, straightened her chic dress, and wore a smile as she climbed off the elevator, holding hands with Mike. Right away the classic music from the fifties and sixties ballroom filled their ears.

A live band was playing with white tuxedos and black bows on a stage on the far left corner. On the wooden and mirror-polished dance floor, most of the men were suited in black tuxedos and the women were clothed in beautiful colorful evening gowns. They watched for a few minutes with a couple of drinks and the numbers changed from fast to slow and then fast again. From slow jazz, cross-step, and the Viennese Waltz to the fox trot, all kinds of choreography by the young to the oldies were visible. On the right side, the bar was buzzing with onlookers drinking and enjoying. The opulent foyer seemed to be decorated with colorful gowns dancing in harmony and spot on lighting was like pearls scattered and shone.

Mike and Tina graced the stage by their presence. The band singer started Billy Joel's *She's Always a Woman*. Mike and Tina danced the Viennese Waltz to full perfection to the song. Everyone was so intoxicated that they stopped dancing and gave way to watch Mike and Tina. It became their show and at the last pirouette that Tina did with Mike's hand, everyone was awestruck. After their masterpiece, everyone gave a standing ovation and clapped almost for a minute. Mike kissed Tina this time with even more passion. John and Shawn looked at each other and clapped. The sound resonated through the foyer.

Down below, Zach and Catherine were making love in their sea-side cabin. Their bodies were entwined and they didn't care about the dance or anything at the moment. Catherine didn't know it would happen so soon. Zach and Catherine's ways parted long time ago when she had quit the martial arts program. She didn't imagine that fate would bring them together again after all these years in such a fashion. She definitely wanted Zach and the last six months had proven to be awesome for her. Initially, Zach did have feelings for her as well but didn't know if she had the same so he kept low. In the last six months, Zach and Catherine had gone on several dates and had romantic dinners. Both had started enjoying each other's company very much and it was very visible to the group as well. Zach knew when the right time was—she had tears in her eyes when a month ago Zach got down on one knee in a restaurant. She couldn't believe she would have a companion for life being in such a business.

Unexpectedly there was a knock on their cabin. Zach was all spent to reply but Zach lifted his torso, looked at Catherine and replied, "One moment please." He sighed and put on his nightgown and partly opened the door. Catherine tucked herself under the bed sheets, even when she couldn't have been seen from that angle with a partially open door and she couldn't see it either.

"What is it?" Zach inquired.

"Sir, there is this envelope for you." And suddenly Zach couldn't complete his words. "Ahhh...what the f—" and he took a few steps backwards and as if inebriated, he lost his balance, swayed, and tripped on the chair without looking. With his hands high in the air, he slammed down sideways on the big bed. He didn't move. Catherine screamed and the door automatically got closed. "Oh...Zach, Zach." She turned him over only to find a shot had gone through his chest, the blood puddled on the floor, and was blotching on the sheets all over. Zach lay there speechless, lifeless. Catherine's vision was impaired due to the heavy tears that were ceaseless and she screeched and screamed while clutching the sheets with her hands. She then again heard a similar thud sound which was followed by a short, manly scream.

She then quickly dashed to the door and opened it to look outside. Right in front of the door was a wall that stretched both ways. The narrow corridor to her left and right was empty which was going to the other cabin rooms. Suddenly, she realized she was naked and her hands were blood soaked. With the back of her left hand on her forehead and wiped the tears off with right hand. She came inside, closed the door, and began thinking. She quickly got dressed and called Mike in his room. She could hear the ringing but he didn't pick up the phone. Then she tried calling John, same result. She then tried both of their walkie-talkies to no avail. She was confused. She thought of going up a couple of decks to the foyer where most of the people were gathered but was worried about Zach. Her mind was thinking about all the possibilities. *Who could have done it? Why did they do it? Was it related to a past vendetta? Why would someone kill my Zach?* Her crying increased and she sobbed and she started dripping from her nose now. *Why do they take whatever I love the most? Why does it happen to me?*

Her rational mind again took over and ordered. *You can't sit here any longer; you are at risk. Go to Mike first.* Again, she wondered, why Mike had asked them all to be separate and not gather all six of them at any time during this job. They could be in couples but not all of them together. But the time had changed.

Catherine arranged Zach's body and covered the bloody bed sheet parts under the blanket and cleaned up the blood puddle on the floor and streak marks off it. Then she quickly stepped toward the door, opened the door, and looked around. Her eyes were hurting and were all red and bulged out. She stepped out and quickly locked the door behind her and dashed to the left of the narrow corridor. At the end of the long corridor which was decorated in wooden panels, she turned left. She then darted toward the outside railing and saw a crewmember. She sighed with relief. She abruptly stopped and called the member, "Hello."

"Yes, ma'am, what can I do for you? Are you okay? You seemed to be rushing."

"Oh, I am fine. I was just trying to get some exercise. But which way is the elevator?"

"Take a right and another right at that light."

"Thanks."

She of course knew the way to the elevator but that was a quick way to avoid a longer conversation. She didn't think that taking the elevator was contradictory to the exercise part nor did she think of her bloodshot, teary eyes. Catherine just rushed to the elevator.

She had to catch Mike and inform him about Zach. She had to know more details on what's going on. She was in shock and several questions looming. *How do I get them all together?* The elevator doors opened on the grand foyer where still some enthusiasts were dancing, and to the right side of the atrium, was an entryway to another vestibule. Catherine scanned the dance floor, the bar area, the musicians, but couldn't find any of the teammates. She then hurriedly stepped to the right side entryway, which was connected to another grand room where a buffet was set up and the sprawling area was crammed with elegant four by four tables and chairs on a plush carpet. She could hear the rattling of glasses and bottles and the screeches that forks were making off of the plates and people constantly chatting. Her nostrils were flared with the food aroma that engulfed the entire terrain. Her senses worked but the mind was fixated only on one thing. Her eyes quickly located Mike and Tina in the buffet line. She had to be subtle. Just when she was thinking of approaching Mike, she thought of calling one more time. She pressed his number from the walkie-talkie from the far corner where she was kind of alone.

Mike was now away from the music and loud sounds and heard the buzz in his tux pocket and picked up.

"Hi, Cat, what's up?"

"Zach's dead."

"What?" he coughed and came out of the line and away from the crowd. Tina noticed Mike. "Who did it?" Mike's shock was evident.

"Someone shot him. I don't..." Catherine stopped short; she sobbed and couldn't keep her tears off.

"Calm down, Catherine. Are you okay? Where is he? How about the room keys? Is he secured?" Mike bombarded questions with evident fright.

"I am okay. I am here to your extreme left. His body is in his room. I've hid the blood under blankets and put a 'Do Not Disturb' tag on the knob. I've got the card keys."

"Okay, we gotta meet now." Mike whispered anxiously and sadly looked at her.

"How? You are the one who said we can't all be together in this ship," she replied through her tears.

"Let me think...Let's meet in John's cabin, it is the farthest one and has only one way to enter and exit. They are sitting to your left extreme table. Let me inform them. I will meet you there, room number 578. We all go there now but separately. Catherine, go after ten minutes and be watchful. If you think someone's following you, give me a buzz but don't take them to our door."

Shawn heard his radio buzzing. He was still casually dressed in an all-formal tux party. He pulled the cell phone from his jeans. John returned at his table after filling up his dish with variety of cuisines.

"Hey, Mikey. What a show you put on?" Shawn said enthusiastically in his usual British accent.

"Listen, Zach's dead. I want all of you to meet me at John's cabin. But we go all separately. Hand over the phone to John."

John could see Shawn's face turned all red and eyes wide open and clearly he seemed to be in a massive shock. Shawn's mouth was wide open when he turned him the advanced two-way radio without saying a word.

"Hello, this is John. What happened?"

"John, I want you to go to your cabin, but before that, disable the camera in your corridor. We are all meeting in your room."

"Okay, but what's the urgency?"

"Zach's dead."

John could now imagine why Shawn turned red and then all grey. John had goose bumps himself but he hid it well.

Everyone's mind was on overdrive with questions of why and who could it be. Mike took Tina in the corner and explained the situation.

chapter

FIFTEEN

Bermudan Imperial Cruise
Room #578(John's room)

Mike paced in a compact room with a large white bed in the middle occupied majority of the space, on top sat Shawn and Tina. John stood near the window on the opposite wall and Catherine sat in the vanity chair near the bed.

"Look, I am sorry, Catherine, for what happened but the bigger question is that are we all at risk here? I think so and that's why I told everyone to be separate. In this case, I can't say if it was good that you were there or not. Did the guy see you?" Mike had perspiration beads forming on his forehead as he spoke.

"He couldn't have. Zach was in the way and only opened the door partly." Catherine said confidently.

"Hmmm...and as you screamed he must not have expected a companion, so he closed the door and ran away?"

"Probably."

"Why did the bloody maniac not come and try to kill Catherine also?" Shawn had to state some of his mind's overflowing questions.

"He probably was not prepared for anybody else. I think our separate boarding and not coming together partly worked." Mike made his guess.

"Mike, I want to know the truth. What's going on? Why would someone kill Zach?" Catherine couldn't stop sniveling, but held back her tears and put a right-hand forefinger on her nose and thumb on her chin.

Mike knew that he had to be subtle and couldn't reveal Mase's event. "Look, I know you are upset. From whatever I know this person could be anybody. A psycho; an old, disgruntled friend; an enemy he made during his car wrecks. Because he was the newest kid on our block, it doesn't make sense that anyone would have anything to do with him yet. Because we've made quite a few enemies but no one fully knows our identity, did he do something stupid? Talk something about his past or our current job to anyone on the ship?"

"Mike, you are twisting it. You know Zach wasn't like that, and of all things, he definitely wasn't stupid. I didn't hear him say anything like it, at least for whatever time I was close to him during the check in and during the games we played." Catherine's tone was a bit fuming at Mike for the accusations.

"Would anyone have seen you with him?" John broke his silence and seemed completely aghast by the bizarre event.

"I mean we were close to each other but not like partners or anything. We mostly behaved as strangers who met and gave an occasional smile at each other," Catherine replied as the tears drip down on the floor. Tina comforted Catherine by patting her on the back.

"What about the body? The housekeeper will come tomorrow." Tina said.

"I've thought of something. Shawn and I will take care of it," Mike responded.

"You can't be seen near the room. If someone or this enemy caught you, it'll be game over," John demanded.

"John, I'd never do such a thing. As I said, I've thought about it clearly," Mike confidently replied.

"What's next for us then? Can we abort this job?" Catherine questioned.

"We are all in a shock right now. You can abort the job, but think about it. You are in the middle of nowhere. What are you gonna do? Here, you can't pull the chain to stop the train. Only when the time comes, our ride will be here. Let's be very careful. None of us will meet till tomorrow and be in contact at all times on radio. Keep your weapons with you. Agreed?"

"How can you say that, Mike? How do we feel safe to continue this job? Who knows if all this is a setup for us?" Tina demanded.

"Tina, as I said, Zach's death is untimely and a complete surprise and shock to all of us. We don't know the source of it or cause of it. If we don't complete our job tomorrow then we definitely will be under someone's gun because we'll lose their trust and they would be unsuccessful in whatever they're planning to do." After a brief pause, he continued, "All I'm saying is that let's not make a rash decision right now. We need to be careful every step of the way from now on."

"But we could just sit idle, lay low, and when our ride comes, we jettison off the ship." Tina picked her brain.

"Oh, and they would let you go free without doing anything. Although they don't know who we are, we also don't know who they are. They still must be keeping tabs on everything. I think the best thing is to complete the job and get the hell out of here. That being said, we'll monitor the situation till tomorrow afternoon and if I sense anything unusual, I'd call to abort it but until then let's treat it as a *go mission*. I need absolute discretion from all of you and it needs to be handled delicately now that Zach has left us."

"Aye, I agree." Shawn nodded.

"That's a start. Who else agrees?" Mike ordered.

"You seem to convince everyone, Mike. I don't care. If I see those bastards or get suspicion on anyone, I am going to kill those mother-fucking cocksuckers with my bare hands." Catherine's infuriated voice got louder.

"Catherine, calm down. You can jeopardize all of our lives," John retorted.

"John's right, please keep your emotions intact. We'll try to find out who it was and deal with it later. Let's all finish our job tomorrow," Mike seconded that. "Hopefully, without any further issues," he added.

"Shawn, come with me. We gotta dispose the body off." Mike ordered.

Shawn nodded.

"Follow me. On the third deck down, I've seen the medical supply room. Sneak into that and get us two doctor's masks, aprons, and a gurney. I'll be waiting in Zach's room. Knock three times and ask for Mr. Powlowski and I'll open the door."

"Got it."

"Come out wearing one," Mike added, as he was leaving.

"Of course, you think I am a jackass, you arsehole," Shawn snapped.

Mike didn't reply.

Shawn quickly descended and got into the room. Successfully, he brought out the gurney and headed straight to the big elevator. Luckily, he didn't have anyone in the elevator late in the night. The elevator opened up on the fifth floor and a crewmember was standing right in front of him.

He asked insouciantly, "Is there an emergency?"

Shawn's face was covered with a mask and a hat on his head. He replied, "No, I need to clean it up. I am going to the wash area."

"Oh, that's on fourth deck. You are on the fifth."

"Oh, I must have pressed the wrong button." He quickly pressed the button to close the doors, but as it was closing, he held one side of the door with his right hand and asked, "Do you want to come along?"

The person shrugged. "I am going up."

Shawn looked at him and could barely say "Okay" before the doors shut down and he went to the fourth floor. Shawn waited there for another five minutes and his radio squawked, "Where are you?"

Shawn replied in his hidden earpiece under the mask, "I had to go to the fourth because of a crewmember."

"Listen, shed the gurney and clothes. Don't need it," Mike ordered.

"What? Mike, this is not the time to improvise mate. I barely made out of the supply room."

"I'm not improvising. They've cleaned up here. There is no body or no other trace that Zach was killed. Nothing. Nada. Zip. It is clean as if the housekeeper just made it."

"Shite! Now what?" exclaimed Shawn.

Mike was really worried but he didn't want Shawn to know that this time he didn't even have a clue what their next step should be. *Maybe the killer came again to look for Catherine but couldn't find her and cleaned up his act, or he very well knew that no one was going to be in the room and it was a perfect time to clean up. But why clean up at all? Why not let Catherine or someone else take care of it? That would have made Catherine liable. Maybe the murderer was worried that Catherine might have seen him, but then Catherine's not out of trouble.* As a leader, he had to instill the confidence in his team, so he said, "Nothing. They made our work easy, but that leads me to think that they also might be worried that an investigation can invite troubles which 'they' also don't want. So, hurry up! Don't talk to anyone and go to your room." Although Mike put Shawn at ease, inside him, the turmoil continued; it churned like a tornado. *What does it mean?*

Shawn replied with an all-pale face, "Okay, then I'm leaving this shitty floor now."

Mike asked everyone to be very watchful and be in their avatars at all times. He recommended everyone to keep low till the morning. Everyone left for their room from John's room with the same thought. *What's up with removing the body and clean up?* Everyone seemed a bit tensed. Although Catherine was tough, today, she wasn't keen on demonstrating her strength or will power. She stated flatly that she wasn't going to stay in the same room where Zach got killed. She requested that she stay with someone else for the night, and since Mike and Tina were perceived as a couple to others, it was either with John or Shawn. She wasn't comfortable with either of them; however, she opted to stay with John.

The next morning the bright sunny skies drenched the decks of the gorgeous, gargantuan ship with ample sunshine as it was chugging along on serene ocean waters. On the center upper deck, a large swimming pool was crowded with young folks who were having fun. A series of lounge chairs stripped blue and white were lined along the length of the pool with aqua blue umbrellas on top which seated a lot of ladies who were craving to get tanned. They were all clad in their fancy bikinis and sipping on their martinis and an on-board masseuse was massaging a lady in the center. The ocean could be heard from anywhere on the ship except here because of the loud party music being played around the pool area. The occasional chirping of birds that travelled across made it feel like they were closer to the shore; however, a full day was to be completed at a mere twenty-eight nautical miles per hour speed of the cruise ship.

The nice warm breeze brushed the cheeks of Mike who was on the extreme right of the pool practicing surfing on indoor, artificially created waves. Tina sat in the lounge chairs with a series of other women in a magenta bikini which accentuated her beautiful body. She lifted her straw hat, peeped through her goggles, and watched Mike struggling with the waves. She wanted to be with him but the protocol was strict and she had to obey it. Although she appeared calm on the lounge chair to the outside world, her mind was on Zach's death. She had a kind of tumult in her head which she couldn't describe. She couldn't concentrate on anything and seemed like she wanted to be with Mike at this moment.

On the other hand, Mike's mind was also battling to forget what had happened last night. He tried to concentrate on surfing to digress his attention to something else other than yesterday's setback and what they'd done to Zach's body. *What if they put his body hanging somewhere visible to the public? What if they put it in the captain's cabin? But then why clean it up in the first place? Who are these guys? Is it even safe for the team anymore? Fuck, there is no other way before our ride arrives.* He had explained to the team that it was better to be in middle of a crowd for safety reasons rather than alone like Zach. A barrage of queries still puzzled him. Suddenly, he fell flat on his face as the surfboard went flying to the backside and hit a fellow surfer. A few kids had a good laugh. He pulled himself up as if doing a push up. He wiped his eyes and gave them a stern look. He turned around, walked, and snatched the surfboard from another surfer who'd helped pick it up from the artificial waves at the backside. Looking at the mishap, Tina all of a sudden came forward from her leaning position and glanced at Mike, who was about to leave for the stall showers. She shook her head. He closed the shower door and turned on the shower. He'd already told Tina to take over Zach's part which was a minor one compared to his trucker's role in California. He still wanted to give more experience to Zach before giving him big assignments. Since he was an expert driver, the California job had made somewhat of sense, and that too was after a lot of convincing by Catherine.

John sat in his room cleaning the tools that were needed for tonight. His mind was also filled with memories of yesterday.

It had been a very tough day for the team and was shocking, especially just before the mission. He was hoping that no one botched today's task on account of yesterday's dreadful event. Futilely, he'd said the same to Catherine at night in his room but she was in no mood. He had tried to console Catherine in vain. She didn't speak at all and left in the morning before John had woken up. Her side of the pillow still felt wet. John stared at it and sighed.

He then looked outside his small window and pondered on what they were really going to do with this hundred-thousand-ton behemoth and the 3,500 odd passengers on board. He also regretted that he couldn't explore the variety of entertainment this vessel provided, such as the spa, the casino, library, and clubs. He would get himself a vacation like this but only with a private balcony from his cabin. Because of the stealth operation, Mike didn't want too much attention and probably didn't want to spend too much either, except for Catherine's cabin which had the private balcony for a purpose. John still managed to check out the pool and the open theater at the pool, hot tub, fitness center, and a Broadway show that the ship pompously advertised. He thought the vacation was worth it, only if it could linger longer.

chapter

SIXTEEN

Mike heard "Ready" from all four of the team members at about 8:00 p.m. on his earpiece. He was now completely sold that no one was going to ruin the task anymore because nothing happened to anyone from last night till tonight. He had to focus on the job at hand, although his mind kept asking the same questions. *Zach? I never thought of it; good that at least Catherine's safe.* He did his best to keep away the doubts and lead with confidence. The first time he was experiencing an unnerving feeling, he felt like he wasn't in control so much, but then he definitely looked calmer today than yesterday. At least some things were out of the question. The call he received from 'The Boss' came across his mind several times today.

"All right, Shawn, you ready?"

"Yes, boss. Are you ready?" Shawn retorted.

"I'm leaving now," Mike replied.

"Just buzz us when you get the access," John said authoritatively.

Mike reached the elevator and went all the way down to the third deck where the passengers were allowed to go. Not much was going on at the third deck, but it was a good spot to find the crewmembers who were doing their daily chores and there were only a couple of people on the other side of the ship's deck. Most of the people were enjoying the Broadway show; some reveled in drinking in the hip club, a few were watching cinema or dancing on the floor while others were busy eating on the upper decks.

Mike spotted one crew associate on the right-hand corner who was tying a rope to the end bar. There was no one around in that hour. Mike suddenly collapsed and bubbles started coming from his mouth. The crewmember saw it vaguely from a distance but he got the hint. He quickly dashed toward the passenger who'd just collapsed. He came and reached down to him and asked "Are you okay, sir?" Mike swiftly thrust his powerful right hand onto the squatted feet of the crewmember and hit it hard. The guy groaned and fell flat on the floor on his belly. He quickly tried to start the radio that hung on his waist but Mike kicked it out of the waistband and it flew across the floor with a thud. Mike then stood up holding the guy's neck with his left hand in front of him and smashed a big wooden block on the back of the man's head. The guy screamed but Mike's hand was on his mouth from his neck before he hit it. And on an empty deck, his muffled screams were drowned in the ocean waves. Mike rapidly dragged the guy into the medical supply room and changed the costume. He now was an official crewmember with access and radio. The guy's nametag read 'Rodelio Retuta.' Mike definitely didn't look like a Filipino so he removed the tag but kept it in the pocket in case he needed it. Mike wrapped the guy's body with the sheets and dragged it to the other side where there was a facilities closet, he opened it with the guy's keys and shoved it him inside and locked the door.

He quickly turned to the elevator and inserted one of the special keys, from the bunch he just got, which went in the side panel which made it possible to access the lower two decks. According to the research, there were other elevators and freight elevators but this one was more toward the back of the ship, a few people knew about it and crewmembers were the only ones who used it. The cruise ships were so big nowadays that not all members knew all other members. There was engine staff, cooking staff, facilities staff, entertainers, bartenders, program coordinators, instructors, musicians, and the list went on and on. It was impossible to remember all 1,100 plus crew members. Mike was still careful after yesterday's event.

He squawked on the radio, "I have the access. Are you guys ready?"

"Yes," Tina replied in the radio. A confirmation was also heard from John. The elevator opened on the third floor and now Tina and John entered the elevator, accompanying Mike. The overall uniform with their checkered trousers and shoes gave them a genuine look of cooks or their assistants. The nametags on Tina's white chef's coat was 'Mila' and John's said 'John.' All three had grave looks on their face.

The elevator doors stretched apart on the second deck and Mike noticed two crewmembers waiting to board the elevator to go up. Mike greeted them and gave a half-hearted smile which was reciprocated similarly. He quickly made a move to the doors to his front and tried to open the door with his card keys. The door didn't open. Mike's hunch that the keys would work proved wrong. Now, he had to find another way. Both John and Tina stood behind him looking at their watches. But to their horror, the elevator doors parted again and the same two members who had just boarded the elevator were back, as if the elevator didn't even move. Mike was now alert and he had goose bumps dancing under his authentic uniform sleeves. He had to think of something immediately. He bent down and started tying his lace to avoid the contact and any further talks. One member said to another, "Wait here, I'll just be back. Don't know how I forgot it?" Mike instantly used his brain and took the opportunity and said with an accent, "Hi, I can't get in, but I asked Jose to come to talk to me outside, can you please let me in? I've brought these guys from the other kitchen as the folks here are slammed and short-handed." The guy stared at it him for a second and then gave a nod. "Thanks."

Once they entered the two massive doors, the guy quickly took something from the right-side front cabin and took off and the door was shut behind Mike's back. Tina and John promptly followed Mike. They could hear the hustle and bustle of a typical industrial kitchen. The murmurs grew louder as they approached and the rattling of the pans, hissing of the flames, the aroma of the food; it all became inescapable surrounding them. They were in fact in one of the giant two kitchens that served this behemoth's hungry passengers. John looked at the huge steel panels and counters, and behind them the chefs and sous-chefs were rushing because the cruise served a buffet for lunch and dinner for a total of twelve hours, along with several elegant restaurants on board. They knew that they were still out of the sight from kitchen members because they could see all the cooks sweating to their left and they were still away from the real heat with a wall that was five feet tall next to them. The kitchen was half-open for more ventilation and the narrow path that they were walking on had a huge ventilation duct above them. To their right there were small cabins. More to their right ahead, Mike saw cabinets more like home kitchen cabinets and he knew that this was what he was looking for. This was the excess pots and pans storage area. He opened one cabinet door and found it full of silverwares. He saw big bags made up of net-like laundry bags lying in the corner which were full of what looked like the uniforms of chefs, bus boys, waiters, etcetera, plus a lot of bags filled with tablecloths, napkins, and decorations. At the end of the alley, to his right, he saw multiple carts. He found the one he was looking for and quickly cleared the way to take it out. "That's what I am looking for," he uttered aloud.

"Isn't it too big?" Tina questioned.

"Maybe, but it'll fit John fine," Mike answered with a grin. "Actually, that's a good point. This is big enough to even fit me. John, do you want me to do this?" Mike asked.

John looked straight into Mike's eyes and said, "Mike, let me do this. I know I can do this. Besides, I know more about this cruise ship than one anyone else." Mike saw an unusual fanaticism in his eyes. Mike raised his brow but nodded to him in agreement and said, "Okay."

"The elevator should be on the other side." John was making a calculated guess. The engine crew was isolated in their area and the public didn't have direct access. But according to the research John did, they had separate elevators, one of which ran into the kitchen. A kitchen staff member could directly bring in the food for the engine crew, which only led to the shaft and mechanics area, then you needed a separate clearance to enter into the engine area. Since 9/11, the engine room tours had been a no-no, so access to the public was completely off limits.

"Tina, get the food. I see there is some prepared food lying outside the door ready to go," Mike directed. Tina moved along the pathway to find a door which gave away some light from the kitchen where carts packed with food bowls were sitting ready to be taken away by the crewmembers to the various food areas throughout the ship.

"I'll get the cloth." Mike hastily grabbed a tablecloth from the storage cabinets.

Mike pulled the cart and placed a large, satin, beige cloth on top of the cart to cover the bottom's empty portion. The top would sit the food for the engine crew. Tina signaled with her hands to come along the narrow pathway and take a right, which was another pathway but dimly lit and going in another direction. She quickly moved one cart from the kitchen side, joining Mike, and placed three to four big bowls that fit on the top of Mike's cart. John hid perfectly inside the bottom shelf of the cart covered on all sides with the satin tablecloth.

"Good luck. Let me know when you're done. Follow the plan." Mike raised his right thumb and started swiftly moving toward where he entered.

Tina dragged the heavy cart to the inner elevator. A couple of kitchen staff had seen them but fortunately, nobody stopped them or bothered them with questions as long as they were doing the work especially in their uniforms. Tina pressed the 'Lower Level' button in the elevator and as the elevator was sinking in the bowel of the ship, Tina's stomach had that same sinking feeling, though she was very much focused. Her luminous beauty had to be dulled somewhat to look like a Filipino named Mila. She had applied slightly darker make up and had dark hair oozing out of her toque-shaped hat. The elevator door opened into a small space from which she effectively steered the bulky cart and took a left which opened into a somewhat bigger cabin area which had some machinery but mostly isolated. As she paced further, she could hear a couple of folks chatting but couldn't see them whether it was coming from the closed doors to her front or from the other side of the walls to her right was a question. She steered to her right and saw two crewmembers talking while noticing the gauges that were in front of them.

One guy noticed the kitchen staff and said "Hi, what timing. We're just talking about you."

"Me?" Tina gave a puzzled look.

"Oh, I mean the food. I was just asking him when it was gonna come," the guy replied with a smile.

Tina smiled back and nodded.

"You look new, where is Joshua?"

"Sir, Joshua was on a break and we're slammed upstairs so I brought it. Do you want me to go inside and place it on the table?"

"No, that won't be necessary. I will take care of it. But usually Joshua brings three carts together. Did you fit everything on one?"

"No, I am going to bring the other two; I didn't know how to get them all together." Tina smiled to hide the ignorance.

"No wonder you put a fancy cloth on the cart. Generally, the restaurants get them. As crew staff members, we are not treated equally." He smiled and continued, "Nevertheless, drop this cart and bring the other two. We'll put this one in. Oh, and don't' worry about the cloth on those two. We'll be fine without them." He smiled and turned back to the other guy.

Tina wasn't prepared for that but she had to improvise. She reluctantly smiled and said, "Okay, I'll be back."

She hurriedly stepped away from the cabin area and strutted toward the elevator. As soon as the elevator door closed, she spoke on the radio. "John, you stay put in the cart for now and if they take you in, finish it. If you are still outside once I bring the other two carts, we'll finish it." John had no choice. He couldn't say a word.

Coming out, she quickly took a right and stared at other carts that were ready to be taken. From inside the kitchen area, a cook noticed someone had come to take the carts so he just waved and Tina waved back and took two carts. She clumsily pulled one and pushed another and managed to fit them in the elevator. She again came down. She took the same route and saw that the other cart was still there, outside the engine room area. John hadn't got the access to the inside yet. She thought of avoiding what had to be done. The men were still chatting.

"Here, do you want me to help carry one of the carts inside with you?" Tina asked.

"No, will do it. Don't worry about it." He turned back and they continued on with their chatting.

"Okay." She turned around to go but she made an about turn that very second, and with lightning speed, she pulled out a tazer gun and triggered it on one guy. The other guy went to run but immediately another shot went at him and he also collapsed. Both men were still shaking and limping, groaning when John came out of his veil and helped Tina tie the guys up. John quickly hurled the guys into a small chamber to the right which held tools in the mechanics area. They accessed the tools room door with their badges and locked them up. John's kitchen staff uniform got exchanged with an engine crew uniform. There was no time to waste. John got back in the cart and with the access card, Tina drove the cart inside the chamber which held the engine room.

chapter

SEVENTEEN

They were now practically in the bowel of the cruise ship. It was an open space and there were ramps up on to their left which probably led to the humongous engine room. She saw a table which had some food to their extreme right. Tina noticed around the room there was another wall behind which there were some engineers looking at the dials and working on the computers. John had briefed the team that this room is always manned even when the ship is on autopilot most of the time. Where she stood, she didn't know what that room was for. The room boasted of some pipes and machinery but only two people were there working on the desk looking at a bunch of screens. There was a big whirring noise in the background and some occasional beeps could be heard. One of the two officers saw the door opening and came to her. "How did you get access to come inside?"

"Sir, the gentlemen outside said you could drop off and leave."

"Hmm. Hey, did you hear that? Those dumbasses said she could come in. Slackers," The officer said to the other guy.

"Okay, I'll handle it. You could leave now," the officer told Tina.

"But, I've other two carts outside," Tina argued, to create a window of opportunity for John so he could do the task."

"I'll get the carts in. In fact, I'll ask those slackers to bring them in. You can go...uh," the officer stared at Tina's nametag, "Mila."

Tina now had butterflies in her stomach. She didn't know what to argue with the officer who was adamant of her leaving the room. If she used any weapon here, it would bring a lot of attention. She and John could take the two men in that area but the ramp to the left led to doors which can open at any time and the glass wall in front of her showed a lot of the members who were working. It was too much risk. She had to comply and rely completely on John now. She reluctantly left the room; however, she had to perform another job to the other side of the inner elevator which she came from. John had heard the conversation and understood the implication.

The officer switched his radio and called the guys but they didn't answer. "Hmm, slackers. I'm hungry," he said aloud and went outside to get the food. As soon as John heard the door opening, he saw an opportunity. He peeked through the cloth and saw that the guy in the room was intently focused in his work and officer who was talking had just stepped out to get the carts. He snuck out of the cart and steadily marched to the ramp up which was about five steps and then took a left. He was out of sight from the man working, but the officer outside could be able to see him on his left once he faced the room if John didn't hurry up. John faced a door on the ramp which he swiftly opened it with his key card that they stole from the engine crewmembers who were now naked without the radio and tied down in the tools room. He swiftly opened the door and the noise was all consuming.

He looked around. It was a labyrinth of iron walkways around the giant space with steep ladders running down. The meshed iron walkway he stood on seemed greasy and filthy but his encyclopedic mind was impressed by looking at seven-cylinder engine, electrical generators, and distillers. He calculated that the engine on an average day would easily consume thirty tons of fuels. His thought was abruptly disconnected by a crackle on his radio.

"Are you there yet? Tina told me about the situation," Mike asked.

"Yes, I'm here. Give me five to ten minutes and I should be done," John replied.

"Be careful. I don't want to lose another...mate today. Get the job done and get the hell out of there. I will see you at Catherine's in fifteen," Mike ordered.

"Okay," John shakily replied and sighed.

John viewed the vast rectangular area. He quickly walked to the other side of the wall and took a ramp down on the iron ladders but couldn't locate the engine shaft that turned the propeller at the stern. He looked around, checked a few pipes, and found that one was running the fuel. He gauged it with his hand but found it too thick to be punctured with his small instrument. He still took it out and started his battery-operated widget to drill down. He turned it on and there was a shout from his far right. "Hey, what are you doing?"

"Chh...chhh...check this gauge out, man. I see high pressure," John shouted back, trying to appear as confident as he could in his engine crew uniform.

The guy was far away and couldn't see John's face properly but he was on the far corner upper walkway taking the ramp down to see John. John quickly shifted to his right where a big, iron-studded, white, round wall that covered the base of the pipes where they rounded off. He hid behind it. The guy came to where he had seen John but didn't find anyone so he turned on his walkie-talkie and instantly John came from the back and grabbed his neck with one hand and hit his other hand to relieve him off his radio. Radio flew inside the labyrinths of pipes and machinery that swallowed this entire area. The guy hit a back elbow and John fell down on steep iron plank that hung about fifteen feet from the floor below. The guy came near, gritted his teeth, and kicked John again to try and make him fall off the plank. He smashed John's hands that he hung from to avoid falling on the giant hot pipes that were going beneath him. John now hung on one hand. The guy stood on top of the plank stomping on John's one palm that'd clutched the mesh. John moaned and groaned. He could hardly hold it. The hand was giving away but suddenly his second hand flew through the air and his Swiss army type small drill whirred directly from beneath the mesh into the guy's left shoe. He screamed and wobbled and eventually fell down thumping his head on the giant pipes that snaked through the room. John placed the gadget on the plank, got a firm grip of his left hand on the plank, and finally climbed up. John hadn't notice that while falling off the plank the guy accidentally hit a valve handle.

Catherine opened the door to her balcony and stared at the stacks of half-rounded, glass-studded adequately lit balconies sticking out of the ship facing the sea above hers to the right side. Slightly chilled weather prevented many passengers from hanging out in the balcony that night. Most were enjoying the shopping mall or were at the restaurants indulging in world cuisine. Catherine was ready with her baggage. Her mind still rushed back to the moments she spent with Zach especially coming to the room had been tough. What could have been was just washed away in a second. She had done it once and she was confident that she'd find the killer this time around as well and put him to peace but she kept her focus today. Today was no ordinary day she thought, and she'd have to do much better than any other day. As Mike had it planned, Catherine's room's balcony was facing the sea and was at the lowest deck possible and was the first one starting from the back but it was still quite a distance from the balcony down to the sea.

A knock was heard on Catherine's room door. Catherine, now extra cautious, asked three times who it was and double confirmed it was Shawn and only then opened the door.

"Hey, how are you holding up, kitty cat?" Shawn asked, looking concerned. He hurled his bag on the small table Catherine had in her room near the bed.

"I'm okay. Are you ready?" Catherine didn't want to reveal her feelings and get emotional at this juncture.

"Yeah, I'm ready. I was just a back up so I had my vacation. Where are these bungholes?" Shawn smirked.

"I got a message from Mike that they are heading here," Catherine informed.

"Oh, but I didn't hear any alarm go off if bloody John had already created the inferno?"

"No, we have a situation. Tina had to leave at one point without revealing our identities so John is still there figuring out to ignite it and she had to do finish the part two." Catherine bit her lip.

"Oh boy, there is no task when we don't have a situation," he paused, "especially with me doing nothing," he added sarcastically.

"Yeah, but on this one we had a big one. Zach." Catherine hid the tears and her voice was again melancholy.

To avoid further conversation on that matter, Shawn abruptly answered it with a small 'yes' but then he decided to change the subject.

"Can you explain me once again how these damn bloody things work?"

"You just turn them on, hold it in whatever direction you want to go and it should work," Catherine replied, learning that Shawn had no intention to talk about Zach and grieve with her.

"Should? It must work," Shawn chuckled at her.

"Yes, Shawn, I've checked them several times and inspected with John. He's got them so should be perfect. But I also think these are the best. Dual Speed with three hundred and fifty watts of power. The twenty-four-volt batteries keep the charge up to about seven miles, or two hours, which should be more than enough for our purpose plus we'll lose our oxygen before that and as a safety measure, it cuts power at one hundred feet of depth but we'd go only about twenty-five to thirty feet deep because our suits are not made for more than fifty feet depth."

He whistled, "I'm impressed. You are the next nerd in our team after John." He looked at her and said, "Catherine, I'm scared since I've never used this kind of idiotic, deep-dive ocean scooter. What about the light in the dark sea."

"It has a light in the front as well but you all can follow me. We can't attract too much attention."

"Okay, sounds like you have it under control, lady. Here's the rope that you'd asked for." He handed the rope and sat down on the edge of her bed. He looked at the floor, breathed heavily, shook his head. Catherine looked at him and asked curiously, "What?"

He looked intently in her eyes, "You know, Catherine, I'm wondering why Mike called to join me in this mission. There was nothing for me to do."

"You do know Mike; there is always a contingency plan. You are his back up." Catherine raised her eyebrow and looked toward the ocean.

"If so, I didn't know about it. Why put poor John's life at risk when I can do it better than him. I was with him all along in this trip in our disguise and he looked scared of doing such an assignment by himself since he's never done it before."

"I think we all have to be capable of doing things that we think we aren't of. John's size made him perfect for this job. Once he successfully does it, he will be a more confident man. And you, mister, are always questioning Mike's leadership and trust so that could be another reason," Catherine replied tartly.

A big couple of knocks broke the conversation between them. Catherine looked at the time and said, "It has to be Mike and Tina". She confirmed, unlocked the door, and swung it open. Mike rushed into the room.

"Where's Tina?" Catherine asked with a baffled look.

"She had to finish another business. Damn! She is late but she assured me that she would come any minute." Mike shook his head in disbelief and removed his hair and makeup and saw Shawn and Catherine clean as well.

They all looked a little bit antsy but in their natural appearance, everyone was now looking better. Two nights with the wig, the makeup, the whole nine yards in the ship made them sometimes wonder what their real appearance really was, but then they were all used to it. Everyone had taken care of their appearance since the beginning of the journey and that too was after very little activity; such as cleaning of some sort, like brushing teeth, bathing, pool diving, surfing the waves, playing games, etcetera.

"Did you guys hear from John?" Mike asked anxiously.

"No, we haven't. We were just discussing our exit strategy," Catherine responded.

"Hmmm...let me radio him back. It is about time and we are running late." Mike turned on his radio and asked, "John, are you there?"

John had to find another way. John looked at his watch with exhaustion and knew that it was time. He had to make haste. The crewmembers could come anytime in the above room to eat and there would be no escape from there. His calculation was wrong for the first time. It really puzzled him that why the auxiliary fuel pipe had been so thick. He thought of a brute force that can break the pipe, but even in this noisy place, it would be very loud thud which would make someone vigilant but then he didn't have a jackhammer or Thor's hammer for that matter. He quickly thought that he could go to the tools room where they had captured the two officers to get something but it was too risky—to go and come back. He started walking on the sides near the pipe and followed it through a maze of mechanical monstrous equipments and finally on the right hand wall he saw something.

"John, are you there?"

"Yes, I'm in a bit of trouble but now I've found it. It is a little bit risky for me to come out of it and the damage could be big."

"Hmmm...well, we don't have much time. Finish it quickly whichever way and come alive out of it," Mike ordered.

"I will try to. Gotta go," John replied, panicking.

John's analytical mind began thinking and he heard again as if it was *déjà vu.* "Hey, what are you doing?"

John came out of the sliding doors in the corner of the big room where he was and turned around. All of sudden he noticed a man in the uniform was standing where the other guy had fallen down and this crewmember was turning a valve. John was sideways so he couldn't see properly but as he heard the voice, John turned and gave away his look. It was a little farther and the guy just asked casually on what he was up to but didn't seem to be as threatening as the previous one who immediately got in to a fight since he accurately guessed John's intention. But how did he not see the other guy that had fallen.

"The pressure has got lower here," John shouted, to be heard over the noise in the engine room.

"It may be because of this valve. I just realized that it was off. The bypass should have kicked off."

Just as the guy moved away from the valve, he looked down slanted and he noticed a crewmember was lying with a bloody face moaning. He screamed and looked at John on the diagonally opposite rectangular chamber but didn't find anyone. He panicked and quickly took the ramp and hit a 'red button' which was to the side of the wall and an amazingly loud alarm and emergency light went off. John rushed to the backside of the room and climbed the stairs up and started dashing on the iron mesh to the other door outside. But just as he reached the door, the door opened and two officers came rushing inside.

"What happened? Who are you?" asked one chief officer.

"Nothing, sir, I accidentally hit the buzzer. I am a trainee under Captain L'gouard." John tried to reply casually in his crew attire.

"Are you kidding me? You scared the bejesus out of us. More officers are coming here."

"Let me inform them and I'll trip the breaker," John replied.

"You do that right away, you moron. I don't understand..."

Before the officer could finish his sentence, there was a shout from behind at the bottom.

"Sir, catch that bastard before he runs. Ramirez is badly injured lying down here near the pipes."

John rushed outside and the officers leapt after him. John took a right and went out from where he came and two officers quickly followed him. While running, John said something on his radio, grabbed a pipe which was lying near the tools room, and rushed to the emergency exit balcony. He hutched it open and a hiss came from the air inside and John jumped without thinking. In the depths of the dark ocean, suddenly everything went blank and quiet, quite contrary to where he had been seconds ago.

A loud explosion rocked the floor of the cruise ship and swayed it from side to side.

"I'll go find him, Mike, you lead the crowd; but don't go too deep or too far, just hang in there about twenty feet near the ship and we'll find you guys. Don't turn your lights on yet. At just twenty feet they'll be able to see them," Mike nodded to Catherine's courage.

John felt the chill as his body hit the water and he sank about fifteen feet deep with his jump. He didn't notice anyone jumping behind him. He quickly treaded water and came up. His wig was floating beside him now. His moustache coming off, he tore it from his face and threw it away. With the contingency pipe he had in his hand, swimming was becoming difficult and, unfortunately, he was on the other side of the cruise ship than the team. *I don't know if they could even hear my last words. It happened so suddenly.* He started swimming toward the other side of the ship from the ship's rear.

The ship was still moving. It was dark and the ship seemed to be tipping over on one side. Because of the tilt and the big explosion, people gathered outside to see if the ship had hit an iceberg or an underneath rock. He went close to the ship and took out his pipe to breathe before going underwater to hide from on lookers from above. Now only the tip of the pipe strutted up in the air above the water and in the moonlight, it was barely visible.

Just before the explosion, Mike and Shawn were the first ones to go down on the rope. With the rope, it was now about a twenty-foot jump with the oxygen tank and the underwater scooter. Catherine followed them. As they slid down into the water, Tina hurriedly entered and wore the suit that was kept aside for her and she jumped last. It was very dark and there was not going to be any talking for a while, so everyone had to rely on their signals and had to follow one another. Catherine submerged in the water and everyone saw each other with the flickering lights at about ten feet deep before dispersing. Catherine started the scooter, which was just a steering and a propeller. She turned it on and the scooter's fan grunted and made bubbles. Catherine was suddenly pulled by the force and moved in the direction the scooter was facing. She quickly turned it left and went straight ahead. She was underwater and had to find John more toward the surface. The darkness made it difficult to see and lights were out of question so close to the ship. She made couple of small circles and one bigger circle but couldn't locate him.

chapter

EIGHTEEN

John thought about his genius at the right time. Inside the cave of the pipes in an enormous span, he found the room he was looking for. But the badge he had didn't work on the doors in front of him. This required additional security clearance. Immediately he thought of the other guy. He quickly dashed to the guy who had fallen off underneath the pipes. The guy's body rested between two fat pipes and one thinner one awkwardly in the middle of the room but to the side, close to the wall on his right. But to reach to him, one would have to know gymnastics or need a downward ladder. Neither of them were available to John and the clock was ticking fast. John went with the former one, but with a twist.

He took off his belt and hurriedly passed through the mesh of the iron plank he stood on and then locked it. Gravity did its work and the belt hung downwards from the mesh. Next to that, he firmly planted his feet onto the plank above, lay on his belly, and slowly pushed his torso over the plank with his hands. The blood rushed to his brain and hands. He was running out of time but he couldn't lose his composure to finish this task. He dangled upside down with his ankles hinged on the plank securely. He swung his hands to reach the guy's badge that hung on his neck but John missed by inches every time. He carefully brought his left hand back to his waist and took out his handy drill without looking at it, shifted the drill to his right hand, and cautiously placed the drill bit beneath the string that was attached to the guy's badge. His grip was at the edge of the power drill to get the length he needed. He lifted the string and pulled it up to make the badge hover slightly higher. Suddenly, he lost control on the drill and dropped it. The drill went down, even further. But with natural reflexes, he held the string with the other hand as soon as he dropped the drill and got the badge. In doing so, he almost lost his balance and the ankles were now just toes that hinged on the plank and it hurt. He put the badge in his mouth and glanced at his slight right, then he quickly grabbed the belt that hung close to his right hand and placed a firm grip on it. It was the most awkward position but that was his exit plan. After dangling like that there was no way he could have come up without someone's help or going down. Both weren't an option. His toes were planted on the plank, he dangled half way, but his torso bent to his right to clutch the belt he had placed appropriately before. He then let go of his feet from the plank and swung for a moment on the belt but swiftly grasped the plank with his right hand and pushed himself up with both hands, there he lay on the plank flat to take a breather.

But there wasn't much time to rest. He dashed toward the end of walkway and turned left where two massive sliding doors blocked his way in the corner. That was a highly secured area where the propeller shaft was running the engine. He scanned his badge, lifted the lever, and slid open a door to reveal the long shaft that ran the ship. He now saw a fat fuel supply line that came in and supplied to this monster. He started drilling into it but it had thick cover and he knew it wasn't going to be easy, and he was on overtime. John knew that it was going to be impossible to come out of this. Either he'll die in this chamber of the cruise in the middle of the ocean or he would be shot by the crewmembers when he tries to go out of this. He thought of worse cases but in either case, he definitely wanted to do the task at hand. He was way too invested and going back wasn't an option. John immediately spotted the bend in the pipe where the cover wasn't so thick and started drilling in it. Surprisingly, once he passed the cover, the pipe wasn't as hard to poke a hole through. He knew that on the dials above him, the crew would be alarmed of the dropped fuel pressure. This caused a switch to trip. Although modern ships are prepared for this kind of setback, John swiftly darted to small a platform near the crank and stopped the small reduction motor, which helps to reduce the RPM of the turbine that governs the propeller. His work was done here and to be inside this chamber for a minute longer was suicidal, so he thought he had to give himself a chance. He quickly opened the sliding doors and he saw the guy. Since the reduction motor couldn't cut down the speed of the crank, it ran rapidly. That, combined with less fuel, caused a massive jolt and forced the ship to abruptly stop. And since the ship was cruising at about thirty knots, the sudden thrust cracked the massive crankshaft and through that busted the generators. The leaking fuel helped in igniting the chamber. *It had to be massive damage. Man! I'm lucky to be alive*, he thought, while still looking for his teammates underwater.

Tina, on the other hand, dashed outside that area and went one more floor underneath where three of the big diesel generators were held. She scanned a badge, slid the secured door, and heaved it open to her right. With a noise that exceeded 120 decibels, she covered her ears with the earplugs that were ideally located at one of the two entrances. She scanned the area and, not finding anyone, quickly climbed up a narrow ladder. After a couple of turns, she located the diesel generators as John had explained. She carefully took out a box-shaped digital machine and a few detonators that were attached to the box, which she wore as a big belt underneath her uniform. She carefully hid the belt underneath a thick, white pipe and entered the number '15:00' and pressed the green button.

Tina traced her way all the way back to the elevators and graciously walked out from the kitchen area and ran toward Catherine's room when it happened. There was a monster earthquake that rippled through the floor and she was flung to a side and could barely hold on to a walkway railing. She thought she heard a huge blast and loud obnoxious alarms blasted in the corridor. She thought for a moment that the time she pressed on the bomb represented minutes and not seconds but then it occurred to her that it was not her, but it was John who was up to that task. With the ship swayed to one side, she tried to find her ground and swiftly dashed to the door and quickly took the emergency stairs and reached Catherine's room just in time.

The ship had lost some of its electricity with the initial breakage but with three backup diesel generators gone in just a few minutes, it had no lights, no air conditioning, no radar, no communication, nothing at the moment. Now it was just a piece of a log floating on the sea.

Inside the water, John's feet felt something gnawing at him. He panicked and swam away and looked down but he could only see a light coming toward him. Catherine appeared from behind the light and he was relieved. She signaled him to take the other scooter that was tied to her oxygen tank. John got the scooter out but his pipe was now in water and he was running out of breath. He slightly bobbed up his head above the water, took a deep breath, and dipped back underneath and signaled to Catherine where his oxygen tank was. She signaled with her hand to follow her. John started his scooter and went deeper to follow Catherine.

Catherine swerved and took two turns and they found the other team members. Everyone was suited except John. Mike and Shawn held the oxygen tank for John. He struggled in the water to wear the backpack straps of the oxygen tank on his back. Finally, he got it. Mike observed the whole situation and doubted that because they had to cover a long distance; without his suit, John wouldn't survive the distance and die from severe hypothermia by the cold waters of the North Atlantic Ocean. He didn't know what to do. He signaled everyone to move quickly. It was 10:00 p.m. at night and they were about seven hours from Bermuda.

The cruise ship just stood there now in a black out. People got panicked and some of them noticed the smoke coming from the back of the ship. Everyone experienced the rocking of the giant ship which created a chaotic atmosphere with screams. The crew quickly started checking the generators. The chief officer was trying to establish communication. The captain ordered that a few boats be dropped and capture the culprit that did the damage. Immediately, six security officers jumped onto two different boats and were lowered; they made a splashing entry into the dark and cold Atlantic waters. The security officers started the engines of their boats. If they didn't find anyone, one boat with two officers had to go all the way to the boat that the radar had captured before.

The utility water inside the ship was cold. People were screaming for hot water, electricity, and their safety. A large number of crewmembers were dispatched to calm down angry passengers. They announced that there was a glitch in the generators and a small fire had erupted but it had been contained and that they should be able to restore everything back soon. The captain knew that it was a pipedream. There was no way they could restore the connection back soon.

Tony was smoking, looking at the clouded sky with moonlight peeking every few minutes from them. He sat there, just waiting. He was thinking of why his boss wanted to work with these folks. He never knew anyone but it was a quick meeting with only the leader of the group and that's it. He had traveled a long ways from Harker's Island. Instead of an impressive luxurious private yacht, he had to take the underwater submarine that was used for undersea tours to use all by himself. But the irony was that he couldn't bring anyone with him, which really sucked; it was a courtesy of his boss. He had sat there for four hours now and was getting bored but he knew that the time had come. *They should arrive at any time now.* There wasn't much in there for Tony to get entertained. He was practically invisible in black water looking at the big fishes through the glass windows. He eyed at one of the posters to a side wall that read, "Enjoy the climate-controlled cabin and explore the underwater wild life just ten feet below the surface. Our semi-submersible vessel will blow your imagination with colorful sea creatures like bass fish, urchins, rockfish, jellyfish, and many more. Join the adventure today, call 1-800—" He stood up and walked toward the end of this small submarine and checked on the small boat that was tightly tied to his vessel. That was the cover. Once they leave the scene, the boat was going to stay there because the vessel would have been detected by the cruise ship.

Mike looked at his compass and signaled everyone, along with Catherine, to follow them. Just before the deep dive, from a distance, Mike noticed the boats that had launched in the water which he assumed were dropped to look for John. John was shivering but he had to continue. Mike didn't have time and there wasn't a way to communicate any changes with Tony. They were far from the cruise ship now and going deeper and deeper. The scooter was at full throttle chugging along at about thirty feet deep now. Only John was travelling at about twenty feet below the surface of the water because it gets colder as you go deeper into the ocean. They covered about two miles from the cruise and Mike decided to check on John. He moved the direction of his scooter upward. The fish moved away from his shaft of light and the whirring of the scooter. The current of the water was perfect, which made the operation a little easier. Mike gave a thumbs up to John and John reciprocated. Mike journeyed parallel to him before he decided to peek above the surface of the water. He couldn't see the boat that was dropped. The cruise ship sat in darkness and was still a giant piece of metal which floated in the water without much movement. The dispatched boats were not too far from the ship looking for someone.

The captain tried to look with his night vision binoculars but couldn't find anyone. With no communication working, no sonar or radar either, even if he found someone it was tough to get them caught. If only he could restore the communication, he could inform the authorities to look for the marauders. The only thing he did was to get some help on satellite phone from Bermuda.

Mike then dove deeper to avoid any potential risks. Mike's head was anxiously thinking if John could survive another hour in the chilly water. He had asked Tony to bring all that was necessary. Tony was Mike's friend and Greg's right-hand man. Mike used to get small assignments from Greg some years back. But Mike liked Mase because he had bigger connections and the money was better. Now that Mase was gone, Mike had called Greg to help since he couldn't trust anyone else. Same as Mase, Mike kept a good distance from Greg and his army. Mike still had the haunting memory of Mase saying, "Don't take any assignments other than me." He actually didn't take assignments from "anyone," but he had to get some help from Greg to get out of this weird situation.

The cold water crawling on John's body felt like he was being pierced with thousands of pointed javelins. He was now numb and couldn't feel much of his body parts especially the hands that held the scooter. The hands got stuck with the scooter and he couldn't let go of it even if he wanted. He felt a sharp burning pain for a long time throughout his body but now his body was just going numb. He was okay when Mike came to check on him, but he knew that he still had another half an hour to go and cover another three to four miles to reach the boat. Even with the light, his eyes were getting tired and the body wanted to shut down. He was at about twenty feet below water and no one was following so his survival instinct kicked in.

Tony was getting ready for dispatch. He looked at his watch. His sub had to be completely turned off because if the ship somehow communicated the problem, he may get asked to check on it or authorities might start coming along from the ports; however, before that he made the sub move its head bob slightly above water so that he can look for the team. The key was the time. Although there was less chance of authorities going from Jacksonville or Newport to the cruise ship because the location where the ship had stopped was ideal, the cruise ship was closer to the Bermuda than from the US coast. But in these difficult circumstances, the United States Coast Guard was always called to help and generally, the dispatches came along pretty quickly. Tony stood up from the tower to see and suddenly he heard something. He squinted his eyes but couldn't see anything, then he heard it back again. He looked through the manhole, this time intently, and heard clearly this time, "Help!" Tony's instincts told him to save the guy but he was on a mission and he couldn't botch Greg's orders. He didn't know who it could be. *A stranded fisherman?* He ignored it but again he heard, "Help!" The guy shouting must be about three quarters of a mile but due to the extreme calmness, it could be easily heard.

Completely oblivious of the fact that John was now in no condition to travel, Mike looked at Catherine and signaled to go up to everyone from the deeper part. The scooters had done a great job. Shawn and Tina followed them. Mike now was about twenty feet deep and couldn't see John around. He signaled other members to stay there while he made a couple of circles but couldn't see John at all in stark darkness. He then directed his scooter upwards to get to the surface. He saw John waving hands shivering half in the water screaming, "Help!" John had seen the black sub sitting about three quarters away and was trying to get it here. Mike immediately pulled out his oxygen mouthpiece and screamed, "Hey, John! Are you okay, man?" "No, I'm not..." His quaking voice couldn't complete the sentence. Mike quickly thought about the situation. He pulled out his scooter and quickly directed it to the sub and turned the light on and off a couple of times.

Tony now was thoroughly befuddled. He stared at the flashing light. He thought he was sitting there for four hours and not a single boat had passed nor did he see any far away except the giant cruise ship about eight miles away. The way the direction of light was coming was as if someone had come straight from the cruise ship to this small sub. It could be only Mike's team, he thought. Then he heard clearly, "This is Mike. Come over." Mike gasped while treading water. Everyone now surfaced to see what had happened to John. They all pulled out their scooters and flashed at Tony. Tony looked at five shafts of lights coming to him and he knew there were six passengers that he had to carry. He was still thinking why there were only five lights but his gut told that it was Mike's team. He climbed down, rushed to the engine room, and immediately started the engine. He didn't know what was wrong but he knew that something had gone awry and the team was not being able to make the last three quarters of the mile. The engine came to life and the worn out passenger undersea tour sub pushed the water behind and quickly reached close to the team. Still no lights. The team climbed up to the tower with Tony and Mike helping John climb up the board.

"What happened, guys? The lights could make them see us?" Tony asked.

"There is no time for it, Tony. I can't explain right now. We had an emergency." Mike breathed heavily and stood up after climbing on board with his hands on to his waist. He quickly shoved the scooter and the tank on the side of the open area.

"Get some towels and clothes. Let's take him to the inside room. Tony, release the boat and get moving," Mike ordered.

Mike and Shawn picked up John and lugged him to a small, lower deck facing the sea with a glass-paneled room. John was now a cocoon and his hands and toes were getting black and shriveled due to frostbite. They quickly wiped him and covered him with warm blankets and wrapped his hands and toes. They turned on the heater. The commercial sub already under ten feet of water started moving back toward Harker's Island.

In a tiny room, which probably held the crew and maintenance equipment, they all sat after getting cleaned up.

"This was a suicide mission. I had told that to Catherine in the beginning," Shawn remarked.

"I knew, Shawn, that you would start with your prejudice again. I am also hurt by Zach's death and John's situation but you know that these things happen, damn it," Mike barked.

"I agree with Shawn this time, Mike." Catherine looked aggressive.

"Okay, now gang up on me, guys. Tina, why don't you join in as if all this is my fault?" Mike gazed in Tina's eyes and squealed.

"Can we please stop fighting? I'm scared and I don't want to lose John. Let's concentrate on the next steps and how we can get John to treatment." Tina's sadness came through her voice. Everyone looked at her and felt a slight compunction. Mike swept his face with both hands and rubbed them go over his hair and to the back of his skull in frustration.

"Whatever medicine we might have on board we'd have to use. We are not reaching Harker's Island for next one and half days," Mike estimated.

"I will take care of John," Catherine replied. "I too don't want to lose John. I've lost enough. He has been a great friend of mine since my karate days," Catherine sobbed.

"Would they get the power back?" Shawn asked with sane mind.

"They had an emergency backup which I destroyed but they have a couple of auxiliary generators so they might be able to restore it but not the engine. Looks like John did some serious damage to the engine," Tina replied.

Everyone looked at Tina so she smiled and said, "What? Can't I say something intelligent?" After a pause, she continued, "Well John had explained to me his plan and I remembered it correctly." She chuckled. "So now you know it wasn't me again but it was John's intelligence." It lightened up the mood a little bit in the room.

"I hope they don't sink the damn thing," Tina sighed.

"I fear that too," Mike replied.

"Well, we'll see. This was ridiculously risky mission with a narrow margin for escape and we lost a teammate and John's lying on a deathbed now. Isn't it now?" Shawn's hostile tone echoed in the room. Again Shawn snapped, "Why not me, Mike?"

"I told you before that this mission was to provide John some exposure and you were my back up, that's it. If John had backed out last minute, I was going to give it to you. Or if the mission had failed, I'd have asked you to finish it. Not every show is Shawn's show," Mike irritably replied.

"You are so egotistic, mate, that you can put your teammate's life at danger. Because it has to be always your way or the highway," Shawn further provoked Mike.

After a pause, Mike breathed heavily but replied confidently only one thing, "Nothing will happen to John. He'll be fine."

Everyone dispersed but this was such a small submarine with plenty of open space to look sea creatures but hardly any additional private rooms. Two floors of glass-studded walls and tiny rooms at the end and that was it. Catherine went to the open area where John lay.

chapter

NINETEEN

After changing two airports—the Beaufort Morehead and Coastal Carolina—from Harker's Islands, the team finally reached the Carolina airport at different times as they all flew in different air vessel. As Mike had predicted, John had survived without any big issues. He was on heavy dose of cold medicines and practically dozing off throughout the journey due to the drowsiness. Everyone was drained, mentally and physically. The mission had taken its toll on the team. Everyone hoped a hefty amount after this suicidal mission but Mike's deliberation went to a completely different trajectory.

The commercial sub was never registered or had never logged where it went from Harker's Islands. Tony took the vessel to nearby islands to make it look like he was just using it for maintenance. On the way, he picked up a girl and enjoyed his catch inside the sub for a couple of more days before he packed his bags to return to Greg, his boss.

'The mammoth cruise ship was stranded in Atlantic waters for about eight hours before the tugboats arrived. The captain was unavailable for comment but the corporate headquarters spokesperson said that it was a difficult situation and they are trying their best to get the help. A few minor injuries are reported when the ship suddenly stopped due to the breakdown of the crankshaft after an engine fire. The cause of the engine fire is yet unknown. The Imperial Bermudan Cruise is giving a refund to all passengers and free tickets for future cruise travel. A passenger who I interviewed said, "It's like, 'See, you didn't get killed, try it again.'" It captures the sentiment for others as well. The passengers were angry because the communication and electricity weren't restored until after four to five hours of the fire. They had issues with emergency generator and people blamed that the crew wasn't prepared for any contingency. The gargantuan, state-of-the-art cruise ship has faced huge damage and now is being drifted via tugboats to Bermuda. The United States Coast Guard was the first to come to the rescue. No other ship was seen in the vicinity that could have helped and since the communication was down, there wasn't much the crew could have done before that. No statement of wrong doings were reported by the crew; however, a couple of passengers thought they saw some suspicious activity as the boats were dropped and search teams were sent. Police has denied any terrorist activity and maintained that it was a glitch on the ship. For RNNC, this is Jane Bricker. Over to you Carrie.'

The message had been seen by everyone at the Coastal Carolina airport at different times. They were all relieved but puzzled at the same time. Nothing had really happened!

At the airport, John was the first one to ask, "Mike, what just happened? They didn't do shi—t." He barely completed it with a big sneeze. He looked terrible with red, tearful eyes and he was sleepy, weak, and covered in two sweaters, a jacket, and a woolen cap. Whatever sparse attendance was at the gate, everyone looked at John like he just came from Alaska or Antarctica.

"I know, John, what you mean but I have the same question and I don't know what to say to you," Mike despondingly replied.

"Whoa, whoa, mate! Does it mean that we won't get paid after this shitty, bloodthirsty mission?" Shawn screeched.

"No, Shawn, we did our job and we should get paid. No ifs about it," Mike calmly composed his reply.

"We 'must' not 'should,'" Tina added, making quotation marks in the air with her beautiful fingers.

"Look, guys, I am sorry that I don't have a clear answer as to what happened and why there was no plan executed as I was told, but there must be some reason or they may have done it for sure. Who knows what they wanted from this? It's not like the Dubai job where we knew that they were targeting Prince Sheikh. We had a contract, we did our job, and we should get paid, period," Mike affirmed and looked away.

After a moment of silence, Catherine yelled, "Those fuckers didn't have the balls to do anything when we took all the risk and lost Zach in the process. Mike, you should not take any job from these guys."

"I need to talk to you guys about something," Mike said, but the conversation was brusquely ended with an announcement

"All passengers boarding flight 351 to New York are requested to arrive at Gate 21. We'll start the boarding."

Mike couldn't say what he wanted. Actually, Mike couldn't say a lot of things he wanted to say. Others were in the same boat while in the same plane. John's mind was going through a roller coaster of his own thoughts and the sedation was not helping either. Tina, Catherine, and Shawn couldn't figure out what would have gone wrong. There were so many questions. What did Mike want to say? Why had Zach died? Where did his body go?

Before they all went on their separate ways in New York, Mike had asked everyone to lay low for a while as usual.

In his posh room, it was dark with all the curtains shading the daylight. With eyes closed, head slanted, index finger and the thumb of the left hand clutching the upper part of his nose, Mike was roiled in his deep thoughts. The subterfuge was successful but at the same time, it didn't yield anything. He wanted to end all of it. He wanted to end it now. He wished he knew the identity of this guy. The turmoil continued with other thoughts like, *Although our masks and make-ups would have worked and the public might not know the real reason of the ship's smash up, the cruise crew would have counted the total head count of the passengers and definitely seen six people missing. The cops would have taken that into account and started an investigation on our fake identity. Airport and ferry logs would have been checked. Our posters would be already in the police stations by now and search would have been started. It is bad and good that we are in New York.* His mind wandered back to the events on the ship. *Why the fuck didn't he do anything with the ship? May be it was just a test. I should ask the team to—*

His thought process was interrupted with a loud phone ring. Mike saw the number. He reluctantly picked up the phone.

"Hello, who's this?"

"Hey, hey, hey, didn't recognize my number, big Mike?"
The voice was raspy and deep throated. The sarcasm was evident.
"I did recognize it but was making sure." Mike was subdued in his response.

"Yeah, it's good to take precautions in your business or you could be killed." A soulless laughter ensued in the background.

"What do you want?" Mike squealed.

"It's not what I want; it's what you want for your job," the unknown person calmly said.

"I want the damn money and want it now. You fools didn't have the guts to do your job."

"I would refrain from using such words, Mike. I can crush you any time I want."

"Why didn't you do anything? What was the plan, to frame us? You asshole." Mike's angry and authoritative dialog made the person give a long pause.

"Wow, I see the passion, but anymore foul word and your game will be over, you little fuck."

"You can't do shit. You don't know who I am. There is no more business with you."

"Oh, believe me; you'd be handcuffed by now if I just release your phone number with critical information."

"You know, whoever you are. I have been in this business for a long time now, and I know who I am talking to and what your motives are. If you would want me to get handcuffed you'd have done it by now but you want something else from me so you can't do anything to me. Oh, by the way, the phone is not traceable and obviously the address is incorrect," Mike smugly answered.

"Hmmm...you have a point, Mike, but I wouldn't count on it. I have a plenty of guys like you who'd risk their lives to make petty money, you know?" The guy said it in the most patronizing manner.

"Come to the point." Mike walked to and fro in his room.

"You fools could have done a better job by not alarming the crew." The voice got louder and angrier.

"Oh, wow, now you will teach me my job. Without alarming the crew, how were we supposed to put the ship in an inactive mode?" Mike yelled into the phone.

"Lower your voice, Mike. My crew has short-listed a few guys and we already know a couple of them guaranteed work for you. There was someone in your group who alerted the authorities. They already knew something was going to happen and my men were completely helpless."

"That's impossible. The crew should have been busy figuring out the engine fire and electricity issues. No one in my team had the motive of doing anything stupid like that especially in the middle of the ocean. You think I am stupid? Now when I come to think of it, from the beginning, this whole assignment was a ghost task where you just wanted to find us."

"Mikey, Mikey, I don't need this elaborate scheme to find you guys. You are trivial. If I put efforts, I can certainly find you. This mission had a dual purpose: to find the mole in your team and to solve my problem."

"We already talked about it. I assigned each member different tasks and all of them were successful. None of them are stupid. I fully trust them." Mike completed the sentence thinking, *except Shawn.*

"Did you know that the cops have already started an investigation on the six missing passengers?" A faint laughter was heard.

Mike thought about it for a moment. *He now knows how many people work with me.* He had no plans of telling him about Zach's murder, but at the same time, he wanted to know if they had killed Zach. It was a delicate matter. Mike regretted that when he took the job, the guy offered the opportunity to find the mole that Mase had talked about and had provided a lucrative task along with it, which now looked like a total failure.

"Any suspicions?" Mike prodded.

"Oh, did I tell you the latest information that cops found a body in the trail of the cruise ship."

Mike's heart pounded and his blood boiled. He screamed, "You fucker, you guys did kill him."

"Thanks, Mike. It was one of your team members then I presume, so sad." The voice echoed in Mike's ears.

Fuck, what did I do? I just gave him the information of Zach. He was speechless for a minute. The silence hung between the lines.

"I think I put you in a lot of trauma, Mike." The guy laughed hysterically and boisterously.

"Hell with you. I want the money or..."

"Or what, Mike? You don't know me. Don't try to exploit any options that you don't have and," he screamed in the phone loudly, "do not threaten me, ever." The Boss sounded furious.

Mike was now sweating. He didn't know what to respond. The fact was that he tried to look for anyone suspicious in the ship but he didn't thrive. He decided to keep mum before he made any other mistake. But then he thought if *this guy* knew that the dead guy was working for him, he couldn't have killed him or maybe he was just faking it to cover up.

"So you are saying that you didn't know who he was? And without any reason you just killed him?"

"Look, Mike, if I had known who he was he would have been abducted to get all of your information plus why would I want to botch my own mission."

"Because there was no mission. You just wanted some kind of revenge due to an old job which we successfully did and yet again your men had failed you so now you want to play the blame game."

"Mikey, I don't have the time for all this. To ease your pain, let's say that the police haven't been able to identify anything out of the body. The body is eaten so badly that just by examining it cops couldn't even tell whether it was a male or a female. However, another big piece of info is that they found a crewmember dead as well."

Mike suddenly had a burst of relief but at the same time was puzzled by the finding of another body. He calculated thus far from the conversation that he had revealed inadvertently that his colleague was dead, most likely not killed by this 'boss,' the mission wasn't completed due to the fact that The Boss's men were alert and found out that the authorities were already alarmed and security was tightened on the ship during the distraction. He was glad that he hadn't revealed any other details and everyone else was safe. However, the questions jumped which he wanted to neglect that who'd killed Zach, who this boss was, and what he eventually wanted. Why there was a crewmember's body was a bigger question. John didn't say anything about any crewmember who might have jumped after him and gotten killed.

"Did the crewmember drown and died?" Mike asked casually.

"We don't know yet, they are still investigating. So you see, Mike, I am not that bad after all," grinned the speaker.

"I want the money. I kept my promise," Mike fearlessly spoke.

"I want the mole. I'll give you the money as I promised." Without skipping a beat The Boss replied with the same fearlessness.

"I don't have any traitor. Damn it! Why don't you understand?" Mike then, with a pause, completed the sentence, "I'll see what I can do."

"That's like a good boy. So far you have been blinded, Mike. How are you going to find that asshole?"

"As I said, I fully trust them but let me talk to them to see if I can find a clue."

"It sometimes makes me think that you may be the black sheep," he guffawed.

"I am not afraid of you. And what are you going to do with my infiltrator? Why should I even reveal it to you?"

"Mike, I'll find you some day and then you all will be exterminated rather than just the leak link. How do you think I know what police found at the sea when it is not even made public at all? Don't underestimate me," The Boss coolly threatened Mike.

Mike had a sinking feeling in his stomach. He thought of ending the conversation before he messed up again. He just said, "Okay."

"You know, Mike, this whole assignment has been a complete waste of my time and energy because of your dumbass, back-stabbing teammates. I gave you this assignment so that we could find the mole and get this job done too. Also, to give you some credit, there are others but you are the best at this job and I pick only the best. I'll have your money sent tomorrow. I expect some leadership from you from now on."

The click that ended the phone on the other side echoed in Mike's ears. Mike could barely switch off his phone. It was the first time he felt helpless. He felt cornered. He was dealing with an unknown enemy who knew enough to destroy what he had created all these years. But Mike knew the 'boss' was right; if there was any back-stabber, he should be captured immediately. His hands were shaking with the phone still in his left hand.

Mike grabbed a bottle of water from the fridge and poured it on his head, as if it would purge his sins and show him the righteous path or clear him from all the anxiety he'd been dealing with. The only thing it did was wet him and the floor, which he had to clean up and change his shirt.

chapter

TWENTY

After Mase's death, Mike laid low for a while but couldn't for long. He started planning to work with Greg, or Mase's other man called Sammy The Slammer. He was evaluating both. Then one fine day, he received an unknown call. Mike clearly remembered the surreptitious phone call on a Sunday evening a few months ago. The voice had been dark and deep. It was threatening.

"You escaped narrowly, Mike. My men almost had you with Mase." The voice got louder.

"Who's this?" Mike asked.

"I am your friend," a cold reply came back.

Mike ragingly raised a question, "Who the fuck is this?"

"An enemy's enemy is a friend, remember? But who are you, my friend?"

"What the hell are you talking about?" Mike asked furiously.

"I am talking in plain English, my friend. You are the one who's confused. I've heard a lot about you but don't you think you should reflect upon your recent jobs," The Boss inquired coolly.

"What about them?"

"That you've messed all of them up and in that, you've messed up mine," a slightly angrier voice echoed.

"Who gave you my number?"

"I found Mase and you, isn't that enough to answer that question?"

"What do you want?"

"I want you to find the betrayer in your group or I will hunt you down and kill you all bitches," calmly but passionately the voice concluded.

"Incapability of your men doesn't suggest that my men are betrayers and you have no idea who I am. I've completed all my jobs successfully and if the ball is in your court, you gotta do something about it," Mike retorted loudly and irately.

"You don't understand, Mike, who you are dealing with here. Let's cut the crap. I want you to do an assignment for me," the speaker squealed.

"Oh, so all this is about an assignment. You could have come to the point straight. Why not contact my contacts? Why directly me?" Mike looked confused.

"Because I want to kill two birds with one stone. You'll find your spy and complete my mission."

"Wow, so you've decided that I have a traitor in my team and you want me to find it. No, I don't want to do the job. Ask someone else to do it. I am not interested."

"Wait. If you hang up the phone on me, I will send this info right to the cops. I will find you one day and then you'll beg for mercy crawling at my feet," menaced The Boss.

"Do what you like, you faggot, I'm hanging up."

"Don't be stupid. The money is great. I will pay you one million on successful completion of the mission. All you have to do is turn over the betrayer and complete the mission."

Mike's ears now paid attention. He thought one million would be a great amount. Mike thought about this guy's motives. *If he surely thinks I have a conspirator, why risk his job with my team. Why not go somewhere else?*

"The job must be risky and would pay you probably fifty times or hundred times what I am being paid. Besides, if you think I have issues in my team why pick me in the first place?" Mike played devil's advocate there.

"Mikey...Mikey, you know, revenge is wonderful. Once you take it, it fills your subconscious with the victorious elixir. I want to take the person out who botched my assignment," The Boss said authoritatively.

"Which assignment are you talking about? Shahab's? That was an incompetency of your men. They didn't do nothing."

"Yes, but it wasn't my men's incompetency, but your men's back-stabbing," came a livid reply.

"How can you be so sure?"

"Because I know my men and what they did. We lost a couple of lives there."

Mike sat down and asked, "What's the guarantee that you'd pay us and not kill everyone during the job?"

"There are no guarantees in life, Mike, but I keep my promises," The Boss replied philosophically.

Mike felt the echo. He usually said that to everyone in his team what he heard from The Boss. "Well, what's the job?"

"I could tell you if you meet me for a coffee?" he chuckled.

"I don't like coffee dates. I am more of a beer drinker, but I can't meet you anywhere."

"I thought so. You'll find a red envelope with all the details in a folded newspaper beneath the garbage can in front of the Starbucks at Times Square."

"If you want me to do the job, I'll tell you where to drop off the plan. Times Square is a very public place and generally doesn't sleep. I can't risk it."

"Okay, smarty pants. I have no problems with it."

"I will call you tomorrow with the location," Mike ordered. Then he continued after a pause, "If I see any of your men straddling around that area tomorrow, I will kill them and the deal is off," Mike strongly stated.

"Don't try to threaten me. The deal is mutual. I see that you are seeking your safety. That's fine by me. I want the job done. We'll talk once you have read the plan. You don't have much time though."

"Earlier the better. Keep your money ready."

"How exactly are you planning to pin down that son of a bitch?" the authoritative voice demanded.

"I will probably limit a couple of people's duties to see if they are botching it and keep a good eye on them throughout the operation."

"All right, let's hope you do it right this time. Don't prove me asinine again."

Mike had called the next day on where to place the plan. "In Subway number sixty-two, coach four. Stick it behind the seat number thirty's support tomorrow. I will pick it up within five days."

Mike picked up the envelope without any problems on the fourth day. He discussed the whole cruise idea with The Boss and decided to tell very little to every member. It was more like need-to-know information for each member. But he knew that the gang would discuss it with one another and will try to get a better picture among themselves.

Mike came back from his flashback and decided something. He stood up and made some calls.

chapter

TWENTY-ONE

John was not in the right frame of mind the least you could say. John had just overcome pneumonia but somehow he still was cold with a few thoughts. Goose bumps danced on his hands as he created a few plumes from a Cuban cigar. Not a chain-smoker but whenever he was tensed, he smoked, and of course, stuttered. He knew he had to confess what he knew. What if the team right away sacks him? The situation was getting complicated the more he thought about it.

Catherine's call last night made him take a stand against his growing concerns. Catherine had done a lot for him when he really needed someone to take care of him. While sitting on his lounge chair, they talked on phone for an hour.

"I can't repay you what you've done for me." John's heart filled with gratitude.

"Don't even mention it, John. What are friends for?" chuckled Catherine.

"Thanks. Do you want anything?" John asked, hesitantly.

"It depends. What can you offer?" Catherine playfully asked.

"Take my share from our last job."

"Oh, why do you guys think always about money?" After a pause she continued, "You risked everything there. You were the hero. I can't do that; you deserve it more than anyone else." Catherine had a smile.

Both were vulnerable and acted like it. Both needed company and solace at the same time. Solitude was killing them both from the inside since Zach died. Catherine pondered if they'd never boarded that ship whether or not Zach would have been alive. She kept swinging between the glorious past she had with Zach and the present when she was getting closer to John. John had a short stature and not exactly an athletic build, but he was brilliant and had a good heart; and the fact that she knew him the most in the group, naturally inclined her toward him. He proved his chivalry as well in the last task. She thought, they say you should love who loves you and not the other way round. Catherine could hide her despondency by bolstering John's health when he needed it the most, and John could hide his guilt for some time but remained on the edge of being hellish and heavenly.

"I need to tell you something; it is personal. Hope you can keep a secret."

"Try me," Catherine asserted.

With a big sigh, John began the sentence. "You know, I know who killed Zach."

"What?" Catherine asked with a big grunt, now intense again, back from her blooming thoughts. "Why didn't you say that earlier?"

"Because I was scared. Because...I...I...I didn't get a chance." Occasional bursts of intense emotions brought stammering.

"John, who killed him? I want to know right now." Catherine was loud, filled with anxiety and fury.

"I am getting a call from someone, hold on." John pressed the hold button on his cell phone.

Catherine shrugged and couldn't believe that at this juncture John would take someone's call. *He could call him or her later. Then she thought maybe to avoid her question, John just made that up. Maybe John was in danger and the call may be regarding that.* She was a little bit confused but wasn't going to trust anybody now.

"This is John, who's this?" John asked.

"Hey, John, this is Mike. Just called you to let you know that we've a team meeting tomorrow. Also, I'm driving to Connecticut. We'll meet at my old farmhouse. Too much action going on here in New York; I need to stay low for a while."

"I see that you are using a completely different number. You're serious about it. Anything to fear?"

"No, just take care. Stay low. Drive to Connecticut tomorrow. We'll talk more tomorrow night."

"Okay, Mike. You take care, man. See you."

John clicked back over to Catherine.

"Hello, Catherine, are you there?"

"Yeah, I am here. Who was it?" Catherine's angst got bigger.

"It was Mike. He should be calling you any minute. Tomorrow we've a team meeting at the old farmhouse in CT. He is already going there but he sounded a little bit edgy. He was using a different number and asked me to stay low and take care."

"Hmmm...I am getting the call right now. I'm not gonna pick up till you tell me the name."

"Catherine, given what Mike said and how he acted, I don't think it would be wise to discuss this on the phone right now, plus I will be more comfortable if we discuss this tomorrow in the team meeting."

"Really, John? Really? What are you hiding? You know what; you just asked how could you repay me. I ask this as my reward." Catherine's frenzy was palpable as she argued with John.

John sighed, "Catherine, come on, I am going to tell you tomorrow. Please be patient."

"I'm coming right now to your apartment."

"Please, don't do that. You won't find me there," John quickly replied.

"John, why are you building the suspense? I thought we could tell each other anything any time but this certainly doesn't seem like it."

"I am hanging up. I can't discuss it any more. Bye, Catherine. I'll see you tomorrow."

Catherine clung to the cell phone at her right ear even after John had hung up two minutes ago. Catherine couldn't grasp what John had to hide from her. She wanted to rush to his apartment and ask him in the face. She was just about to get out of Zach's demise and still grieving when John again scratched the deep-wounded bruise. Catherine had no choice but to be patient.

She thought of driving together with John but Mike's instructions were clear that no one had to be close until this investigation dies down.

John had finally come to terms with it and decided to take a plunge.

Mike was fighting his own battle of thoughts on how to put this to the team. The two reasons we had called the meeting for were to ask everyone to move to a different location for now and that someone was a betrayer. If he threw away his best hand of knowing that there is an intruder in the group, he'd be an idiot. Once he thought of laying it down there in front of everyone and to see how everyone reacts. But that would lead to a total chaos and the group would be dispersed and the knowledge would be gone or someone could get killed in the mayhem, in the heat of arguments. He didn't want the blame-game; the whole idea was stupid. He had to think of something clever to test the members.

Shawn pondered over Mike's call and was bewildered. He had no idea that they were in grave danger. *Location change? Phone change? Why did Mike change the location all of a sudden? And to my question if we should change the location, he said to discuss it in tomorrow's meeting? I mean we're keeping low, why the fuss? What bollocks?* Even though Mike's perspicacious judgment, time and again, had proven to be correct, Shawn was already disenchanted since with the last two jobs he wasn't getting much action. He knew something was going on and Mike somehow didn't give him meaty roles like he used to. Shawn didn't believe if Mike had known about his venture.

John's call had created a real ambiguity for Mike. Mike didn't know what to believe anymore. He had his own secrets. Now, he knew that everyone had their own little secrets. During talking to Tina, she confided completely unknown information to Mike. Mike couldn't justify John's action but had to believe. Why had John not told that before? What caused him to come out now? Why did Tina hold the information? Why is Shawn acting like that? He'd more questions now than he thought after he called everybody. In a way, he was relieved after talking to John. It was a tricky situation, every leader at one point in time has to pass through these and it emerges them as even greater leaders if they can successfully deal with them, so he thought.

Of course, Shahab escaped, but the CIA captured him right away and the governor had been on surveillance ever since that incident.

The FBI corroborated the story but couldn't link what had happened to the governor when an attack had been launched against him near Elk Grove, California. After a week of this attack, Shahab had escaped successfully during a turn over from one state prison to another in southern California. If it were not for an anonymous tip, the FBI would have lost Shahab. Fortunately, they were successful in capturing him back. The governor had maintained that the police got right on time after a couple of terrorists killed his chauffeur and were about to attack him. He never knew why they tried to attack him. The FBI and police had some doubt that transferring Shahab from one penitentiary from another was unnecessary because he was going to be moved eventually to Guantanamo Bay anyways. However, the governor had vehemently defended the move, stating that it was only to get him to a more secure location to avoid further thrash and that his escape was a complete miss from a law enforcement side. Police and the FBI had not been able to track the attackers since then. The attacks were messy in terms of damage and visibility but overall clean in terms of not leaving any tracks except one.

The truck that rolled off from the bridge was stolen day before from Los Angeles, California, from a wash area. The large pipes were fitted somewhere else, which again were stolen from another truck. The FBI investigated both the truck drivers and their employers but didn't find anything obvious. They decided to keep a watch on both of them to track their movement. The FBI still thought the motivation was to get the governor in captivation in lieu of Shahab's release.

Shawn had stolen the truck from Los Angeles and had driven on I-5 north in the night. Mike had waited for Shawn in the interior part of Bakersfield near a farm where they detached the trailer of the stolen truck to another stolen truck and changed the number plates. It became a brand new truck. The police didn't get called till next morning about the other truck that Mike had stolen.

The original plan had been to stop over in a pipe factory and steal them in disguise with fake paperwork but on the way, Shawn decided to take a short cut when he saw exactly what they wanted on another truck. Mike wasn't keen on it. But this time the driver was there—alive and awake sitting on the shoulder about to take a break. Shawn took a break as well and parked behind this truck. He befriended with the driver and started drinking with him. Mike never came out so to the truck driver it seemed as if Shawn was alone in the truck. Shawn then gave a drowsy drink to the driver with a Rufus. The driver immediately dozed off and was not going to wake up till another ten hours. It was already 4:00 a.m. and they were still three hours from Sacramento. They again changed the trailers and the number plate and embarked on their remaining journey. For the last few hours, the truck was hidden in an old ship storage near Stockton. Zach had arrived there on time. The mission was completed without any issues except that the last driver, when awakened, didn't find his pipes and went to the police.

chapter

TWENTY-TWO

There was a half-moon floating in the dark sky, partly covered with clouds, and the cold breeze that swept past Mike's legs was just right. He stood outside taking long drags and making wisps of plumes in the breezy air with his back leaned to his car trying to calm his mind down. He somehow felt that it was all getting to an end now. Maybe it was the decision but then maybe it wasn't. The perfect tautology—to be or not to be. But the place was just right. The car was parked in the front of an old farmhouse which he'd inherited. A few neighboring farmers had tried to acquire it over the years, but he had been reluctant of selling it. He always thought this could be his safe house but other than that, he always thought of living a country life once he retired and wanted to spend time peacefully here.

There was not much farming done in years and the place was just decrepit. Weeds had crept up all around the area. The smell of a putrid skunk in the vicinity was overpowering. The overall air was filled with the smell of cow manure and vegetation. It was awfully quiet. The road to the house was also made with dirt and stones in the old time and was filled with moss on the stones and weeds had found life in every tiny crevice of the path. Mike had it cleaned twice a year, but it wasn't the time yet and spring had just passed.

The area had a small country road going in from Highway 179 and split the two sides in green farmland. After a couple of miles to the east, there sat his semi-modern farmhouse which had some necessities like electricity, a heater, and water. Mike had never paid for the phone line; there was no use, so it was cut off long time ago. The cell phone coverage was enough for his once-a-year getaway place. This was completely in contrast with where he was used to living in New York, yet he cherished it.

He extinguished the butt with his rugged black shoes and went inside the farmhouse. The house was centrally located, however, close to the back fence of the farm. The house itself was clean and tidy since he seldom came over and had it cleaned. He checked the hot water and heater and both were working fine. He checked out the rooms and all of them had old but comfy beds. The bathrooms looked good. He was all by himself for tonight before the gang arrived tomorrow. He thought of calling someone, then he shut himself off. *Why ruin the peace?* He crashed and soon was snoring.

The next day everyone had arrived except Shawn. Catherine was dying to know who killed Zach. She'd already asked

John twice. John looked nervous, so did Tina. Shawn finally arrived in the evening.

"Here comes the devil. As always, late." Mike made the comments as he stood on the front porch looking down to Shawn's entry.

"Aye, Aye, I heard that, Mikey," Shawn jokingly yelled when he was still far away lugging his bag.

Everyone had a cup of coffee in their hands and was nervous as to what Mike's next move was. Catherine poured a coffee for Shawn while he settled.

John perched on the railing of the porch and others were on scattered chairs in the front porch area sipping their freshly brewed coffee. It was drizzling a slight bit and it produced an earthly aroma from the sand surrounding them. Everyone shared the contradictory feeling due to good ambience but uncertainty about the future.

"Welcome, gentlemen, to my grandfather's farm," Mike announced.

"I've called this meeting for two reasons, but I'd like to ask all of you first if you need to share something with me. Let's start with Catherine," Mike stated.

"I'll be clear and honest. I came just to hear the name of Zach's killer and then whatever you have to say."

"What?" Tina gasped. "Mike, you know who killed Zach?"

"What the bloody fuck, Mike? Why didn't you tell us all before? How come Catherine knows about it and we don't?" Shawn echoed Tina.

"Shhh...calm down, people. John, now is the time." Mike held his hand and pointed his open palm toward John.

John looked as if a young boy was asked to give his first speech in front of a large audience. Moreover, he looked all red and guilt-ridden. He gave a quick glance at Catherine, mustered the courage, stood up, and walked slightly away from everyone.

"People, hear me out first and then judge me."

Everyone looked astonished and quickly glanced at one another. Nobody spoke a word.

"Once we arrived at the cruise ship, everyone had to be separate. The plan was that Mike and Tina would appear as if they met at the ship and bonded, same was with Zach and Catherine. Shawn and I were to accompany each other. But of course, we couldn't gel as well with each other and ended up spending a lot of time alone during the cruise. I checked out the whole of the ship during my solitude. Zach's room was one deck above mine."

Everyone rapt in attention, listening intently, looked at John. Catherine somehow had the hunch and she already was feeling knots twisting in her stomach.

John continued, "On the day he died, in the morning, I heard him calling someone from the cruise phone which is not entirely secured."

"Where did you see him calling from? Who was he calling?" Shawn interrupted John.

"Yes, I was coming to that. He used one of the passenger's satellite phones outside in the corridors. He didn't use one in his room which made my suspicion grow. I couldn't understand a word from where I tried to hide, but I didn't want to give away my position. I first thought that he could just be talking to his family but the way he was whispering made me doubt his actions. So I followed his activities except when Shawn and I were doing a couple of activities together." John looked exhausted and drained and the intensity with which he was telling the occurrence made his face all red and he had sweat beads on his forehead, even with the cool morning breeze on the porch. "His day went overall with normal activities like any youngster by himself will have on a cruise ship. He took a few drinks and sat at the top deck's big swimming area and checked out girls. He made a couple of impromptu girlfriends there. He then went for a lunch with a couple of ladies at the fancy restaurant in the food court area near the shopping mall. In the afternoon, he was in his room for a couple of hours most likely with one of the girls from the cruise."

Catherine heard all of it without any interruptions. She followed Zach as well and she could vouch for most of it except the last part. She wasn't comfortable with it. It was a direct innuendo that Zach was not faithful to her. She couldn't stop herself.

"Wait, you don't know that," she snapped.

"Yes, I don't know for sure which girl was there. I know for sure that there was someone because I heard the noises coming from the room.

Catherine looked away in disgust and tears rolled down her face because she knew that she wasn't around at that time with Zach. She was with him more in the evening when he died. Now she remembered a few girls waving and smiling at Zach when they both were going from the restaurant to his room to which he reciprocated. When asked, he'd replied, "Casual encounters."

John continued, "But in the evening after his debauchery and getting highly noticed on the cruise when we were supposed to downplay our roles, he was alone and started going to the bottom deck to which I was surprised. I followed him."

"Wait, what time are we talking about here because you were with me in the evening?" Shawn intervened.

"Yes, but listen first. It was around 5:00 p.m. Again, I heard him calling from a secluded passenger satellite phone, and this time, I was very close—hidden in a passage closet near the booth. It was brief but I heard almost the entire conversation." John paused and lifted a water bottle and poured it in his mouth. Nobody moved an inch or uttered a word. "He said, 'Hey, it's me. This is my last call. Mike and folks are going to blow this up tomorrow night. Be ready. We can catch them red-handed. I've gained their full trust. Don't worry.' Then I heard a couple of yes's and no's and at last, 'see you tomorrow' then he shut off the phone. I couldn't believe what I just heard. He was about to blow our entire operation. I didn't budge until he was gone. I was scared and worried. I didn't know what to do."

"My god, that son of a bitch." Shawn shook his head.

"I can't believe he'd do such a thing," Tina responded.

Catherine didn't speak a word. Her mind had enough material to process than she could develop. She simply didn't believe that her Zach could be a traitor. She was just disgusted with the thought.

"So did you hear any names to which he called upon?" Mike inquired.

"I heard the entire communication, but didn't hear any specific names."

"What happened then?" A weak sound came from Catherine. Her heart was filled with distress and some sort of load got heavier on her chest.

"I thought that he could be working with the cops, FBI, or who knows, some other governmental secret force or the gangs who want to unmask us. So I quickly thought of telling everyone but that meant direct contact with you all, which was a no-no for the operation. Then I checked the time and I had to meet Shawn at the dance party, followed by a buffet dinner. So I went and sat with him, but my mind was constantly hovering on what he was gonna do next and how to solve this mystery. Then I decided to do one thing. I could surprise him because I had the upper hand now. So I took off from Shawn and went to mm...my...my room." John's anxiety crept in.

Everyone's mind was working toward where this was going. They all kind of knew but their minds didn't accept it; so keen to hear the next words from John, no one spoke although their expressions spoke a lot. An occasional cry from dog was heard as morning turned into afternoon. The chirping of birds and buzzing from the insects filled the background sound. Apart from that, it was jarringly quiet. John wiped his face, took another sip of water, and tried to continue.

"I...I...then went to my room and wore a makeup of a black guy and wore a uniform of the crew member which I'd brought for our ttt...ttt...task. I took my pistol."

"Whoa...whoa, you just took your pistol like that?" Mike now screamed.

"L...let me speak first. I decided to surprise him and pin him in his own room. The plan was to catch him by surprise, don't rrr...reveal my identity, and then tie him in his room till I contact Mm...mm...you and others."

"Why didn't you speak to Shawn about it when you knew about all this, you were with him during the time?" Tina asked a good question.

"Forgive me but I wasn't in my right mmmmm...mind. Plus, I didn't know who to trust. I wanted to contact Mike first but there he was dancing with you. I buzzed twice but either he ignored or didn't hear. He would have decided the next steps but I had to take charge. So I knocked on Zach's room's door. And he asked, 'What is it?' and I replied, 'Sir, there is this envelope for you.' He opened the door and beneath the envelope, I hid my pistol. I had caught him by surprise, but at the very moment, at the end of the long corridor, one of the crewmembers shouted, 'Hey, who are you?' and I was in a complete shock thinking he had discovered me. The second I had looked away from Zach, he'd seen my gun, which still hid beneath the envelope, and he immediately started closing the door on me. I had to react and, accidentally, I fired the gun. I had no intention of killing him. I was just trying to uncover him but I messed up; I messed up." Tears welled up in John's eyes.

Everyone was flummoxed. Catherine had covered her face with her hands and was shaking her head in disbelief. Tina's eyes grew bigger and her mouth remained open. Mike looked away in what seemed like darkness even in a bright day outside the porch. Shawn's hands were behind his head supporting it, which he tightly squeezed, and said, "Wow," and blew some air out.

"I was going to bring him in but couldn't. I killed Zach and now we had lost the source of his cccc...ccc...contact as well. I messed it up big time. I didn't have the nerves to tell you guys the truth. I was completely flabbergasted. I didn't know what to tell and what not to in the middle of an assignment. Now, I see myself as a k...k...killer." A lump formed in his throat and finally John broke down.

"What happened once you shot Zach?" Mike questioned.

John breathed heavily but continued, "I was going to go in but heard a scream from Zach's room, and I dashed to the side of the corridor where the crewmember stood. I had to shoot him right there and then. I already had taken out the camera in the corridor but the crewmember could ruin the whole mission and it was a great risk. I held him on my shoulder as if he had trouble walking and supported him to the closet door closest to us and shut us inside. I used his access card to get in. It was a tiny supply room where the housekeeper kept everything for the guests in that corridor. From a tiny glass slit, I saw Catherine running madly to the elevator and her encounter with a crewmember who probably came to fix the camera or heard the muffled shots. The crewmember left quickly for tools or a new camera, and assuming that Catherine's going to talk to you folks, I rapidly put on the housekeeper's dress and apron and took out the cart. The cart had small doors inside which it held everything from soaps, tissue papers, towels, and other toiletries. I took out the adjustable metal shelves and took the cart and went to Zach's room. I used housekeeper's master key and cleaned up and fit him in the empty cart and took it quickly downstairs in the crew elevator and took it to the backside of the bottom deck and since it was dark I just heaved his body in the water along with the bloody bed sheets. Then I quickly removed my makeup and returned to Shawn at the buffet dinner trembling. My heart was racing like a rocket."

"What happened to the crewmember you killed?" Tina questioned.

"Once we were informed of Zach's killing downstairs. The meeting was going to be held in my room and no one was going to Zach's room except maybe Catherine I thought. So I rushed and took the elevator to the fifth floor and took out the crewmember's body from the closet and heaved him similarly into the water. It was clean. Nobody had tracked me. I had to hurry because if real housekeepers came in time, it would have been a mess. I was worried about the missing crewmember with regard to the cruise team identifying a missing person. But then I thought that Mike might call off this mission due Zach's death, and we may not have to go through the mission where the crew is already looking for a missing crewmember. I hoped that we as a group wouldn't talk about Zach's death of course if we continued." John paused.

No one spoke or looked at each other.

"I don't know if I did the right thing or not. I mean killing wasn't the intention but it happened and I am at fault, but at the same time, I decided to risk everything and make the mission successful. You all praised me for the mission for which I am grateful. Now the decision is up to you guys of whether to include me or not in future missions," John concluded.

"Hmm...I'm surprised by your speed with which you cleared the blood of the crewmember," Shawn commented.

"I'm too. Life is a bitch. In panic, you want to save yourself and your survival instincts kick the fuck in," John replied unabashedly but calmly looking at the sky. His reply seemed a bit defensive.

"Well, I think, it was an unfortunate event but hey we lost our traitor which we didn't know was there so that can't be bad, can it? You proved your mettle in the assignment no question about it. I'd still prefer if you had talked to me first rather than taking any action. You ruined the element of surprise because Zach didn't know that you knew about him. Nevertheless, what's done is done. Let's talk about the future missions." Mike chimed in after a pause. He took another pause remembering The Boss telling him about cops finding another crewmember dead.

Catherine still couldn't believe that John had killed her Zach. Tina was dumbfounded by the whole event. But Catherine's temperature was rising, and she couldn't bear the composure with which Mike was handling the situation. She decided to take control in her own hands. She just stood up and dashed toward John and started slapping him hard and incessantly while screaming as tears rolled down her face, "Why the fuck did you kill him, John?" Her voice felt sodden. John didn't react and stood like a statue, his eyes didn't meet hers, they looked down—his face all red and guilt-ridden. Mike held Catherine and asked her to stop and eventually she moved away and started weeping in the corner of the covered porch. She knew that John was right on so many levels yet she couldn't keep her emotions intact. She was a strong woman, it was unlike her, but love made her do bizarre things. Zach did matter to her so much. She was befuddled by the infidelity and betrayal of Zach. Mike thought that she knew that she brought him in the group and she was partly angry at herself for bringing him in and went to a guilt trip for getting him killed. Shawn tried to soothe her from the back, holding her from the shoulder. It was unlike of Shawn doing such things but sometimes he showed that quality, too.

chapter

TWENTY-THREE

Mike's mind was working overtime. He was thinking about long-term repercussions on what John had said and done. Mike could safely now say that there was a threat of a mole and that they had luckily found it and got rid of it, but he detested the whole situation. He saved his thoughts.

"I will come to each of you but I need some answers from Catherine when she catches her breath," Mike ordered.

"John, whatever's happened has happened," Mike dryly said.

He glanced at all of them and said, "To everyone in the group, next time, should such an unfortunate event occur, I want you to be careful and consult me first for the next step."

"John, another thing, because of your stupidity of not telling or not having guts or whatever you wanna call it, you might have wrecked our whole operation because of the crewmember's search. I saw the search happening but they kept it quiet. No wonder now the police are looking for us desperately. With twelve hundred crewmembers, it will be hard but not impossible to track everyone. But who knows who this guy was and what position he held. We could have been in real danger especially not knowing that they were looking for suspects while searching him." Mike was loud and clear.

"I…there wasn't enough time…" before John could finish his sentence, Mike held up his hand in the air hinting to stop. "It's not like he was the only person harmed in this mission, there were several others hurt, locked, and a couple of them were unconscious. I'm not gonna dwell on it. These things happen in our business. But, fuck, we gotta do better than this."

Mike looked at Catherine and directed at her, "Catherine, I am sorry this all happened but you're a strong person. I need you to handle this calmly and with an open mind. Zach was a traitor. If John had not killed him, I would have." At those words, she looked up at him and he continued, "But only after knowing the source he'd been working for. But I want you to tell me, how much information did you provide him of our previous jobs? I know that he didn't just join the group out of the blue. He must have cajoled you in getting the position in this group and I know that you aren't gullible but because you had a soft corner for this guy, he took advantage of your vulnerability and attacked us from the back—that son of a bitch backstabber."

"I would have been naïve, but I don't advertise our secrets out in the market. I didn't say much about the missions. Before he joined the group, he used to meet me and we used to go out on casual dates, not like date-date. I told him about how we provide cover-ups for the big stuff. He sometimes used to annoy me with every little piece of information he read in the newspaper and asked whether we were behind it. I told him that I wasn't going to reveal any of it. He got me eventually, I will give you that," Catherine stoically responded.

"Think if you said anything about the Shahab's case," Mike probed again.

"Why are you asking it now? Why does it matter?" Catherine bounced a question.

"Uh...uh..." Mike took a couple of minutes before he thought of a good response. "I'm just thinking that could be the reason that particular task resulted in a failure for the 'party,' so to speak."

"I don't know, I can't answer that, Mike. Who knows? But I did tell him a little bit about our Shahab's case when he probed me a lot during one of his post racing celebrations."

"This was after he read it in the newspapers or before the mission?" Tina chimed in.

"Look, I was drunk. Now leave me alone. It doesn't matter anyways." Catherine started walking on the dirt road toward the main gate.

Mike eyed Tina and shook his head as if to say *stay away*—that she shouldn't have meddled. Mike thought Catherine was either really not in the right frame of mind or she was covering something advertently. Mike didn't speak and swept his hand to everyone when everyone faced Catherine's back to prevent them from speaking.

Without saying a word, Mike started walking along Catherine. Both walked silently and didn't speak until they reached the middle of the road from the gate to the house. Mike tried to break the silence, "Look, Catherine, no one's blaming you. We all have made mistakes. It is just that if we know what you'd told about it, we know for sure that he may have messed it up for the party. Some people are not happy with the outcome of that job."

Catherine swiftly turned and curtly replied, "Mike, don't patronize me. I told you my answer. And if some people are not happy then they themselves should have the guts to complete the job after we made it so easy for them."

"I understand it. I am not saying that we won't get any new jobs or our name is soiled or anything of that sort. These things happen in our line of work and neither of us can blame one another for a failure. These are real risky jobs that we do, and these things are bound to happen but we want to avoid such things, so now tell me what you told Zach before the assignment." Mike came in a roundabout way to get her to say what she left off with when she said she was drunk. He didn't want to reveal that someone was on the look for them, but when he said that some people were not happy with the outcome of that job gave a hint to Catherine. Plus, his sudden move to the farmhouse and a different phone with a new scrambler obviously beaconed some trouble on the horizon. Catherine wasn't as dumb as he thought.

At the porch, the tension wasn't leveled. Nobody spoke to each other first. Shawn rocked in on an old rocker, John leaned there taking the support of the railing, and Tina slept sideways in disappointment on a large chair with her feet hanging down touching the floor. Finally, Shawn asked, "John, man, you should have told us."

"I told you, I wanted to pin him and confirm what he knew and then I was going to..." John snapped, but was interrupted before he could complete his sentence.

"You wanted to become a damn hero, is that it? That's why you were hiding it from everyone else. What a dumb fuck you are? This is critical information and has to be shared with everyone. '*I didn't trust anyone,*'" Shawn angrily made fun of John's impression and bombarded John with a barrage of questions and advice. "What the fuck were you thinking? I mean come on; for God's sakes, we've been doing this for ten years now."

John avoided the conversation because he knew that the more questions he answered, the more questions he was going to get. He had already told his story and nothing was going to change.

Mike and Catherine were walking toward the gate, away from the house. The clouds had scattered away and the sunlight shone on the glistened stones that were drenched by the drizzle earlier. It was still quiet.

"He'd called me just before the day of our kidnapping mission. It was a big celebration and he'd won the *Fast and the Furious* type illegal race near the downtown area and didn't get caught. He asked me out for dinner. We had great food and I enjoyed his company. As a matter of fact, I'd always enjoyed his company and he probably knew that. I was hammered with the drinks and I can vaguely recall that he suddenly dropped me a couple of questions on our next mission. I think I told him that we are going to help rescue someone and cover up by trying to rob a bank. I don't think I said anything more than that."

"I see." Mike nodded. *This was probably enough for him to put two and two together. But then why even create all this drama?*

"Did you tell the place we are going to do it?" Mike asked

"Of course not, I remember it correctly that I never mentioned Shahab, the bank, the Twenty-First Precinct, New York, downtown, or any of those sorts of things that would have given him the clue. But it might have been obvious because I was with him till midnight so it was probably obvious to him that I wasn't travelling outside of California or something like that," Catherine fired back.

"But did you tell the time when we were going to do it?"

"I think I may have mentioned inadvertently couple of times just to get out of his company. Not the actual time but like 'tomorrow' so he knew that it was going to be somewhere in New York in the morning or noon."

"Hmm...interesting," Mike concluded. His deliberation was still stuck to the fact of why he had not tried to ruin the entire operation. Was he late in understanding the details? Is Catherine hiding something? To keep it from arising any suspicion of two suspects? Was Catherine helping Zach? Or it could be just as simple as he created a small perimeter near a few of the precincts where the possible rescues could be attempted with some dangerous suspects and might want to catch the entire team. The bigger question was if John was telling the truth. *Could John be the traitor and Zach somehow knew and so he had to kill him?* Mike thought. *But If Zach knew about John, he would have told someone, at least Catherine. She was with him. He didn't say anything like that. And even if that was the case, why would John come forward and declare all of this. Doesn't make any sense. Fuck!* With all the above reasoning, he was going with the current story for now.

"Do you know if he tried to follow you anytime?" Mike stopped at the gate, turned around, and guided Catherine to take some steps back.

Catherine confidently disagreed, "Nope, he knew that I was sharp and I would come to know if someone was following."

"If he really was connected to the police, then he might even have placed a bug in your apartment or your car or somewhere," Mike questioned Catherine.

"I don't think so, but I can check plus I always used to drive my car to his place. Also, during those days, I'd not allowed him to enter my apartment."

"Mind you he was the best driver, so he may well be following us throughout and not be seen." Mike raised his eyebrows.

"Impossible, I drove the van and I was constantly on check for any followers and I could have recognized him immediately even from a distance," Catherine affirmed.

Mike didn't say anything. He was lost in his thoughts nearing the porch.

At the porch, Shawn looked pissed, John disinterested, and Tina now sleepy. Mike was digesting all the events and although John managed to rescue the mission in the midst of an intruder's perfidy, he somehow didn't like John taking the charge upon himself without consulting anyone, and mostly him. But Mike was relieved in a lot of ways. He could now focus on the work and probably the team got a lesson on how important it was to not trust anyone outside the group. Although his guts told him that Catherine couldn't have been partners with Zach, he decided to be vigilant about it.

He mulled over the anonymous calls and threats he got and the fact that he was hiding here in Connecticut in a remote farmhouse much to his chagrin. He'd never done that, he had always confronted his opposition, but this time it seemed a bit risky. This guy or gal had enough clout to turn the authorities against him if he didn't remain extremely astute and adept in leaving no trails behind.

As much as he didn't want to, he doubted himself today. He had made some grave errors by not being a better leader. *I am at as much fault as John or Zach. I should have never allowed Catherine to get Zach in. I should have listened to my gut. Maybe Shawn's got a point that I am not leading very well. Now by telling them that I was forced to put them on a damn suicide mission, all will be alarmed and wouldn't like me for that. They will doubt my leadership.* His mind somersaulted from pallor to rosiness and thought about how successful he had led the past missions and all the strategies that had worked because of his shrewdness and spur-of-the-moment thinking. He immediately decided. *I can't let that happen. I think the peril's unveiled and I don't need to sell a stinking fish anymore. Let's tackle issues at hand.*

Mike reached John's shoulder and patted him without saying anything. John looked in his eyes and nodded and looked guilty as hell.

"All right, you guys. You might be thinking why the hell I asked you to come all the way to Connecticut to discuss this matter. Right?" Mike announced, eyeing everyone.

All came back from the trauma, siesta, fear, etcetera, and focused on what Mike had to proclaim.

"Well, I heard from our sources that the bodies were going to be identified soon; that the cops retrieved them from the sea and that cops have a new detective who may be linking these cases, so I am just being cautious. An extra prudence didn't hurt anybody. Agreed?"

No one spoke. They looked at each other like *whatever.* Mike was surprised that nobody showed if they cared.

"Okay, I think, you guys had to sink in a lot of info today and everyone's tired now, I suppose we can talk tomorrow." Mike tried to pull a smile hoping to make everyone feel relaxed. Mike saw Shawn with his corner of the eye at the end. Shawn's edginess was palpable.

"It means there is more to talk about? No more surprises, mate, let's get over with today whatever you've got, Mike. Come on; just lay it out on the table." Shawn waved his hands sideways to gesticulate.

"Hmm...everyone agrees? I'm fine discussing it but seems like everyone's exhausted," Mike replied.

Everyone was curious now as to what else was still left. Catherine finally broke her silence, "Yeah, let's get it done with it. Please, Mike, we've handled a lot worse before."

"Okay, there are two things I need to discuss with you guys. One that I want all of you to move from your current location and find a safer place for some time. And the other..." Mike was cut abrupt.

"Why?" John demanded.

"Because, as I told you—precaution. Because prevention is better than cure. I just told you the reason why I decided to change the location." Mike peered into John's eyes and replied, which John found somewhat esoteric.

"Why are you all of a sudden afraid of the police? We never used to be. Is there some other threat which we don't know of?" John pressed on the issue.

"As I said, detectives are not just sitting on their butts doing nothing. I've heard from a source that they are gathering information from all the past events, pictures, fingerprints, DNA samples, witnesses, and phone calls. Also, a special team has been assigned to us. Of course, we were in a getup in those pictures, but I think they may have found out that there is a 'cover-up team' creating chaos and allowing the huge tasks to get carried over. Someone probably is clever enough to connect the dots and make a case out of it. I am not saying that they've found us, but take precautions. Use a new phone with a different SIM card and scrambler program. John, you should get us all a state-of-the-art scrambler so no one can trace our calls. Does it all make sense? And to answer your second question: no, there is no other threat," Mike explained. He deftly avoided the mention of The Boss who controlled him currently in some regard and that he provided this info to him.

"I think one thing we never discussed is that how much Zach had told to the police?" Catherine gazed at Mike while Tina tried to keep her eyes open.

"If he worked for the police?" Catherine looked at Tina and added.

"Yes, those are all good questions which we'll never know, thanks to John. But I'm not going to let John go free from this. I want every detail of Zach's background—who he talked to, where he went in his free time, phone calls, bills, bank statements—every damn thing that'll give me the info on who he worked for." Mike walked, got close to John, and gazed straight into his eyes.

"Look, I said I'm sorry several times and I'm not gonna repeat it for anyone now. I will do the research and give a report on Zach soon." John's face was agitated and red.

"Okay, and what's the second bloody fucking thing?" Shawn looked angry. Shawn thought about hauling his ass somewhere else with all the stuff and changing his neighborhood, phones, and every other piece that completed any jigsaw puzzle police were putting together. He didn't like it a bit and made that very evident.

"The second fucking thing is you, you motherfucker," Mike screamed, gazing his eyes and moving closer to Shawn.

Everyone was alerted and stood up. Shawn stood up, his eyes widened, and his face had a look of part astonishment and part guilt. But before he could open his mouth, Mike pounced again.

"You asshole, you are going behind my back to Greg. What do you think of yourself? I'm a fool and won't know anything?" Mike drew out his 0.357 Magnum revolver and aimed it at Shawn.

"Hold on, hold on," John intervened, standing with his hand held across in between the two gangsters.

"What's going on? Can someone please tell me?" John demanded, his eyes ping-ponged between Mike and Shawn's eyes.

"Tina, why don't you tell what happened?" Mike ordered, still yelling with his eyes red and the revolver still aimed at Shawn's belly.

Tina was caught by surprise. She seemed scared. *How the hell did I come in between?*

"Uh...uh...I saw Shawn discussing it with Tony in the cruise that they are going to work together soon." Tina stared at John and said as fearlessly as she could and sighed.

"What?" Catherine questioned. She was now shocked and thoroughly confused with what was going on on this porch.

"Yes, he's teaming up with Greg, who was one of my resources in older days, or should I say my younger days." Mike gazed at Catherine; he seemed a bit mellowed down.

"What the fuck is going on? Does anyone work for this team anymore? Zach probably worked for the police, John kills Zach, Shawn's working for another team, and you and Tina are hiding facts. I think it's enough for me." Catherine blatantly gawked at Mike and argued. "I'm pissed, you bastards. I'm through with this. I don't want to talk to anyone anymore."

"You know what, Mike, yes, I think you are a bloody fool and you didn't know anything. Just like you didn't know anything about John and Zach. You had your good days, which were very few. Since the last five years, you've made blunder after blunder and you are digging a hole and dragging us all into it. You are a complete disaster, mate, that's what you are. I am not afraid of your gun. You don't have any guts." Shawn stared at him, looking intently in his eyes just inches apart.

"Don't push me, Shawn. I'm tired of this shit as well..." John again pushed Mike away from Shawn before Mike could complete his sentence or tick the trigger.

"Why did you do that, Shawn?" John screamed and looked at Shawn.

"It beats me, do you still need an explanation, mate? This guy can't lead. He's done. How many mistakes can you make? I want to live and lead."

"Is that your reason for leaving this group? To do business with another team, after all these years?" Catherine's gaze narrowed and her voice was high.

"Yes, and if you had noticed, Mike's given me the most petty jobs I've done in years in these major tasks we recently completed, or could barely complete. Why did he have to risk John in the engine room when I was there? We all know that John's an enabler; I'm the implementer. He is a brainiac, for God's sakes. I am strong and the most experienced and would have bitten my arm off to get that work done. But no, he didn't give me the meaty roles because he keeps a bloody grudge on me and doesn't trust me. Why should I work for him?"

"Oh, so you are proving your fidelity by joining another group?" Tina scowled at Shawn.

"Listen, I'm not scheming anything here. Tina created a Chinese whisper. I have just started talking to Greg and he's offering me to lead a bunch of tacklers who he knows and some I know. It's simply a better opportunity," Shawn put it casually in his British accent.

"Shawn, you know our business. How can we trust that if you got captured some day you won't leak our information, or tell Greg about our missions? You know the drill, Shawn, come on. There is no going back in this business." John questioned Shawn intrepidly.

"Didn't Mike used to say, `There are no guarantees in this line of work?' Just kidding." Shawn paused and continued, "But you can trust me because we've worked together and I've no grudges against you guys. You know where to find me. In fact, I wasn't planning to leave. I thought I would work here if a bigger opportunity came up. "

"How stupid can you be, Shawn? There is no way we can trust you if you left the group and hell if we let you join again on anything," Mike retorted, still inches close to Shawn.

It was evening already. The birds' chirping that filled the background was getting quieter now. The noise that they didn't enjoy was fleeting with occasional tractor sounds, trucks that passed through the main road, and heavy-duty sprinkler's going on in the nearby farms. The light that was peeking through sparse clouds and inching closer to the porch was now going away as everyone's trust.

"Look, wankstains, I am not contractually obligated to work with you guys if you think so?" Shawn attempted to crack a joke and grinned.

"Fuck, Shawn. That's what you got? Next time, take my task or any task that you like," Catherine gaped at Shawn, seething.

"That's not gonna happen, Catherine. Things have gone too far. You're right. It doesn't seem anyone's working for this team anymore. We all have differences of opinions, but we work together to achieve a bigger task. Shawn's decision has changed a lot of things. I don't want to deal with this anymore. Shawn, you are out." Mike moved away without looking at him and just waved his hand with the revolver ordering to leave.

"What are you ssss...saying, Mike?" John couldn't stop himself from gazing with wide eyes.

"You, John, are another bigger fucker..." Mike was furious and screaming at the top of his lungs but tried himself vainly to stop abruptly. He fired a shot from his 0.357 Magnum.

A few remaining birds all fluttered away from the sound. It was quiet once more. Heads turned and eyes were on Mike. Mike's eyes were boiling with rage. The bullet went past John's shoes inside the porch floor making a big hole with wood chips flying aside. An occasional shot wasn't uncommon in this part of the country where farmers or animal owners did fire in the air to keep the birds away or shot a wild animal.

"Just leave, everyone, I am dispersing this group," Mike announced with his hand held high and motioning to leave.

"Those are big words, Mike. Do you know what you are saying? Have you thought about what you are going to do?" Tina was the only person who could venture in who Mike probably wouldn't hurt, even when he looked wrathful.

"Just go, Tina. I'm disbanding everyone, including you." Mike didn't dare to look into Tina's eyes.

Tina's big beautiful eyes were tearful in a way that John and everyone noticed. She didn't say anything. Everyone headed to their rooms to get their luggage. No words were spoken. All left, leaving Mike to his solitude.

chapter

TWENTY-FOUR

A Few Weeks Later...

Kamal Khan looked through the window of his tenth floor Langley office in his pinstriped gray suit. His still eyes gazed at the rain that messed up a few schedules for every one today. It reminded him of his tempests in his early days. His broad chest and tall stature seemed imposing. His receding hairline was a mix of gray and black and he wore weathered wrinkles on the forehead, giving him a personality to his tanned skin and his rather huge appearance.

His vast office was smothering him today. He had orders from the who's who. He had just talked to the NRO chief and he heard that Mr. President himself might engage in this affair. The politics was huge and he was not ready to budge. The president was under pressure since the Dubai act had come to his door. They had tried to sweep the dust under the rug but rich Middle East partners wanted more than just a bone that was thrown at them. Mr. Khan's best officer was in the works but Mr. President was not ready to have one more act of terrorism, or any kind of attack, that could jeopardize the party's upcoming election for his second term, even if it meant future annihilation. At the far corner of his modern, semi-circular desk, a huge LED monitor blinked with a few yellow sticky notes stuck at the base. The case files were littered all over the desk. Important fax papers and other paperwork filled in the gaps in an attempt to cover the entire area of the table. Mr. Khan moved and heaved himself on the ergonomic chair, picked up his phone, and with a sigh, dialed a number.

"Let's take him down now," Khan said.

"No, sir, the business is still unfinished I think."

"You think so? This isn't a game anymore; do you understand that? We've lost so many people and this is getting messier every day." His authoritative voice was deep and loud.

"Sir, with all due respect, although he's abandoned the group, he'll strike back with some other team. I still have a chance."

"Look, officer, you've been dragging this too long. I've got calls from NRO twice this month on this matter and the vice president also is getting itchy to get this resolved as soon as possible, and Mr. President himself is now interested in the outcome. There is a lot of politics getting involved; there's a lot at stake. I can't risk it anymore."

"I'm doing my best, sir. Now, if he does involve others, it will be a setback and we'll have to keep a close eye on him. I think we can nail the guy," the officer answered with confidence.

"You better do it fast and right because the water's above the head now and I'm pressured from the top level. I can't keep you on one case forever. We've got a shortage of people in Iraq, Sudan, Namibia, Egypt, North Korea, and places you might not even have heard of. There are so many cases I can use you on," the official demanded.

"It's not like I've been sitting idle here. Due to 'this,' you've gotten so many leads and successful operations which without me would have been completely out of you and your officers' hands, so give them dogs some bone." The voice had an air of smugness.

"Do you think I haven't told them about our success stories? Without that, you'd have been off the case long time back. Because I trust your abilities, I've been fighting with my superiors, and to some extent my subordinates, for a long time now, but they are breathing on my neck now. Besides, covering up your ass in so many police investigations has not been a walk in the park either," gasped Mr. Khan.

"Hang this carrot again on the donkey and hope that they'd still take the bait. I assure you that soon we'll nail this guy."

"Hope that's the case. I would need a twice-a-week report from now on. You take care, officer." Mr. Khan sounded tough but soft at the same time.

"I will. Thanks for your support. Bye."

Present Day
Detroit, Texas

It was mid-day of June in downtown Detroit. The heat
was scorching outside but one couldn't miss the suits of the government officials that walked toward a few judiciary buildings
around the area with one hand on the phone and the other carry-
ing a coffee or a briefcase. Under the green canopy of Peter's Café,
despite the heat, Shawn sat under the umbrella outside watching
people go by, minding their routines. He was wondering where
Greg had been. He'd called him a couple of days ago to meet in
Detroit and had confirmed yesterday to meet at Peter's Cafe. He
jolted out of his thoughts when his phone buzzed in his pocket.

"Dude, Greg's out. Yesterday, the cops picked him up from
the Coco Bar." Tony was gasping.

"Fuck, Tony, are you toying with me?" Shawn stood up
with his phone. A couple of old folks who were having snacks
outside behind his table looked up in Shawn's direction. Shawn
realized that he'd screamed in panic.

He lowered his voice, "What did they arrest him for?" His
voice was almost a whisper, but with aggression.

"I don't know, man, but I tell you to just lay low for a
while. I've known Greg all my life, he wouldn't sell us out no
matter what. You couldn't be in this business if you are not thick
skinned; you know that, right?"

"I'm not worried about that. Okay, he flew me up all the
way here and now he's stuck in a New York jail," Shawn sighed.

"Where are you?" Tony casually questioned.

"Don't worry. I'm safe, bloke. I'll talk to you when I reach
there. Phew...crikey Moses! Thanks, Tony," Shawn said, with
enough ennui.

Shawn knew that he couldn't trust anybody. He was even wondering if any of the suits with black goggles on the phone were actually watching him. He scanned the surrounding. The café was at the corner of a crossroad. Straight across from him was a bookstore in a brick building. The right-hand corner had a florist and next to it the board said: "Department of Criminal Justice." To his diagonal corner right ahead was a city court. Three cars were parked in front of that against the parking meters. None of them had left since Shawn was sitting there. Right in froʃnt of the road was a line of parked cars since parking was scarce in that area. An occasional mom with a stroller was seen, a few people were hanging out nearby. Due to the courts, people constantly stopped, went in and came out of the court. It was a busy street. None of that mattered but all of a sudden, he was scared and suspected everyone. One had to be vigilant in this business. *Probably Mike was right on laying low for a while.* He felt the urge to leave the town immediately.

chapter

TWENTY-FIVE

Four Months Later...

John was almost as happy as he was shocked to receive a call from Mike. It was a nice breezy day and Boca Raton, Florida was just awesome. John put his sunglasses aside on the lounge chair. The waves were pretty high and kids were enjoying surfing. The lean and tall palm trees swayed to their sides and the clear sand at their feet gave a picturesque scene. Sipping on his beer next to one of the trees, John thought about what Mike had said. He was enjoying his vacation as he had dreamt about. He would have wished to go to Hawaii but staying here meant he would be closer to his mom who lived in a retirement home here in Florida. He had everything with him here except one thing. He missed Catherine. She hadn't forgiven him since then. It was a long separation and his heart always had this void.

"Hi, Catherine, this is Mike," Mike greeted her with enthusiasm.

"Hello, Mike." Catherine's insouciance was palpable on the phone as well.

"You are still mad at me, huh?" Mike kept his patience and tried to probe her.

"You've done nothing wrong, why would I be mad at you? Actually, I'm happy now that I'm off the group. As if a burden has just lifted off, you know, Mike?"

"About that, we need to talk. I know I was out of line before but I need your help."

"No, Mike, I'm not coming anymore. I'm happy as I am. Just leave me alone and don't call me again." Catherine sounded uneasy and her eyes narrowed.

"You don't understand, Catherine. John misses you a lot. He's told me that he'd only work if you were ready to do it. And I need both of you. This is the last..."

"No. Sorry, Mike, I'm done with it. Tell John to go to hell. And it's never the last; you will always have the greed to do one more job every time we do one. It's not about the money; it's the thrill you seek from these adventures; playing hide-and-seek with cops and winning it eventually. Come to think of it, you are no better than Shawn," Catherine screeched and breathed heavily.

Mike exhaled, his eyes red now. "Catherine, you'd never have to work after this job, I promise." He tried to keep his cool. "Besides, John didn't tell you the truth about Zach's death. I will tell you once you complete the job."

"What is it, Mike? What's he hiding?" Catherine was puzzled. Her hunch was tingling.

"Catherine, come on. I'll tell you when you complete the job," Mike offered. Mike just threw a bone, he knew that John didn't know any better but if this made her join, nobody would mind. Of course, she'll be mad once she knows there was nothing to know, but it was worth a try. He'd already discussed this with John as a contingency plan.

"What if we can't do it successfully?" she inquired.

"A promise is a promise. I will tell you no matter what the outcome of our job," Mike affirmed.

"What makes you think that John wouldn't tell me before that?" Catherine's voice had that naughtiness.

"Same answer as before—a promise is a promise. I've got one from John that he can't tell anyone before the mission's over. So are you on board or not?"

"Okay, I'll do it just to know the truth. Where do I meet you?" Catherine agreed half-heartedly.

Mike gave the address and she noted it down carefully.

Mike hung up and watched the magnificent view of the musical fountains in front of him from his posh and luxurious Bellagio balcony. The panoramic view of "the strip" accentuated with the images and lights being reflected on the Bellagio pond was breathtaking. He watched the crowd that gathered surrounding the pool to take a glimpse of the dancing fountains. People stood still and heard the music and watched the fountains in plain awe. He gazed to his slight right to see Paris's replica of the Eiffel Tower in golden light. This city indeed never slept he told himself. There were people wondering in the street even on a weekday or any night. He saw a few limousines entering and getting parked under the grand porch of the Bellagio. He chugged his beer and sat there on the patio chair wondering what he could have done differently.

He asked himself how he had messed up. Life a few months back had just not been worth living. *The friends, my team, all had turned against me, me? Shawn was right; I haven't been a good leader. But this time I will straighten things all right.* His eyes were still fixated on the fountains.

Then he heard a ring from his plush hotel room that he'd been waiting for. He glimpsed down if he could see a particular car. His eyes had been seeing the glitz and glamour of Las Vegas but deep down he was looking for someone special on the road. He pushed to his feet and opened the balcony door inside to get into what might be termed as the "royal suite." It was actually a honeymoon suite for Mike. He had planned it thoroughly. He picked up the phone.

"Hello?"

"Hi, sir! I'm calling from the concierge's desk, there is a guest coming to your room. I just wanted to inform you as instructed." A sweet decadent voice came through.

"Thank you. I appreciate it."

"Thank you, sir. Enjoy your stay at the Bellagio. Anything else I can help you with?"

"No, that'll be it. Thanks."

"Okay, you have a wonderful night, sir." Click.

The suite was about two thousand square feet. It had three guest rooms, an office, and two full bathrooms. A large living room with wall-to-wall high-end brown carpet with blue and orange floral design wowed the guests with its opulence and grandeur. One-of-a-kind designer lamps shone light into the room. A huge, red, curved day bed lay in the center of the room next to a wall which a widescreen LED TV hung. On both sides of the day bed comfy but intentionally worn-out brown leather recliners rested. A small kitchen and a round glass dining table were at the end of the room at the northeast corner. A small crystal-bead chandelier made kaleidoscopic images on the glass table that was guarded by four red and brown leathered chairs that matched the kitchen counter top and the bar area next to it. Close to the entry but to one side, a large Jacuzzi bubbled, which was flush with the floor so you had to climb a couple of steps down to go in from the room floor. Below the TV an enormous, cherry-colored contemporary chest held fresh white and pink lilies in a twisted glass vase. The recess lighting enhanced the ambience, which was accentuated with smells like Cool Water perfume.

"Come in, please," Mike welcomed the guest.

"Wow, I'm impressed. You've done quite well for yourself. Did you have an escort service coming in daily?" the guest commented.

Mike was devastated after everyone left his farmhouse. The plan was to convene everyone at the farmhouse and talk about The Boss but that didn't come up due to all the other issues going on. He simply felt it wasn't important at that juncture and felt like his leadership was in question at that time.

He'd had days where he would just go surfing on the beach during the lull period or self-imposed exile for keeping low. He'd always had an athletic build and loved the ocean; however, after he "disbanded" the group, his heart grew fonder of it. He even travelled to California for its San Diego and Los Angeles beaches; also, once to Hawaii but he couldn't focus. He just felt that something had emptied him; he had this hollow feeling. His mind fast-forwarded a few years and he thought that what he'd do next in his life. He had never thought of quitting this "profession." He really didn't pay attention when he'd told Tina that he'd do something big and be done with all this.

In retrospect, he thought it was good to be alone for a while and understand what he really wanted. Time for reflection was essential. His life had changed. All of a sudden, positively, he felt relieved. He was not under pressure of a deadline to finish a job. From his numerous hotel rooms, he observed countless minions who rushed to meet ends while he guzzled his beer and romanced his retirement. After a fruitful conversation with himself, feeling satisfied yet unsatisfied, Mike came back to his New York loft.

He did have a feeling of apologizing to Tina and the others for not being a great leader and letting them down. His conscience was guilt-ridden but his mind would play tricks—sometimes feeling apologetic and at times revolting. He'd say to himself, *Nobody cared for me, why I should have a burden on my shoulders?* With this ping-pong being played in his mind, he would just pass time watching TV and going places. He met and greeted a few new people but wasn't fully getting out of a partial depressive phase of his life that he'd never experienced before. He could relate now to some of the celebrities who he watched on the gossip shows. Celebrities whose lives had tremendous fame when their star was rising and a few flop movies, albums, or a television series and they sunk badly with the sunset of their careers. No one would even bother to call them, as if a black hole just engulfed them into obscurity. He thought that he was probably missing being popular, being in command, being able to complete the job successfully, and pleasing the party that paid for it. He missed the feeling of that fulfillment.

What a lot of forceful soul-searching couldn't do, a phone call did. As fate would turn out, he got a call from The Boss.

"Congratulations! You got your traitor!" The Boss greeted.

"I'm in no mood of talking to you right now, you fucker. It's all because of you." Mike just blurted whatever he thought was right to say.

"What is because of me? I helped you. You should thank me. I saved your ass, you punk." The Boss's voice grew louder.

Mike then realized that the guy on the other end of the line doesn't need to know what happened at the farmhouse, or that he's disbanded his team. "Why have you called? And how the hell did you get hold of this number?"

"Oh, so now you are in the mood of talking again, bi-atch?" The Boss mocked.

"I don't have time for stupid talks. What is it? How did you know that I'd still be available on this phone?"

"I thought we always talked on this number, didn't we? But the real answer is greed, my friend. I understand that greed is the biggest vice and I can help you fill that. That's the reason you pick up my phone even though you may have changed your number looks like." The Boss slowly uttered the words.

"What's the job?" Mike came right to the point bluntly.

"Ah, I knew that you'd be willing to listen to my offer. Here's the deal. If you successfully do this, you may not have to work again. We need some distraction in Las Vegas." The Boss carefully laid it out on the table.

"Where exactly?"

"This job is not just creating a simple distraction; we need the power grid off of a couple of casinos for a few minutes."

"Impossible. They have backup generators that will fire up immediately. There is no way you can make it through the casino without getting shot at. But it is good to know that you are an overall petty thief."

"Call me whatever you want but I'm doing it for a cause and I'm smart about it. You're telling me that these casino owners are not thieves? They don't steal money from middle-class families? They rob them of their hard-earned money and deprive their families of stuff they could be really buying instead of wasting it in that whorehouse. If I have to rob a thousand casinos, I wouldn't have a drop of regret and will do it willingly... *insha'Allah*."

The last couple of words slipped from his mouth but The Boss continued, "I don't have to give a philosophical lecture to you right now. It is hard and that's why I've come to you again. You have to do the job; plus, I have an idea for you."

"Again, I don't like that tone. I don't work for you. I will do the job but at my own terms like before; that is, if I like the job and if I want to," Mike ordered. Mike knew that he needed a job but didn't want to sound needy.

"My friend, you'll have plenty of money for your seven generations, how about that as a term?" Mike could hear The Boss grinning.

"Okay, I'll do it but don't want the details on the phone," Mike replied.

"Should I post it on Facebook then?" The Boss's chuckled. His sarcasm didn't bother Mike.

"Here's the plan. In the New York Public Library's 'Gubernatorial Document' section on the main floor, there is a section about the Civil War. Pick the ninth edition of *The History of Civil War* and place a piece of paper on the exact details, names in code words, tomorrow at 8:00 p.m.," Mike explained, as if he'd thought through this before the call.

"You like to play games, huh?" The Boss chortled.

"Don't try to catch me. If I sense any scheme going on, I'll kill you." Mike's calm voice didn't project his fast heartbeat.

"I like your style. We'd be a good pair I tell you. Let's do that," The Boss affirmed, and hung up.

The next day, on a busy E Fortieth Street with taxis honking, the wind had picked up and was getting chillier from afternoon to evening. Close to Fifth Avenue, Mike sat on a bench in Bryant Park next to the New York Public Library reading a *New York Times*. He had his overcoat and thick spectacles with big black side-burns and a black hat. He looked like a Jewish rabbi more than anything he might have thought of doing but the getup worked. He looked at his expensive Bvlgari watch which showed 7:32 p.m., the sun was trying to hide in the horizon but wasn't successful yet.

He flipped a couple of pages and glanced at the soccer players that passed the ball from one player to another. He extinguished his cigarette butt on the corner of the bench and pushed to his feet. He then folded the newspaper, placed it under his armpit, and started walking toward the library.

The exterior of the building glistened in the orange light. He went past the majestic lions that guarded the library, climbed up the massive span of stairs, and went through the center entrance. He went straight to the clerk asking for help with a historical document and the clerk pointed the way through the main reading room. Mike wasn't new to the grand room. He heard a guide whispering to tourists that "this room measures seventy-eight feet by two hundred and ninety-seven feet. That is roughly two city-blocks' length."

He went past the group and went straight to the bookcases and looked up his one of a kind watch which displayed 7:42 p.m. There were a lot of people scattered looking up different books which were stacked on the sides of the main reading room. He picked his aisle and stood next to the ornate bookcase and started searching for a book. He was uncertain that if the library had multiple copies of the book then he'd have a hard time finding it before someone else got it. He couldn't take any chances.

Then Mike saw a guy in his mid-fifties with black leather pants and leather jacket come up to the section. He had brown hair which was mostly covered by a red bandana and glasses that hung high on his forehead. His teeth were all brown, and the face was freckled with dirty fingerprints like a mechanic. He certainly didn't belong in a library. Then he picked up *The History of Civil War.* Mike's back faced the guy's front on the other side of the bookcase. Mike watched the guy's reflection on his cell phone mirror while searching for a book on the other side. As soon as the guy turned, Mike picked up the book from behind, shook it open, and placed it back. A piece of paper dropped when he shook it, he bent down and safely placed it in his pocket and headed out.

The bandana guy turned back and looked at another guy who was sitting in the far corner reading the London Herald. He shook his head and the guy clenched his teeth and started walking toward him. The angle at which the other person was sitting he could clearly see someone picking up that book from the front as his partner had put it, but if someone were to take the book from behind and that too replace it so fast, it was impossible to detect. The chicanery worked again. The Rabbi left the library and called a taxi. The Rabbi looked at the quickly passing objects through his window but his mind was in a piece of paper that was in his pocket. He took out the paper and looked at the map and the instructions. He nodded his head and was shocked with his palm on his right cheek as if he secretly admired the bold plan The Boss put together. He knew that they both didn't trust each other much but the guy had put enough faith in him to give him this kind of operation. The timeline and distraction concerned him a bit.

"Mike, you are still the dreamy one!" The guest tapped on his shoulder from the back which jolted Mike back from the memory. He was still standing in his luxurious suite in Las Vegas.

"I apologize, Tina. I should have behaved better with you. You know these past few months have taught me a lot about myself." Mike poured Tina a glass of red wine and one for himself. He toasted and continued, "I think I just needed that seclusion from you guys to think properly. I think this is it. The time has come." He took a sip of the wine and enjoyed the taste on his tongue. "This will be our last big one." Mike just realized that she'd changed already.

"I hope so." Tina put her hand on the back of Mike's neck, pulled him in front of hers, and gave him a smooth, silky kiss.

Mike took Tina's hand and pulled her in front of the room where the warm Jacuzzi bubbles welcomed. He disrobed her bathing gown. He just stared at her in her orange bikini. Her figure was like a goddess, lean but well maintained in certain portions. Her beautiful face was radiating, along with her long legs that glistened with the shimmer. Her flat belly enticed Mike. She pushed a lock of her silky hair from the front of the face and asked cajoling, "What's your plan, Mike?"

Mike looked into her eyes and pulled her toward him and replied, "What do you think?"

"That this is our last big one," she laughed, and moved away from him.

Mike laughed at the joke and replied, "This isn't going to be the last one." He pushed her along with him in the hot tub. They splashed water at each other and enjoyed the evening doing what they enjoyed doing.

chapter

TWENTY-SIX

FIVE MONTHS BACK…

He had read the note again. He had digested the plan but his gut hadn't allowed him to do such a thing. He just couldn't believe this guy's plan. He had to admit it was brilliant but really damaging. *Do I really want to do this?* His mind started playing games with him again. After a long, forced sabbatical, this was his chance to end it all and start a new beginning with Tina.

"I can't do that. It is too risky. The distraction is not possible," Mike said loudly on the phone.

"Are you really saying that? The Mike I knew never hesitated. My friend, that's the reason you get paid so handsomely. Work is yours, you can use whatever means, but that's my idea."

"Firstly, we don't know if it will work after putting in all the effort, and second of all, it'll have a huge impact. I don't like the odds here," Mike offered.

"It's entirely your call. If the job's not done or we are not successful then the deal is off the table. You get paid zilch. I can help you with the equipment and stuff, but at the end, you need to do it. So make your judgment call," The Boss haggled.

Mike got the feeling that The Boss didn't want to do anything with his area of expertise but his idea was hard to pass up. He just needed to figure out how to make all the things work together. Mike did like the idea of a massive distraction, or should he say destruction, but couldn't swathe his mind around the idea. The idea was real demonic, no question about it. "Leave the distraction to me, you do your part. How about that?" Mike suggested.

"Well, I am not so sure about it this time. You have failed me before, but I trust you because you were let down by a mole in your team. This one is a difficult one and if you don't agree, I have others to do the job."

Mike wanted this job badly, he couldn't let it just pass. *It will be a morale booster; a moneymaker; a maniacal mission.* "No, I'll do it. You should have enough time to complete your job," Mike said.

"That's like a good boy. Just ring me if you need the equipments. I have the whole gamut." The Boss hung up.

Mike tried to get the identity of this guy. *He sounds like a fifty-plus guy, all-American accent with his phrases and he had the equipment to do all of this. But that could be bought or looks like he may have used it before somewhere else. No, can't be because otherwise, why would he involve me? Oh, also, he inadvertently once had ended his sentence with 'insha'Allah' in one of the talks. Is he a Muslim?*

Mike desperately needed John's help on this project. This was going to be a huge project which would take months of work to just get set up but the uncertainty lingered if it will work or not. *Or could it be done faster,* he thought.

After a hiatus, if he wanted everyone back on board it had to be something simpler. He wasn't sure if the guys were rusty. *Do I want Shawn back?* He didn't trust him, but he was ideal for a job this big. *Would Catherine, Tina, and John approve of this?* This very question had bothered him from the day he read that note. He thought they might but his heart had always said no. His mind teetered on the tautology: to tell or not to tell. And he thought of the repercussions of not telling and telling. He decided not to tell since it wouldn't get approved by anyone, except probably Shawn if he was on board because the guy simply didn't care. But the others were more humane and hence there was no reason to say anything about it. It would be hard to get everyone on board and not give the information on the distraction but that's where his leadership and trust would get tested, so he thought. Mike decided to go with his gut this time.

A Couple of Months Later
Near the Nevada Desert

It was a pitch-dark night. The Moon's partial crescent had just disappeared behind the roaring black clouds that seldom hover over the Mohave Desert. Tonight, however, felt like a different night. It was raining in Nevada near the desert. The city of Henderson was about to go to sleep after its routine business. The city of Henderson has about 250,000 people; it's not a very small town, but not a huge one either. Henderson was perfect for the next distraction. Mike's car stopped at the foot of McCullough range where a huge boat storage-like structure towered in front of him and he could see the city lights behind it. The range rose 3,800 feet above the ground and hid black rocks all over under its belly due to a volcanic explosion some million years ago. Like a lot of other lesser-known Nevada towns resting behind the glitz and glamour of Las Vegas, this obscure town once boasted to be the hub for war machinery material. The town served a great deal during World War II with its hugely popular magnesium that was used in missile cases, airplane engines, and other machinery. But Mike wasn't here to steal magnesium; he was following Antoine Bryant.

Antoine's car stopped at the exit gate of the tower structure. The gate opened after he scanned his badge, and he immediately rolled up the window to avoid getting wet. As expected, he was the last one to come out of the building. Mike had studied him for a few weeks now.

Mike's black Range Rover followed his silver Toyota Camry. A long narrow road outside the city snaked through the range and joined the bustling city. At night, there was nothing but emptiness surrounding the area. There were no cars coming this desolate way. The road going away from the city led to more desert to the east. Generally, no one bothered to venture that way because it was a dead end after a few miles and the overall area was tightly secured by law enforcement.

Antoine picked up the phone and called his wife. Mike could barely see a glimmer of light in Antoine's car through his cars' sweeping wipers, which were barely helping in pushing water from the windshield.

Mike was alone and couldn't take any chances. He had to catch the guy before he reached the entrance of the city. As soon as he saw Antoine's phone light was off in the car, Mike suddenly swerved his car to the left as if overtaking the car in the front. Antoine looked at the car to the left but the low visibility and rain made it difficult to see who was in the black Range Rover. Unexpectedly, the car on the left accelerated slightly ahead and suddenly took a sharp right turn, swerving it on the road horizontally and blocking the Camry's path. Antoine immediately braked and came to a screeching halt. Mike swiftly jumped out of his vehicle. He looked taller in his black overcoat, water dripping off his head. Before Antoine could make any calls or do something damaging, Mike immediately pulled his 9 mm with silencer and shot his windshield. Antoine was aghast. He tried to get the phone from the phone holder, which was hooked to an auxiliary cable and playing soothing music just before the shrill sound of the glass breaking. Antoine fumbled to dial but

Mike dove onto the hood and placed the muzzle of the 9 mm on Antoine's forehead.

Antoine froze. His face, originally pale black, was now partially red. He seemed to be in his mid-forties with a few wrinkles on his face. He kept an unkempt French beard and had a buzz-cut afro. He appeared slightly older due to a pair of Kenneth Cole, black-with-silver-trim rectangular spectacles that looked like two, attached magnifying glasses. He seemed tall, even when sitting behind the wheel. His hands were up, his body shivering, and a couple of tears rolled down on his cheek.

"What ddd...do you want? Please don't kill me. I can give you my wallet, cell phone, and this car." His hands trembled, as did his voice while speaking.

Mike pressed the muzzle harder on his forehead while both got wet from the rain that was now dripping inside the car from the broken windshield. "I'll come straight to the point." He took out a photo from his overcoat and flashed it in front of the driver. "Recognize her?"

Antoine's face turned white as snow. He couldn't believe where this was going. He was in deeper shit than he thought. "Yes, what do you want?" quivered Antoine.

"Shhhhhh...just answer my questions. Don't ask too many questions? If you want to celebrate her birthday that's coming next Monday, you'll do whatever I say."

"I'll kill you if you do anything to my daughter. I don't care who you are or why are you just barging into my life," Antoine screamed.

The weather was getting stormier. The thunderstorm growled and the lightning was visibly razor-sharp against the stark contrast of the black sky. Tonight, the Mohave Desert would quench its thirst, as if it wanted to squeeze every drop from the clouds before they rolled away.

Mike clicked on the trigger and pushed the muzzle hard on his head, piercing his skin. A streak of blood appeared and rolled down his forehead. "You can't do shit, but I will do whatever I want. If you tell anyone about this, even your wife, then I will come to twenty-three hundred Connor Way and kill your daughter and wife. If you go to the police, the same will happen. So listen carefully, meet me at 'The Fountains' at ten a.m. tomorrow near the café; I will explain what I want."

"I am not going to do anything. Kill me right now," Antoine blurted, after mustering up the courage.

Mike shot another round and Antoine skipped a heartbeat. "It's not about you, it's about your daughter and your wife, do you understand?" The bullet went through the driver-side window, breaking the glass into a spider-web pattern. Shards of glass flew onto Antoine's lap, and a couple of slivers got stuck in his face. He was staggered; no words came out of his mouth. With his hands still up, he just nodded his head violently, tears flowing down on his cheeks.

"Good, that's like a good boy!" Mike patted on his head with the 9 mm in the same hand. With his left hand, Mike pulled out the keys from the ignition, put them in his pocket, and jumped off the hood sideways to the driver-side door. He motioned for Antoine to come out by waving his revolver sideways. Antoine, still with his hands up and shocked, slowly stood up and clicked open the door.

Mike, fully drenched, handed him his car keys and said, "Use this car. Tell everyone that you've given the car for service and this is an interim rental car they have lent you. Be casual, don't look suspicious, fearful, or threatened, and never ever disclose our meeting to anyone or else you know what I am capable of." He placed Antoine's phone in Antoine's pocket. "If you don't come, I will call you and hunt you down."

Antoine thought that the idea of not showing those feelings seemed utterly impossible. Still oblivious to what this guy wanted, Antoine had no choice but to surrender and obey. He couldn't comprehend his wife and daughter getting shot. He nodded and took the keys. Mike motioned for him to go toward the Range Rover, "Go, now."

Mike took the already ajar door of the Camry and heaved himself into the front seat. He smashed the remaining windshield through with his leg and the window's spider-web with his elbow. He turned the key and the engine roared to life, but he waited for Mr. Bryant to start his before following him through the sinuous road toward the city. Mike followed Antoine to his house and left with a salute, which was the ultimate threat.

The threat had worked. Antoine was a simple guy and his life had suddenly changed today. Antoine had no idea who this guy was, but he definitely knew a lot about his family, where they lived, where he worked, when he came out of work, and his daughter's birthday! *This guy definitely is an insider or knows an insider who probably is helping him. Gosh! Damn it! I don't know what he wants.* He drove the car into his driveway but just lay on the steering wheel for a good twenty minutes in order to come out of the shock and appear normal to his wife. Suddenly, his phone rang. He picked it up and pressed the green button in terror.

"Remember, ten a.m. at 'The Fountains' or else." Then he just heard the dial tone. No number appeared on the screen. He shut off the phone with his hand on his forehead and, startlingly, another ring came. He looked at the phone in his hand, and to his relief, it was his wife—or was it a relief really, he pondered.

He declined the call and reluctantly came out of the car scheming up things to say to her about the car, why he was drenched, and any other details that might come up.

The Next Day
10:00 a.m. at The Fountains

The Fountains was a huge, ultra-modern café with a seating area as large outside as inside. Beige, rounded umbrellas with gold poles decorated the hexagon glass tables with Plexiglas chairs surrounding them with matching brown cushions. The frames of the chairs were all beige to match the umbrellas. People ordered pastries and their famous mouth-watering cakes and enjoyed them near the large chocolate fountain, which was nicely located inside the café but seen outside from a giant glass window. Mike sat their sipping his macchiato in his black and black combination when Antoine appeared in a white tee and blue jeans looking for someone. His face appeared as white as his t-shirt—grave and shocked. He tried to seem more relaxed than the other day, but he couldn't hide his emotions well. Mike signaled him outside to a corner table. He pulled out the Plexiglas chair and sat opposite to Mike.

"Good morning, Mr. Bryant," Mike greeted.

"Look! Whatever you may want, do not touch my family or I swear I'll kill you. I haven't had the courage to kill a bug so far, but I swear if something happens to my daughter, I'll hunt you down." Antoine's voice echoed low but enraged.

"Calm down, Mr. Bryant. Stop dreaming when you are not in a position to do anything of the sort. And nothing needs to happen if you simply obey as I tell you," Mike suggested.

"What the hell do you want?" Antoine tried to whisper but still others could listen as he got louder with anger.

"Stop yelling or Maggie will be gone. If I just make one phone call, my sniper will take a shot from the window and both your daughter and wife will be dead. Now, listen carefully. On next month's first Thursday, when you go to work to operate the plant, you will go to forty thousand PSI at a full 4.2-mile depth. Comprende?"

chapter

TWENTY-SEVEN

"Half the job is done. I'd need the drills in Tucson, Arizona tomorrow. I will give the exact address tomorrow. " Mike stood in a public booth while Tina was sitting in an open café looking at Mike. She seemed curious as to what Mike was planning and who he was talking to.

"I'm proud of you, Mikey boy. You never trust me, huh? You are still keeping the site a secret. Okay, I'll play along as long as it's gonna work. Hope you don't take three states all at one time." Mike could hear boisterous laughter. Immediately, Mike pulled the phone away from his ear. The voice continued, "I'll be around to see your work this time. We may be able to meet. Insh—" The sentence stopped in between.

"I'm doing your work but on my own terms. I will give you your distraction," Mike stressed with gusto. "Plan for next month's Thursday. Ciao." Mike shut off his state-of-the art cell phone and got out of the public booth.

Tina was concerned and watched Mike getting out of the booth and walking toward her. He was wearing a black suit and looked dashing, as she had always found him. He had kept a short amount of stubble, which Tina loved. He pulled a chair next to Tina on a tiny, white table made of ornate iron. On top was a small candle, and it was almost getting dark. Mike ordered tagliatelle pasta with pesto sauce with focaccia pugliese biga bread and Tina ordered an Italian salad with Italian dressing. "How cliché?" Mike smiled at her and returned the menus to the well-groomed waiter.

"Mike, honey, what are you up to? What are we doing? Why are you so secretive this time? You look so tensed. I've never seen you this tensed before." Tina put her hand on Mike's hand and asked curiously.

"Trust me, Tina, I'd love to disclose this right now but we still have about a month and I'll let you know when the time is right. I think half the battle is won but I need others on board, and that's what's bothering me." Mike drew his hand through his ruffled, spiked hair, tapped his other hand on top of Tina's, and looked into her eyes.

"Oh, that's no problem. I will talk to John and he'll convince Catherine. It shouldn't be that hard," Tina candidly replied.

"I hope so. I'd need everyone's help here. I will have to talk to Shawn bi-atch myself."

While picking her salad leaves on her silver fork and shoving them into her mouth, Tina replied, "Oh, Mikey, I forgot to tell you. I talked to him a few days back. He said he's gonna do a big job with Gary. He didn't talk much but said something about the Caribbean Island; said he was gonna be there for a couple of months. I didn't hear from you and I needed some money, so I'd contacted him. I'm sorry." Tina put her fork down and looked into Mike's eyes.

"That's all right; I wasn't of much help either. It's not your fault. Sorry for treating you like that once again, love. I am lucky to have you back. But that puts me into a precarious position. I need one more person to do this job, which means they need to be hired and tested immediately."

"Can we not finish this one with four people? How big is it?" Tina asked.

"It's big. Baby, it's show time; no time to play around on this one. Let me rethink the plan because I thought it with and without Shawn, but I would have been more comfortable if he'd been in. No worries. I've got it under control," Mike replied with a smile, rubbing her forearm.

"Look, Mike, we are in Vegas. If it's big, it's gotta be something related to stealing from the casinos, and we are creating a distraction for that. Did I guess it right or what?" Tina whispered with a slight grimace on her face, still chewing.

"Yes, you are partly correct; but this time, we'll have a bigger chunk, trust me. I'll let you know everything," Mike said, taking a big bite of bread into his mouth.

"Who were you talking to?" Tina said while finishing her last bite and rubbing her mouth with the white, satin napkin.

"*The Boss*. I don't know him and I don't trust him. He had the idea but he didn't know how to execute or have the right people for the job. This time I might catch him in the action, but I don't want to be caught in the action at the same time. I've spent more than six months of my life on this project; believe me, I will not let anything happen to us and will tell you everything at the right time." Mike's blue eyes grew wider and Tina could feel the honesty in his reply. Tina nodded.

"By the way, John's on board and he's on special duty already." Mike winked at her while finishing his dish. Tina raised her brows displaying a dislike that John had already been a confidant.

"Tina, make sure you directly call Catherine. We need her on board; I'll see what I can do with one less man."

Antoine remembered the day at The Fountains. Antoine was aghast as soon as he realized the apocalyptic plan. "Are you fucking nuts? That high pressure and that depth can cause chaos. We haven't done that before. That can actually cause..."Antoine abruptly stopped and just stared with his eyes wide open. He couldn't believe what this guy wanted him to do. "There is no way in hell I'm going to do this. You can kill me right now." Antoine's face was in rage and terror.

"Antoine, just look at this video." Mike took out his Smartphone and showed him live video telecasting his home. The video showed his wife in the kitchen and daughter Maggie playing in the backyard with their dog. Antoine started sweating like a pig. He was completely befuddled. He now understood exactly what this guy wanted to create, an earthquake!

Antoine was a geothermal power engineer and had high authority controlling the experiments they did underneath the rocks of McCullough Range near Henderson. Advanced geothermal techniques involved drilling deep into the hot rocks and then injecting them with high-pressured water. The propelled water made it into the Earth's shell creating crevices in the rock and absorbed that heat. Then they pumped the heated water back and used the ensuing steam to turn electricity-generating turbines. In the United States alone, the Department of Energy had given more than $100 million to enhanced geothermal projects. But the drilling was done only up to one mile, or a max of two miles depending on the state of the Earth. Deep drilling causes fractures in the rock to interact with seismic activity in such a way that could produce huge quakes. Antoine remembered correctly that one of his idols, Markus Haring from Switzerland, had caused more than thirty earthquakes in December 2006, with the largest registered earthquake being a 3.4 on the Richter scale.

Mike was talking about much higher pressure and drilling up to four and a half miles, a depth that can cause extensive damage. It could wipe out Henderson and could even wipe out Las Vegas as a whole. *That's just insane*, he thought.

Snapping his fingers, Mike said, "Antoine, I've done a rough calculation. It will give about a 4.0 earthquake on the Richter scale for probably only ten to fifteen seconds at the most, in a radius of about a hundred miles. That's like being in Southern California where Mother Earth shakes and stops at her own merit. You will just be mimicking Earth in a different area. What do you say?"

"Rough calculation, huh? Whatever your name is, mister, you are completely out of your mind. I'm not doing it, period. You can do whatever. I'm leaving and going to the police straight away. If you want to shoot me, shoot." Antoine pushed to his feet.

Mike, cautious of his surrounding, calmly showed his hand to stop, pressed a few buttons on his phone, and turned the phone toward him. He could again see his wife in the kitchen window and suddenly saw kitchen window breaking and his wife fell down by the impact. Antoine was so infuriated he punched Mike in his face and the phone flew away and everyone looked at them. Mike calmly picked up the phone while Antoine looked down angrily and anxiously. Antoine felt helpless. Mike guided his hand to Antoine's elbow, pushed him outside of the café, and started walking with him.

"Look, fucker, I'm not kidding, do you see that? Mike's eyes were now red with a slither on his face from the hard punch. You'll pay for this, you punk-bitch. Do you think I'm kidding here?" He pushed Antoine away and punched a few numbers on his phone. He again put the screen in front of Antoine's eyes. Now, he could see his daughter playing with the dog in the back-yard. All of a sudden, the dog got shot and he lay flat on the ground in front of his daughter. His daughter started scream-ing and crying. The sound wasn't so good but he could feel his daughter.

"You motherfucker." Antoine pushed Mike hard and start-ed punching him in the stomach and face on the road and people just looked at them. "That's it, baby. You all are going down; first your wife, then your daughter, and then you." Mike's voice was menacing to him but still low enough that others couldn't hear. He immediately called a taxi and pushed him inside the taxi with him. Antoine started crying vehemently. He crouched down, shoving his face in his hands. Mike gave a hard elbow on his back and Antoine moaned. "Hey, whatever you guys have, take it outside the taxi," the driver yelled. Mike was so mad that he could kill both of them, but he kept his calm. He knew he needed this big distraction. The driver dropped them where Mike had instructed. It was the southern end of Henderson, and nothing much was going on there. Away from the bustle of the city, it was quiet.

Mike gave the money to the taxi driver, but the driver felt something was wrong. The place where he dropped both of them seemed remote, but he just minded his business and went away toward the city.

"This is the last chance; are you going to do this or not? I'm asking you this last time and mind well that this is not a request. Your wife's not dead; it was just a stone through the window. And the dog's been shot with a micro tranquilizer, but both of them could have been shot by bullets. Say no, and I will show you your family getting killed right now. Then I will kill you here. End of story. Do you think I can't find someone else to do the same? I can actually find a few engineers and they can even be bought by money. I don't want to create huge damage, and you know the drill much better than the others do; which is why I am choosing you. If I only cared about the quake, I could have talked to anybody, but then it won't be a controlled experiment, would it? Think about Bob Marsh, Ajay Mane, Chung Wo, Harry Pierre, Joy Moore." Mike spoke confidently and tried to raise some good questions in Antoine's mind.

Antoine's phone rang. Of course, it was his wife, as he expected. He looked at Mike. "Pick it up, but tell her to remain calm," Mike demanded.

Antoine told his wife to calm down. The stone that broke the window could have been some rowdy teenage kids and the dog must have gotten a heat stroke or something. He should be back on his feet soon. Soon enough, while he spoke to her, the dog was getting his senses back and his wife seemed appeased enough. Antoine hung up the phone and turned to Mike. "Do you fucking know what forty thousand PSI and a four-mile deep drilling means? First of all the director wouldn't authorize that at all. My hands will be tied. Secondly, this could even mean we could have a quake that's a five to six on the Richter scale. And that would be for a prolonged period of time, depending on what seismic activity gets stimulated. It's impossible to structure and control once you have induced the fractures this far into the rocks. There is no stability or control after that. This could annihilate the entire city of Henderson, Las Vegas, and other cities. This is completely crazy. It will kill my daughter and wife and myself anyways; it will destroy our property completely. Why should I do it?"

"*Now, we're talking.* First of all, you'd add earthquake insurance and make it worth a million dollars. Then you'll send your daughter and her mother to a safe location. Once you trigger the operation, you don't need to stay there. Take the company's helicopter and fly away. You'll get your cut also. You don't need to suffer. It won't be that big, I've seen so many calculations."

"What makes you so sure? Those are paper calculations."

"Because I've spent two months studying this in Switzerland. I have observed the scientists and even stolen the research papers. I've done whatever I could to understand this." Mike's stare pierced Antoine's eyes confidently.

"So you've killed more people doing this." Antoine shook his head in disbelief. He continued, "Even if I want to do this, we don't even have that type of drill. We have only drilled up to one mile. Just the drilling alone would take a month, or even two to three months depending on if the drill breaks or some other equipment malfunction, which is common in this field. This is not something you can learn in two or six months and just start dancing with it. I've spent my entire life studying this. This is a science which is still not exact. You need years of perfection, and still you can't guarantee the result."

"That's why I've picked you. I've brought the drills, specially imported. You will allow them to go through as a special supplier and convince the director to go deeper; don't tell him about 4.2 miles. In the daily report, publish a false report of 2.5 miles, but I want you to reach at least four miles by next month. If you don't, I will kill you and your family. I have also shortlisted three other engineers, Harry, Joy, and Ajay. I will pick them one by one to do this same job, and if that isn't successful, I will go inside with fake documentation. I know you guys are always in search of good geothermal engineers. Once I get access, I will do it myself. So you see, if you don't do it, I have so many other alternatives to do it. I'm asking you since you are the expert and can minimize the damage. Choice is yours, and you get your benefits rather than dying."

Fuck, man!" Antoine just squatted down, looking at the ground furious with his choices. He shook his head for a long minute while picking up twigs from the ground.

He stood up more confidently and said, "How much will you pay me? I don't think I'll have any future after this in this industry. They will hunt me down, then where's the protection?"

Mike squatted in front of him and looked into his eyes. "I'll guarantee your and your family's protection once you do this, and then I'll send you to Canada or Mexico—your choice of country with fake passports. You would have enough money to do nothing, or start your own business if you decide to."

"I know I can't trust you but I'll do it, and I will make sure that there is only a small quake." Antoine's eyes were red with tears and he shook with anxiety, fear, sadness, and anger.

"I'll tell you the volume we need for the water on Thursday. You don't start injecting water till I tell you on Thursday," Mike said.

"But there is no way this can happen in a month and a half from now," Antoine responded.

"You will make it happen." Mike looked into his eyes and put his hand on his shoulder. Antoine removed it with a thrust.

The sun was on top of them and it was a complete contrast from yesterday's rain. The heat was scorching and the tan was palpable on Mike's face. Both started walking toward a lonely bar, which seemed infinitely far from them. The air, the heat, the mirage, the daunting task in front of Antoine was making it difficult while he was stodging. Mike finally had a breather since he had won the battle. He knew he'd played a gamble because he didn't have a real shooter the day before at his house, but he thought the threat itself would be enough for him to not contact anyone. He'd put a radio-frequency transmitter in the living room so he could hear the entire conversation in Antoine's place. He kept a good watch so that Antoine didn't do anything stupid. John, in an orange shirt and green, fluorescent vest with a white helmet, was equipped with a micro-tranquilizer gun and sat perched in the cage of an electrical company's truck. There he pretended to fix a light pole and was advantageously located having a clean view of Antoine's backyard and the kitchen window from high up. Mike had to be very careful because he couldn't let this guy buckle under the pressure or elope with his family. It was time for the ultimate threat.

After a long, and what seemed like endless, walk under firing heat, both stood in the parking lot of a bar. Mike said, "Here's the deal, Antoine. I trust you, but my people and I will be continuously watching your family. If you change your mind at any point—or after going to work, you tell someone about this—I will find out. Currently, the choice is that I've allowed them to stay with you during this month, but I can simply kidnap them anytime and keep them captive until you finish the job; keep that in mind. At no point does the plan change until I say it changes. Understood?"

Antoine, not eager to enter into another debate recognizing his limited choices, just nodded with his hand on his stomach. He was in pain after a long walk with an empty stomach, a mouth dry as hell, and a back that hurt because of Mike's strong elbow knock.

chapter

TWENTY-
EIGHT

After reaching the hotel room, Tina called Catherine and explained the whole situation. Catherine was tentative and hesitant. However, Mike threw the bone to Catherine about the truth behind Zach's death and assured her that this was going to be the last job everyone would do. Catherine definitely took the bait, reluctantly agreed, and showed up at the hotel finally. Mike had already informed John that he had made a false promise to Catherine to join and John had to play along. John was initially reluctant and was really bothered and confused, but then he agreed.

Mike then left a message to Shawn on what Tina had said and that he was interested in him being on board for a new job. Mike couldn't count on him anyways, so he couldn't wait. He was ready to do this operation with four people as long as Antoine supported it.

Mike had done his research this time. Antoine was the chief officer directly reporting to the director and he had a couple of engineers working for him. Antoine had put a lot of thought into this. He knew that Mike was right. If he didn't do it, Mike could make others do it. And if he had spent as much time as he said he had, he could get in the control room and do it with a few of his men, but he still would have to go through all the password locks and other digital barriers.

A couple of days after he'd agreed to do the job, Antoine entered and exited the control room more often than ever and kept his sights on every bit of information. He quickly generated a fake report that there was a huge steam pocket a mile below and he'd have large success if he drilled one extra mile.

In the dimly lit conference room, in his black suit and with all the confidence he could muster, he pointed to the infrared foil showing the pressure, heat, and deep pockets of air within the rocks of Henderson. "Gentlemen, I bring you the mother of all steam pockets and the surrounding area through which we could generate enough electricity for all of Henderson." The director, two assistants, two engineers, and a couple of technicians looked flabbergasted.

"But, according to the graph, it shows additional one mile deep," the first engineer questioned.

"Yes, that's correct. But as you can see with the new drills that I've ordered and this report from a Swiss lab, you could easily go to that depth without disrupting anything." Antoine tossed the report in front of the engineers.

"Antoine, you're a fine engineer. I respect you, but this is not a university lab where you can perform this type of experiment. You know this is highly dangerous if we go too deep. You know the consequences and yet you want to attempt such a stupid plan. You don't seem very confident in the plan that you're proposing, are you?" The director raised his brows and spoke with a high voice.

"Here's the detailed plan." Antoine went on explaining where they would puncture and how deep they would go with the titanium drill and swiftly thrust high-pressured water inside the crevice to generate and then pump it back. The whole plan was foolproof. After a lot of negotiations, the director ordered that he could do 0.2 miles per day and send him a direct progress report via email, as the director was leaving for a tour of Europe. Everyone left the conference room but Antoine was sweating like a pig and was shaking in his chair. However, he had to act positive. After the meeting, he gathered a little bit of faith that the plan was working. The challenge still was that he had to go two additional miles deeper. Plus, before sending the report, he had to send real reports to Mike. He wondered if Mike would understand anything of his infrared scatter plots.

The next day, two brand new trucks arrived at the property and, as expected, the security prohibited them to enter the geothermal station. Antoine got a call from the officer. After a few briefing questions, they allowed them to enter. Two military-like, black trailers entered the enormous, well-lit premises.

It looked like a huge warehouse, and the ceiling seemed like it was touching the ozone layer. There was a huge caution sign, and barricades stopped the vehicles on the concrete flooring. Flexible walls prevented anyone from seeing any further what was going on. Loud noises of underground construction echoed in the hall. A big whirring sound with occasional hissing and a continuous salvo of digital beeps filled the room; no wonder all the engineers and technicians were wearing ear-muffling headphones.

Mike and, John in their new disguises, sat in the truck just to study the facility. Antoine and the engineers ordered their laborers to crane the drills from the truck. Antoine looked at the drivers, but he didn't see anything noticeable. One driver jumped off the truck to go to the restroom and immediately the security guards stopped him. Without security clearance, he wasn't authorized to step into the premises. He wasn't allowed to go to the rest room. Once they were unloaded, both drivers picked up and left the area.

Antoine immediately ordered that the drills be installed. One of his sharp engineers felt like Antoine was in some kind of a hurry. Antoine was in a hurry to save his family and himself, but at the same time, he was a respectful and kind human being who just couldn't understand the malicious intentions of others. He started reading about the new drills. He made sure that he was present for every calibration and every foot they went deeper. The engineers also felt some kind of bizarre change in Antoine's behavior. He was now micromanaging them, actually the whole facility all of a sudden. They talked to each other, "Must be the discovery. He probably wants to hog the glory all by himself." Antoine wanted this to go as smoothly as possible while also fulfilling Mike's request. He was doing his best.

Mike got a good idea about the location and the facility, although they didn't allow him to go far in the big arena. He noticed that the security was sparse. McCullough's hills were not like Yosemite's mountains where people flocked every day. The range sat in total obscurity and relative anonymity, even though it was close to Las Vegas. Nobody usually came to the facility except a few governmental agencies to study and a few geological engineers. The black suits came with their own security. The place didn't have any valuable items except the technology itself and one couldn't damage anything in a day's time, so it made sense that the government was saving money on security. From inside the truck, he noticed a few cameras at different locations outside the building and inside it. This preparation was needed if Antoine was to bail on them at the last minute somehow.

Mike and John got reports daily and they made sure they were authentic. Every week Antoine would find some kind of a threatening note like a cat killed on his driveway or the side yard door would be open when he would go home. Often there would be a hole dug out in the dirt next to the concrete pathway and on the concrete, with dirt, it would read, 'Deeper Faster or Kill her.' He would rub it off with his shoes and then ask about if someone had come to do the yard work. His wife would always reply, "No." The threats were made strategically so that the wife or daughter didn't notice. The dog had to be killed a few weeks ago to do all these things. Antoine bought his daughter a new puppy. After three weeks, he found a note pinned between the wiper blade and the windshield of the car. "Good Work. Keep it up. Liked the yellow railings, grey tall walls, and the height at which you sit. Will call you." Antoine hurriedly looked around only to find silent houses nearby and immediately went inside the car and drove. As soon as he passed the city area and was entering into no man's land, he received a call.

Mike sounded joyous. "Hey, good job, Antoine. Glad that the insurance worked out and the depth's reaching. I hear that your wife and kid are leaving soon."

"Look, I've done what you've said; but going deeper is risky. The temperature is getting higher and the engineers will soon figure out that I'm going way farther down." Antoine wiped the sweat beads from his forehead with the tissue from his car.

"You have to make it work, Antoine; you got no choice. Also, make sure that your wife and kid leave just before a day. Our men will be there to escort them and make sure they reach their destination safely."

"No, you never said that. They will be free to go. I'm doing what you said, let them go." Tears welled up as he thought of his helplessness in saving his family.

"I'm still saying that they'll be allowed to go free once you have done what you are supposed to, or until I am satisfied. Then let it do its magic. As I said before, you can take the company's bird from the top floor and leave to your wife's location," Mike passively ordered, with a threatening tone.

"Fuck, man, why me? Why did I get involved in this?" He parked aside and slammed on the steering wheel with teardrops wetting his pants and the seat.

"Don't be afraid, Antoine. You are doing pretty good. I didn't say anything that'll harm your family as long as you do what we said. They will still go to your in-laws' place. My men will be just outside the house as an added security, which you'll explain to them why they need it, fair?" Mike sounded condescending and he knew it.

Antoine's fingers wiped the tears from underneath his spectacles as he looked around from the car. He just nodded softly and said, "Yeah." He hit the gas hard. Antoine thought that he already knew where they were planning to go and he cursed himself for being such an idiot to choose such an obvious location. *I could have chosen a friend or some other relative, or a motel for that matter. Shit!*

chapter

TWENTY-NINE

Finally, the day arrived. Still only John and Mike knew what was really going to happen. Mike was up early and looked down from his balcony puffing his cigar. Tina came from behind and embraced him.

"Couldn't sleep?" Tina asked lovingly, resting her head on his back with her palms resting on his chest.

"Un-huh. Same with you, huh?" Mike replied after he took a long drag and looked at the water of the pond beneath them that sparkled blue-green in the early morning light. He turned around and kissed her on the forehead. "So are you ready for today?" Tina was lost in thoughts already.

"You don't seem to be in a good frame of mind, Mike. Something's different about you. I miss my old Mike." Tina looked in his eyes with intensity. She knew that it was going to be big but it puzzled her why Mike was being so secretive. She felt that Mike didn't like to be vulnerable, and that's what he had experienced with his team before. He wasn't taking any chances this time around. He seemed closed. He seemed excessively worried and didn't share the responsibilities till now. But she supported whatever she was told to do. "Mike, be positive. I believe that whatever you do, you'd have well thought it out, especially this time."

"Tina, people change with time. I've probably changed. Maybe a lot's going through my mind." Mike defended himself and looked away again at the sky puffing the last stub of his cigar.

"Well, I hope you are fine. I trust you, Mike. I'll do whatever you've said. Now, let's get ready." She seemed afraid. She seemed vulnerable and she knew that Mike was hiding something from all of them. They didn't know what and she didn't display if she cared to know. While she left the balcony, her mind wandered onto yesterday's talks.

Yesterday, in the plan briefing, Mike mentioned the whole plan—that there was dynamite placed underneath the sewage lines. One would trigger another and at about a one-mile radius near the strip, it would rattle, especially near the Cosmopolitan and Bellagio area. The plan was to cripple their power supply so that the "other" team could get access to the casino vault area.

The dynamite blasts were going to provide enough of a distraction to take down their power supply and emergency generators would have to kick in. During the switch, The Boss's team would start their plan and enter the Cosmopolitan Casino's treasury area. They might need more help inside the casino if they start beefing up the security force. Mike's team would again distract those folks.

The mastermind, Mike, was going to play a dual game here. The plan was that at about 1:00 p.m., two of the casino's cash trolleys are taken to the casino vault which served for the whole of slot machines. Those huge cash trolleys would stash at least a couple million dollars, especially with the big weekend going on. Catherine and Tina would be the only people who'd carry the trolleys but instead of going to the treasury area, they will go to the outside exit where two armored truck will be ready to go right after the rattle. It will be chaotic and people will start running around once the explosion happens underneath. Once the pandemonium reins the area, using that chaos, they will start dragging the trolleys outside. John would be somewhere else handling the detonation. Mike would be inside the casino playing blackjack. He'd use his gun if needed and provide a backup to the ladies during the bedlam.

Mike would have brought the armored truck just before the detonation. Shawn had not called and he wasn't coming, according to Mike. Everyone was going to communicate through hidden pieces of walkie-talkies as usual. Tina had a hard time learning dealing blackjack. She had to be very accurate. Catherine picked up very quickly and looked professional. Tina, however, fumbled throughout and was warned by Mike not to mess it up during the show. Sometimes she forgot to give the money right away as soon as someone gets a blackjack or would forget to ask someone to put the minimum bet, and if someone asked to split the cards, she got all confused. She had good practice last night though.

A warm shower sprayed across Tina's curvaceous body and the mist covered the transparent glass shower. Mike stood there watching Tina bathe until the mist covered the door. He sighed and went to get ready. As the shower hit his head, thoughts poured in his mind about why he had lied about Antoine and the whole geothermal energy part. From the beginning, he'd been very discreet and never showed his documents or anything to Tina or Catherine. He was worried that John would open his mouth to Catherine because he noticed that he was getting too friendly with Catherine again. They had even gone out a few times to dine in expensive Vegas restaurants and clubs. He strictly warned John that Catherine reluctantly joined and if she knew that they were torturing a family and going to do massive damage, she might quit or mess up the mission, and so might Tina. This time he was playing too many games at one time and he had to be very accurate in every move. He didn't want to talk about what could happen to anyone. This was his game and he wanted to go big this time. Once and for all, he would do or die. His bravery, his intelligence, his confidence that bordered arrogance had led him to this and he wouldn't change it for anybody. Not even for Tina.

It was a big mission that he simply couldn't afford to miss. He had persevered for this one for over a year and he just didn't want to miss on any part of it. He'd given the sacrifices and for just a few sentiments and emotions, he couldn't let it go. He didn't care about the damage it could produce and the people it could kill. This time, he simply didn't care. No matter what, winning was in his mind, and winning big was something that he'd planned. He was short of men this time; he knew that. John was handling Antoine's family. He had to play the part of bringing the armored truck as close to the exit as possible without getting evicted. He had to change, and then play cards as well. Catherine and Tina were to get the trolleys. Everything was perfectly set. He still wondered how The Boss's men were going to enter into the treasury without getting zapped with the laser or the alarm or the huge security force. And even if they did, how were they going to break the 256-bit encrypted digital combination of an titanium built safe. *And even if they entered, how are they really going to transfer the money and escape. It's a suicide mission. Well, it's there problem.*

Tina and Catherine started walking toward the parking lot. After carefully studying for a week, a couple of hours before the whole operation, Mike had captured two lady card dealers who were similar in body structure and facial features. It had been a rather easy task. John got one at her own house because everyone else left early for work or school and Mike got the one who went to a nearby church every day before going to work. Tina had done her makeup to look similar to the dealer she would impersonate, and Catherine's shirt tag displayed the name 'Camilla.' Both took their respective cars as they were briefed and headed toward Cosmopolitan. Tina scanned her badge at the backside entry of the employee parking lot and entered. Catherine and Tina entered the employee locker room, but both were ready. They both went to their tables as explained before and replaced the dealers.

Mike killed the engine and looked to his left. He had brought the truck that looked similar to Cosmopolitan's armored truck, which he had painted a couple of days ago and kept it underground. He was asked by the front security guard why he had come so early. He had replied that it was the new time and route he had been given. He showed his paperwork. The guard reached to his back, took out his walkie-talkie, and started heading inside with the paper.

Mike promptly followed the guard, went inside, and stood at the entrance. Mike looked at the time on his watch and said to himself, "Come on, Antoine!" His eyes met both the dealers who were opposite to each other on different tables, both clad in their black and white. Suddenly a hand from behind tapped on Mike's shoulder. "Where is the driver for the other truck?" another guard suspiciously asked, looking at Mike's badge. Mike said, "Uh...uh...he must be in it, or maybe he's in the back of the truck checking something." Mike observed that the trolleys were rolling toward the casino treasury area through a maze of walking aisles on a plush, flowery carpet. There it happened.

It was a huge shake, and the ground shook violently. The massive, glittery, and expensive chandelier close to them shook crazily, glasses and beer bottles jangled. It threw off a few folks from their barstools and the lights flickered for a moment. Mike signaled both dealers right then as he hustled and gave a big punch to the security guard in his stomach, who was now off to taking cover under a table close by. Tina and Catherine suddenly showed the shock of the shake and moved quietly to the trolleys that were going in, now with hurried pace. Then it happened again. This time it was even bigger. This time it really shook the ground and a big crevice started forming right in the middle of the casino floor. The management started hurrying the collection to go toward the vault area and stopped all games. People started screaming and rushed violently toward the exit. Before others could go and block the exit, Mike had to hurry. Mike used his .45-caliber pistol with a silencer and quickly shot two of the guards pushing the trolley. The other two at the door were shot from the other side by Tina and Catherine. No one even noticed what happened in the commotion. Mike dashed toward the exit and directed everyone to the other exits saying, "Ramp's broken; exit from the south or the west exit." He quickly allowed Catherine and Tina to bring both trolleys through the ramp toward the truck. The plan was that Mike and Tina would be on one truck and the other will be driven by Catherine. Mike had said to them that they would pick up John. However, he hadn't noticed The Boss's men, but he definitely heard the emergency generator kicking in. The alarm was buzzing and the security started beefing up from all directions within the casinos, and one of the men saw them taking the trolleys outside. A few men rushed toward that exit.

Once the trolleys were out, Mike blocked that exit. Mike's quick thinking helped there. Due to the quake, a big sign from the restaurant next to the exit had fallen. He heaved and dragged the sign to block the entrance. The truck stood slanted as a big piece of road underneath was tilted, but fortunately still connected to the other part of the road. It looked like a jigsaw puzzle piece not quite fitting with the other pieces. Tina and Catherine were finished rolling the large cart into one of the trucks, and suddenly from the armored truck's back window, a shot was fired. Mike took the bullet in the backside of his shoulder. Mike screamed and suddenly Tina and Catherine, who were moving to get another trolley inside the other truck, took out their guns to fire back but were immediately surrounded by two security guards in black suits. The guards signaled for them to get in the truck immediately. A barrage of fire started coming from different balconies and windows from the casino toward the armored truck. The other truck remained there, as did the other trolley.

The doors were shut and the driver gunned the engine, swerving past the broken pavements and fissured road. At one cross road near the strip, the road's gap was so wide that he had to make a turn one way or the other to avoid going into a huge pothole. The buildings were still standing but a lot of damage was seen on the road. Some of the glass buildings were shattered and only the metal framework remained. The van careened and bobbed and weaved to avoid the ups and downs of the road. Emergency sirens were omnipresent. People were running, a few rushing to go to their families. A few people were helping folks who were in deep trenches and under the debris of weakly constructed buildings. The city that sparkled with lights galore was now sparsely lit. Smoke seemed to be coming out of a lot of places, and people were screaming and rushing toward the roads and away from the tall towers and buildings. A few fire hydrants were sloshing water all over the road and with upside down cars, electric poles, and downed palm trees blocking the road, the driver performed amazing maneuvers, as if he had been an F-1 driver.

While the van took a sharp turn, Tina noticed a large, red tower-like structure made of iron mesh blocking their way, which she thought she had seen before. The driver passed by it through the curb, avoiding a jam in the intersection, and then it hit her. To her horror, she realized that this was the Big Shot ride from the Stratosphere's top that was broken, lying on the ground, and now blocking their way. As the driver quickly moved, a huge iron rail swayed from their right directly toward the van. The driver was either very skilled or they were very lucky as he swerved to his left to avoid the gigantic rail from crashing into the van. He also magically avoided the wall to their left. It was the outdoor rollercoaster rail that had just flung out from one side and swung in their way with an ear-piercing screech. Traffic started jamming as people didn't care about any signals and just thought running was the best idea. It was a massive earthquake! While it only lasted for a short duration, it tore apart the city. Aftershocks were still felt; however, the way the maniacal driver was driving the van, it wasn't felt inside it.

With a big bump, Mike moaned and shook off, slowly opening his eyes. It seemed to him that he had passed out. Mike, now half-conscious, noticed that the path the driver was taking was not where many were going. The driver was rushing toward the McCullough Range, toward Henderson.

Mike, now in great pain, lay down near the clanking trolley with two armed men. Tina and Catherine sat beside him supporting his shoulder and blotting his bleeding with their dealer coats. All of their weapons were seized.

During the insane rollercoaster ride they were having, they had noticed that a few shots had been fired at the truck, but they hadn't noticed that an S-333 and two cars that began to follow the truck from the casino were shot down by a bazooka near the casino area.

"Who are you?" Mike moaned, adjusting his feet.

One of the armed men removed his helmet and mask and put his FNH in his holster and said, "Aha, got you, Mikey. I told you if I find you, I would kill you."

"Who are you?" Mike slightly slouched and took support of the back wall with the help of Tina and Catherine. Then, suddenly, it clicked to him, and it hit Tina and Catherine as well. "My God. You?" Everyone seemed in utter shock.

"Yes, my friends. My name is Troy, and I'm 'the boss.'" You would have thought I was just the kid of a multi-millionaire businessman. What's he gonna do? You should remember me from our Queens encounter. That was just a sham; I wanted to get kidnapped by you fools. But I gave you a hard time in that as well. How's the thigh, Mikey boy?" Troy laughed, crazily.

"What? This is for a revenge, you stupid fuck?" Tina growled.

"Relax or I can relax all of you with this," screamed The Boss, brandishing his K100 semi-automatic. "At a finger snap, my man will shoot all of you at the same time. This is not for revenge." Troy's blood-shot eyes scowled at them.

"But I created the distraction for you; that's what you wanted. What else do you need?" Mike winced.

Looking at the money trolley and banging his hand on it with his pistol in his hand, Troy screamed, "And this is your bonus?" After a pause, looking at everyone with red eyes, he added, "This is not about any of this." He suddenly jumped to Mike and put the muzzle of the semi-automatic on his forehead, "Tell your man to give a very pressurized jet and another .2 meters deeper."

"What? What are you talking about?" Mike acted with a groan.

"Don't fuck with me." He immediately shot Catherine's leg. A grinding thunderous noise echoed inside the truck. Catherine screamed and leapt forward, flat on her belly, on the truck floor next to the trolley and Troy's man. Her face bounced as the truck recklessly rushed on a dirt road with continuous ups and downs.

"Fuck!" Mike screamed. "What do you want?"

"I want total annihilation; destroy Sin City completely. Give him the order or I'll shoot every one of you. If you haven't noticed, we are heading toward that facility. If he doesn't, my men will do it."

"What? Mike, what's he talking about? Why did you shoot Catherine?" Tina asked vehemently.

"Long story, Tina. I'll have to tell you lat—" Mike was interrupted immediately.

"Shut up. Enough of your drama. Order it now or you guys are done." Mike noticed Troy's eyes were red with fury.

Mike realized that he had to call Antoine once he was satisfied with the distraction. Mike took his cell phone out while almost dozing off due to pain. Mike knew that if he called Antoine, Troy might snatch it from him. Even if he doesn't, how can he ask Antoine to do what this nut has just asked for? Mike was running out of options. He pressed a few buttons.

"Boss, there seems like a huge number of vehicles parked in front of the facility," the driver questioned with a tremor.

"What? What vehicles?"

"Looks like some sort of Army Humvees and tr—"

Before he could finish the sentence, a UH-60M Black Hawk suddenly weighed down in front of the driver and shot pallets of rounds toward the truck and quickly shot upwards.

"What the fuck?" Troy squealed.

"Boss, they are firing like crazy." For a second Troy and the man looked from the back door's glass window. Now the drone was following them, hovering very low, and again firing rounds at the truck from behind. Suddenly a big thump came and Troy's head was squished against the glass with what seemed like a shoe and the guard got a hard elbow in his stomach. Tina showed quick moves in such a tiny space. Catherine helped by pulling Troy's leg as she was laying flat on her stomach. Tina again punched the other man but struggled to get the gun from his hand. The van made big circles in the open area to avoid the bird that was following. It was a bumpy ride. Troy couldn't hold his ground and fell and Catherine quickly pushed and smashed the trolley onto him. He was now jammed between the back door and the trolley. His pistol slid away toward Mike. Mike was still seated, half consciously, with the support and couldn't move. The white wall of the truck behind him was all smeared in red. The floor was red with Catherine's leg bleeding all over. The truck was taking a turn instead of heading toward the army of vehicles and the Black Hawk was still following. Tina took two big punches from the guard and was still fighting to clutch the gun from his hand when Catherine finally got a grasp on the K100 that had slid on the floor. Catherine screamed, "Drop it or I will blast his fucking head off." Her gun was pointed at Troy. The man stopped with his hands up. "Now, give the gun to Tina. Come on, hurry up." Tina quickly grabbed the pistol from the man and shot Catherine in the other foot "Tina!" Catherine screamed. "What the fuck?" She fell unconscious. Mike was partially awakened by the scream and the loud shot. Tina then quickly shot the guard. Troy was still jammed nicely. The truck was still rushing toward nowhere with the drone following them and still firing. The driver had noticed shots being fired inside the truck, but he had no choice but to keep driving. Thankfully, the truck was armored.

Even the area surrounding the facility was quite broken. It had wide cracks and the open ground did show wide openings in certain areas; but not big enough to engulf the truck, so far as the driver avoided going very near to the epicenter.

With her boots on Troy's now flat body on the floor, still pinched between the door and the trolley, Tina held to the sidebars and carefully opened the back doors. With the truck running on a bumpy road at ninety MPH, the trolley flew in the air and the hit the ground, bouncing for a few meters. With it, the guard went flying down and hit the ground. The trolley's fall was broken by the guard's body. Tina held Troy underneath her boots, holding him down to the ramp bar next to her with her left hand and pointing the gun to his head with her right hand. The men in the drone immediately followed the destroyed trolley and looked at the truck's doors ajar. The driver had observed some of the drama unfolding at the back of the truck, but he had no choice. He continued swerving and driving at ninety MPH in the open desert area. The ground was cracked and hard with crevices created by the quake. The UH-60M lowered to look at who was inside and Tina signaled them. The drone came close and hovered to the side and started firing at the truck tires. It punctured both left side tires and the driver felt the sudden force, the friction. The truck groaned and whined and ran fast with imbalance. With the tires tearing beneath it, the rims grinded over the cracked ground as the truck kept making rounds to escape. Then the chopper came in front and hit the other tire. A man next to the pilot used a megaphone to warn the driver that if he didn't come out, a bazooka was going to hit him. The driver looked back and thought about his options with three flat tires. He thought hard and finally decided to make a stop. A few Humvees were following him closely, and he was quickly surrounded by green Army Humvees while the bird still treaded in the air on top of him. He jumped out of the truck with his hands up.

EPILOGUE

Mike woke up with a frowning face and moaned in pain. Tina sat there and helped him up. "Good morning, Mike."

"Where are we?"

"In a hospital," Tina replied, smiling.

"Where's Catherine?"

"She is in the next room. You need to relax, Mike. Don't stress yourself," Tina offered.

"Wait, I saw you firing at Catherine before it got blurry again for me. Is that right?" Mike asked curiously.

"Yes, that's right. It was to protect you," Tina replied.

"What?" Mike was fully awake and looked completely surprised. "What are you saying, Tina?"

"I'm just kidding, Mike," Tina smirked. "I left out some details. You are in a police hospital and under arrest." Mike looked completely puzzled. "Yes. Sorry, I'm an undercover agent working for the CIA. I was with you on this assignment for more than five years now. I myself didn't know if I was a good girl or a bad girl anymore." Looking down as she completed the sentence, she moved a lock of her beautiful hair behind her ear.

Mike looked away and didn't say anything for a moment. He then sighed and said, "I trusted you the most, and I *loved* you. And you betrayed me? You were the traitor? You were the mole this whole time staying under my nose? So you and Zach were both together in this?"

"Unfortunately not. There is a lot to explain to you; you weren't as sharp as you might have thought you were. Initially, I was also baffled why John killed Zach. But it was a pity story. John got very close to Catherine and then suddenly Zach came on the team. When Catherine got close to him, in fact very close to him, John's envy, the jealousy, spiraled out of control and got the better of him. He had to do something about it, so he killed Zach when he got a chance. Love makes you do such things." After a pause she continued, "As you did." Tina smiled and moved away from the bed to get a glass of water.

"Then why not tell the truth to the team? Oh, because he was worried that if Catherine knew that he killed Zach just because of envy, he'd lose her forever. Whereas, portraying Zach as a traitor would be easy and he would just look better in Catherine's eyes." Mike answered his own question.

"Yup, I'm sorry I had to do this." Tina's eyes couldn't meet Mike's and she took steps to leave.

Mike was now lost in his thought. He smiled and told Tina, "Do you remember what song they played on the cruise when we danced together?"

Tina looked back and said, "No, how does it matter?"

"It was *She's Always a Woman*. If you know the lyrics, it goes, 'She can kill with a smile; she can wound with her eyes.' And later it says, 'And she only reveals what she wants you to see, she hides like a child.'" Tears welled up in Mike's eyes and he looked away to a blank wall.

Tina acted tough but those big beautiful brown eyes sparkled with tear that were about to fall from her eyes. She remembered the song. Her heart had been seesawing till the last moment. At one point, even the CIA officer began to crack. But after the farmhouse where Mike had left her, she went back to the office and with her routine, the good memories were fading away. Mike definitely carved a soft corner in her heart and she no longer knew what she'd do about it, but the last devastation that Mike created, and the length he now went to achieve success in his jobs, was the trigger point for her. That sealed the deal for her. She knew that in this business you can't have friends or be friends with the Mafia. She turned her back, wiped the tears, and stepped out of the room.

"Tina, before you go," Mike said, as he raised his hand to stop her. "How did you come to know about the facility and that I was using the geothermal plant? You still owe me some answers."

"Oh, yeah. Man, you had kept it from us for a long time. As soon as you told me about the sewage bombs beneath the surrounding casino areas, I had my men check it out. But we couldn't find any clues, or any bomb, so I knew that you were lying about the bombing. But I could guess that you were going to have some kind of distraction for sure." She paused and then continued, "I searched in the hotel room but couldn't find anything. I had carefully noticed the unlocking pattern on your phone though, so I started snooping in your phone the night before and found a couple of videos that you had saved from the live video feed. I saw a house and the backyard from a top view where a lady was seen through a window working in the kitchen and a little girl playing with her dog. I saw when the dog was shot."

Tina smiled and continued, "I had a hunch that the distraction was somehow connected to this family and John was there for this filming and shooting. So I sent the video to my team to see if we could find this house in the vicinity. This was the day before yesterday night, but very early morning. After that, I didn't have much time before the job. I watched the video for almost half an hour and suddenly noticed that when the camera panned and zoomed to get the view of the backyard from the side, the post box in front displayed the number on it, which read: 2–3–9–7."

Mike nodded in disappointment. "Then the search was finite. We found the house and did background research on the family immediately and found the facts of the family. This was when I was driving the car to Cosmopolitan. I connected the dots and immediately ordered that it Antoine was the target. I knew he might do something in the geothermal energy plant that could rattle the ground, so immediately an Army force was sent there. Even Mr. President was informed about this. I have to commend you on the master plan. But since we got the information a little late, Antoine had already triggered the first attack, which was measured to be a 5.2 on the Richter scale for a few seconds. Before he could do more damage, the SWAT team arrested him and started putting off the pressurized water. They tried to do damage control, although it can't be undone. But Antoine was careful by not putting in a huge amount of pressurized water, and thankfully, he didn't go that deep. You were sent the reports that showed higher depths, but his conscience didn't allow him to."

Tina patted on his leg. "I'm surprised that you just let it happen this time. I thought you were careful about not hurting more people and the whole premise of our group..." She bit her lip and continued, "Your group was not to hurt a lot of people and still make a lot of money and remain anonymous."

"Greed, arrogance, and the last defeat that I suffered prompted this one. I couldn't satiate my appetite; I wanted to show everyone who's *The Boss*." Mike paused and asked, "But what happened to Troy? Why did he want to destroy Las Vegas?"

Tina sighed, "It's highly unfortunate that a millionaire's son gets in with the completely wrong company. Troy was brainwashed by his young, racist friend who, in fact, was working with a terrorist whom you know very well."

"Shahab-Al Hasan?" Mike shook his head.

"Bingo. First, you helped him escape from the prison. Shahab belongs to the Hezbollah terrorist organization. He started small and wired money all over the Middle East to feed the terrorist organization through stealing cars and electronics. He actually was big on infant formula. His brother was the key contributor in stealing the infant formula from all over the US, Mexico, and Canada. In fact, the government statistics say that over a quarter of the stealing that still occurs is of infant formula; it is called 'powder gold.' This was easy money and was becoming close to black market drugs. Think about it, if you get caught with a couple million dollars of drugs versus Xboxes or HDTVs, the punishment is much less severe. So theft gangs had become larger and more powerful. Anyways, his organization made tons of money doing this and wired most of that money overseas. But here's the kicker: his brother got caught in one of the big bank robberies in South Carolina. Nobody could take the charge in their group. I am assuming that Shahab was told not to risk it since his brother was gone. The organization needed him for other things. After a few months, the money was really diminishing and with the police and FBI cracking each operation one by one, they started feeling the pinch.

The organization looked for every opportunity to get into wealthy Americans' business, technology, and especially money; Troy was perfect. Young Troy met a friend through an acquaintance in a party and thereafter, slowly but steadily, they brainwashed his mind completely. He was a Catholic, but his friend Jamal converted him. Troy is still in a complete trance, it's like some sort of voodoo. Whaddaya know; Troy came up with the plan of getting captured by us. And with the fake signature, they got a lot of money in the stocks of United Web. But he needed more to feed the terrorist organization, and they'd captured the right goose to lay golden eggs every time. Troy's father caught wind that Troy wanted a huge amount of money wired offshore for some weapons transaction, so he denied him and changed his will immediately. After plotting and scheming for a couple of years, it was like intoxication to Troy. He enjoyed the games. He became an expert and Troy's hands went deep. Then Troy had to plan something else, so he came up with another scheme. Troy had this huge cruise ship under his name and if he sank it, he'd get a boatload of money from the insurance. So he planned the whole thing nicely; where Zach was killed and I actually informed the authorities about the whole scene and they were on the boat. He was informed by one of our informers that they had a mole and security was everywhere. That's why he didn't do anything at the time; it was to avoid the catastrophe and killing thousands of people."

"Why Las Vegas? Money?" Mike moved with a grumble.

"Nope, now they had enough money and the organization got money from other countries as well, but Troy had his own sadistic idea of generating an earthquake for destruction. Las Vegas was the experiment. He put his resources everywhere to research the topic, but what he got was that it was extremely difficult to set up their own shop. And even if they did, there was no guarantee it would work. The governmental authorities would immediately catch wind that someone was drilling deep into the Earth's crust. It was almost impossible to do without proper technological knowhow, that's where you came in."

"And I was so stupid to think that he just cared for money; hence wanted the distraction." Mike shook his head again.

"Las Vegas was his play ground. If he succeeded in this, he was going to do this world over in places he thought Muslim's were in trouble. The radical Islamic group, the fundamentalists, brainwashed him into believing that Muslim's were troubled everywhere and they needed to get it right for once and all. They convinced him that someone had to fight for the rights, and that the annihilation the West was creating...someone had to pay for it. Las Vegas was the perfect target; with it being destroyed, so much wealth would have been destroyed. Building all this would cost billions of dollars. He would have pulled off a major victory and created a major setback for the US. Then he would have used you to spread the technique to Iraq, Iran, Israel, Saudi Arabia, and so on in a controlled fashion to destroy the anti-Islamists and some moderate Muslims. His plans were very devious. It's good that you helped us catch him now." Tina winked and took a deep breath after looking into Mike's eyes.

"You were not there to catch him. Did you even know he was coming?" Mike questioned.

"No, I got lucky. You had hinted to me that he was gonna come, so I signaled the personnel that were watching the trucks at the casino that I was gonna be in those trucks. My guess was that he would catch us this time because he knew exactly where we would be and what distraction we were going to create, and my hunch was right. He is bright enough."

"Huh, bright enough? How can a young guy be so naïve to join a terrorist group?"

"I agree, but it's possible. In my personal opinion, at a young age, your brain accepts a lot of things that as an adult you might not, maybe due to experiences. There is nothing wrong to be part of a particular religion. In fact, Islam teaches piety, purity, and compassion to others, like any other religion, but it is the most misunderstood religion. Troy got into bad company partly because he was so rich. He was unlucky that he got brainwashed with a tormented and murky version of the truth from an extreme fundamentalist who met him in college. The fundamentalist convinced him that his people were facing oppression around the world and that they needed help from someone like him. He was an easy target—the money, the age, and the busy father were all in favor of this extremist. Mike, it's not the *religion*, it's a handful of *people* who are to blame."

"Well, you seem to know a great deal about this?" Mike retorted.

"You know, I shouldn't be telling this to you, but my boss is a reputed Muslim. He is the most amazing man I've ever met. He even risked his job to do what was right." Tina had a twinkle in her eyes while saying that.

"Oh, I have no issues with any religion. You know that, right?" Mike smiled and looked at Tina.

"Yes."

"Okay, but how did Troy come to know about the location?" Mike continued his series of questions.

"You underestimated him. He hid a lo-jack circuit on the drills themselves. Even though you switched the trucks in Arizona because you didn't trust his trucks, he was clever and put the tracking device on the drills themselves," Tina patiently replied. She wanted to leave, but at the same time, she was enjoying her conversation with Mike; partly because she felt great and partly because she might be seeing him for the last time.

"Wow, hmmm. What happened to John then?"

"As soon as we found out about Antoine's house, we sent teams to all of his relatives to find out if someone was being held captive. Because his track record was pristine, we knew he would not do it without being coerced. His wife's family was an obvious choice to check. It's a good thing that you didn't message him during our struggle with Troy; we would have just missed him if you had. We approached Antoine's in-laws' house directly, with SWAT in a chopper, and John didn't run or oppose. He was caught with no problem." Tina adjusted Mike's bed sheet and stared at the monitor that hung above Mike's head on a steel rod.

"And you didn't arrest me before just to get a major catch?" Mike looked intensely into Tina's big eyes.

Tina looked away and said, "Yes, that was the whole point of the mission. You started this obscure group which I got lucky to catch wind of and join in the early stages. Of course, my beauty helped." She smiled and continued, "Therefore, I used to goof off and say silly things during tense situations. But my goal was very clear: to reach the ultimate people. Fortunately, this whole thread pointed to Troy, and I was fortunate that we could catch the source."

"Now what?" Mike questioned.

"Nothing. You, Catherine, and John will serve your sentences and we," she continued with quotation marks in the air, "as in, 'CIA team,' will get closer to the terrorist organization by interrogating Troy."

"What about Shawn and Gary?" Mike asked.

"Mike, you ask a lot of questions. I am not worried about them. Once I finish with this, I may do something similar. Now, it's easy that I've proved my loyalty to this group, which Shawn's already noticed. He'll not know about what happened here. Oh, one more thing, that beautiful-looking neighbor of yours, she was a mole too. Sorry, we had to..." Tina shook her head and looked away as if feeling guilty.

Mike closed his eyes and laid there. She started walking toward the door. Her black, beautiful hair swayed both ways and she looked as stunning as Mike had always found her.

Even in pain, even after being betrayed, as she left, he could hear the song in his head. *She can kill with a smile; she can wound with her eyes...*

THE END

Forthcoming novel...
By Maulik Sompura

DISTRACTERS
—The Reversal

Thursday, September 13th
Macau, China

Jutting out in the ocean, Macau dazzled like a pearl at night. Macau, rightly called *Oyster Mirror,* attracted people from all over the world; mainly due to its mirror image of Vegas casinos. However, today people had gathered for a slightly different reason, it was the first night for its grand Shopping Festival. Leong Wong, the Chief Executive of Macau, had just inaugurated the greatest mall called "The Earth." The mall boasted the biggest replicas of Mother Earth's known falls, caverns, jungles, volcanoes, and seas. In the midst of this unique theme, designer shops, trendy restaurants, spa boutiques, and more were embedded throughout. The only thing that the chief executive would have changed was the outer semi-transparent globe that engulfed the whole mall to literally look like *the Earth*. There couldn't be a better day for the inauguration of the mall than the beginning of the huge Macau Shopping Festival, which was now religiously followed every year since 2009. This year's festivities were starting here on Friday evening, and Mr. Wong was going to be comfortably seated for the opening acts and numerous shows that were going to follow. Of course, he wasn't going to be there for the entire extravaganza.

Three people couldn't sleep the night before. Mike wallowed in the bed of a trendy MGM Grand Hotel near the new mall. He lay awake hoping he would hear some good news at least by tomorrow. So far, they had been unsuccessful. He remembered briefing a few days ago in Maryland when three different angles of three different men filled a floor-to-ceiling screen. "This is Nikolai Klopov; this Anaxagoras Soto; and this is Batista Lira." The officer chuckled and looked into the audiences' eyes. "These all are of one and the same person." The man in the suit removed the laser pointer from the photos and again looked at everyone. He continued, "Gentlemen, we have been looking for this guy for more than four years. Interpol warrants him in sixteen different countries. Abu Dhabi bombings, the Mumbai blast, Paris mayhem—all somehow linked to this individual. He has Russian origins but spent more time in Spain. Through his profession, he knows more than ten languages. Our informer and overall report suggests that he's had professional military training. Precision shooting, combat tactics, camouflage, and flying modern fighters are just some of his specialties." Mike now sat on the edge of his bed with his hands aside staring at a long blank wall in front of him. Suddenly, his mind merged those three pictures of this beast to make a morphed version into one. To him, it was surprising that they still couldn't find the Spaniard. *Why they are being so secretive? But it doesn't make sense. Damn! These guys are not telling the whole story. How many times do I need to prove myself?* It was impossible not to draw parallels between the Las Vegas showdown that he had created a year ago and Macau.

A few miles away, in a rundown motel in the old Guangdong province, Anaxagoras's motionless eyes were still looking outside at the gorgeous skyline of Macau from the balcony. As he stepped inside, with a deadpan face, the six-foot-five-inch Spanish commando knelt down and prayed for a few minutes. He then stood up, and with meticulous care, took out his Magnum from his backpack and looked at it as if he was looking at it for the first time. He flipped it over to look at its shiny other side, opened the magazine, and again made sure it was full. He slipped it into the case and thought through his plan while lying down on the bed. A street light that peeked into his room, an occasional TV sound from the motel's other tenants, a few honks from the street below, a neighbor's squeaky door—none of it bothered him. He was at peace; however, he couldn't sleep.

Chief Executive Leong Wong had been under pressure a lot recently. In his ornate mansion, darkness engulfed the entire space. He poured himself a fine Italian red wine and sat on his chair near the bed. It was quiet. Chinese government made sure his allegiance was toward People's Republic of China. The United States had its own agenda. Political ground was shaky. His popularity as a leader in Macau and his Western ties weren't viewed courteously by some countries. A couple of incidents in recent months had given him jitters. Tomorrow was not going to be any different, even though he had beefed up his security five times since the last two attacks. Remaining present in community events was vital to maintaining public belief in safety; and safety was the key to rule. He never used to be worried, and this time it wasn't much different; however, he was slightly concerned. He decided to be alone that night.

In the bed, Mike saw those words floating in the air in front of him.

Eres Hermosa, eres la vida
Donde hay madre, no le es
Usted puede ser claro, puede ser vago
La muerte es imprescindible en su ausencia

Those words were the only clues that were intercepted during a phone call to Anaxagoras or Nikolai. But before the authorities could locate the call, the phone was cut. According to the debriefing, the hint was of either the killing spot, a weapon he could use, or something that connected his job. If they cracked it, somehow they may have a better chance. Mike was no scholar in Spanish but a few classes at a young age and a search on the Internet had helped him to at least understand the words. The team had spent some time today to figure out the answer, but there had only been some clues like "light," "air," "father," and "love." Nothing was fitting; nothing was pointing to what the assassin had planned. *They can't even fucking trace the full thing. This ugly, half-written riddle is their clue? I don't even know if this is real. Damn, I need to find some answers.* His brain translated the words over and over and finally hibernated.

You are beautiful; you are life
Where there is mother, there is you
You could be clear; you could be vague
Death is imperative in your absence

The next morning John groggily woke up and immediately dialed Mike's number.

"Hey, did you get it?" he curiously asked.

"No, what time is it?" Mike inquired in a muffled voice before his eyes could focus on the blurry image of the alarm clock.

"It's five past nine. But I think I got it," John enthusiastically replied.

"Shoot." Mike slid to the side of the bed and took a sitting position with his hand on his head, still pulling his eyes wide open.

"It's as vague as it can be but when you relate it to today's events, there are certain elements that match with the verse."

"Like?" Mike interjected, while walking toward the sink to get a glass of water.

"Looks like he's going to abduct his child," John replied.

"What?" Mike squeaked, now completely woken up.

"Think about it," John smiled.

Mike recalled the words...*You are beautiful; you are life. Where there is mother, there is you. You could be clear; you could be vague. Death is imperative in your absence.*

"But...but *clear* and *vague* doesn't make sense. Also what about *death is imperative?*" Mike argued.

"Well, yes, but a child could be clear or vague when he does or says something and emotionally it's a death. What do you say?" John defended.

"Okay, let's meet at lunch with the others and discuss it further, but I need more info on his children's whereabouts. I still need some coffee before I can crack this preposterous puzzle that's just been thrown our way. Are those idiots doing anything by themselves? I was hoping for a good riddance call from someone this morning." Mike's voice caught the peak of the crescendo.

John hesitantly replied, "Since you've not gotten any calls yet, I assume that they haven't found anything, nor has Tina. I'm already working on the child part. Will update you more during the lunch."

Anaxagoras remembered. He wasn't going to just kill someone; he was going to emancipate human kind. His teacher had taught him well to serve the greater good. He looked outside from his broken window. The light now swept the whole room. He heard the morning chanting and shower noises from the neighboring tenants. He pushed to his feet and walked downstairs to get some tea. As he stepped outside, a group of children suddenly whisked past him playing street soccer and he balanced on one foot slanting backwards a little to make room for them. He stared at them till the group's noise was inaudible and they vanished out of sight. He crossed the road to reach a tea stall opposite to the street only to view the children playing street soccer on the other side. He said, "Xie xie" and left with the tea to his room. He took out his cell phone and said, *"La emancipacion se inicia hoy."*

Friday, 12:00 p.m.

At lunch, everyone stared at the piece of paper and tried to figure out the message, but they couldn't.

"Shit, okay, here's the deal. We gotta stick to our plan. We are somehow going to stop this assassin so we can execute our plan about the CE. John will perform the opening act as planned. And I wouldn't want to get your rehearsals wasted," Mike chuckled. He paused and when no one seemed to care about his joke, he continued, "Catherine, you'd also be in the spectators and I am going to include myself now. Tina and Lee need to be doing other stuff for *our* plan. Any questions?"

Everyone looked at each other and shook their heads in disbelief. The mission was already in jeopardy before it even took life. It's just hours away but this was their kind of first challenge within a challenge.

Tina looked at everyone and with full energy, she concluded, "We are going to find this damn guy if no one else does. No matter how difficult this one is. We can do it. Time is of the essence. Everyone on to their duties."

Friday, 2:00 p.m.

Nikolai prayed for the last time. He was going to die today for his country. He thought about all the years he had served his country so well. He will now die serving his country well.

John dressed up as a giant shopping bag with green and yellow colors and a matching tall, coned hat and lined up with the troupe backstage. The spectators were lining up at the Earth Mall. There was a grand seating area made available right in front of the mall where the huge parking lot boasted more than seventy-five thousand temporary bleachers. There was a long rectangular water fountain in front of the globe's entrance where the prince and other dignitaries were seated. Red carpeting wound down from their seats to the fountain, which extended in the middle throughout the length of the parking lot. It was by far the most expensive musical fountain installed, with dramatic lighting and features, and it was going to be inaugurated with this opening extravaganza. The water was also covered with fake lilies, lotus leaves, and lotuses. Bright, colorful light shone through the space between the big, round, green lotus leaves and made a dramatic effect. The music began with a laser light show.

Tina announced, "Team one, in place?"

A voice in her earpiece responded, "All go."

"Team two, all set?" Tina asked.

A second voice replied, "Getting there. No signs of him as of yet. Any clues?"

"No, no hints as of yet. Keep a tight watch," Tina ordered.

Mike was dressed as a security guard and looked through his binoculars for hints of the assassin. Catherine was dressed as a casual visitor and was doing the same, but without the binoculars. She was moving from bleacher to bleacher to see if she could find someone. She stared at a young lad in a black jacket who looked out of place and was nervously walking on the empty bleacher. She noticed that he suddenly took out his cell phone and dialed some numbers. What he said made him a definite no. Mike concentrated on a few ladies because he thought they might have just completely ignored the ladies as a possible assassin. However, nothing seemed fitting or interesting. All this time at the back of his mind he was still rehearsing the verse: *You are beautiful; you are life. Where there is mother, there is you. You could be clear; you could be vague. Death is imperative in your absence.*

It was getting late. "Are you ready, John?"

"Yes," John replied, stealthily so as not to give away his dancing bag wear.

"Any clue?"

"Nope, as I told you before, his children are in America enjoying their vacation and have plenty of security. Don't know if he's gonna blow up this thing, shoot from somewhere, or what."

"This one's a goner. If we don't stop him from doing something stupid, making CE go to another opening is gonna be impossible. The security gets alerted and we fail. We can't let that happen. Keep your weapon at all times," Mike sighed.

"Well, I checked all the bags here and none of them look like one with a gun inside." John's chortle could be heard on the earpiece.

"Well, be alert. I'm getting another beep, must be Catherine." Mike pushed the other button while staying away from the public to avoid any eavesdropping.

"Anything yet?" Catherine asked.

"Nope. Hang in there. Will inform if I find something," Mike quickly replied.

The first bugle and drum roll happened. Everyone was on their feet. Mike gazed through his binoculars and as he scrolled through his lenses horizontally, the middle fountain spit a tall spike of water as a sign of the beginning of the show. Mr. Wong, a few businessmen, a couple of bankers, and a large number of security forces covered the equator and half of the globe. They looked pleased with the proceedings.

Then it hit him like a rock. A lump formed in his throat for a moment. He stared at the globe and looked at the fountain and he realized it then. *Damn! How did it not occur to me before?*

He quickly moved to an alcove and barked on the radio, "John, you there?"

John was now lined up as one of the bags bordering the fountain as it had slowly begun dancing with the lights and music. John sneakily replied, "What? I can barely hear you?"

"It's the fountain, I mean it's the water," Mike hurriedly replied.

The music, people chanting, and the water were not helping in hearing. While making different poses and turning around with the group, John asked again, "What?"

"It's the fucking water," Mike screamed, and then moved away to another location to attract less attention.

Mike continued walking. *"You are beautiful; you are life. Where there is **Mother Earth Mall**, there is you. You could be clear; you could be vague. Death is imperative in your absence. Comprende?"*

Mike again squawked, "Tina, I don't want team one to get engaged. I think John can finish the business but it is up to you." Tina replied positively.

John continued his steps with the other dancing shopping bags, but the hair on the back of his neck raised and his eyes widened as he realized what Mike had just said. He sighed and replied, "Got it. Let me think of something." He completed a pirouette. His eyes were now completely focused on only one thing: the fountain. The dark water that it held glistened today with the lights shone from beneath and the sides.

"Try to do it so no one gets alerted, and let me know if you need anything from me." Mike shook his head. He felt helpless. He quickly radioed Tina and explained the same.

"Fuck, my act ends now in a couple of minutes," John squawked. The only logical thing was that the assassin had to be within a range of a couple hundred meters to take a shot at the chief executive. That meant that he would have to be very good. John quickly estimated that the guy couldn't have a shotgun or a rifle; he would have to carry a 9 mm or a Magnum. The idea brushed passed his eyes: the guy swooshing up and bobbling his head from the water, waving the gun, and taking three shots at Mr. Wong before quickly making a dive to escape. While making another pirouette and exchanging a clap with his neighbor, he focused on the fountain's entire length, but he couldn't locate a breathing pipe due to the fountain's mist and a host of lilies and lotus leaves. *Damn! What should I do?*

Mike tensely called John again. "What are you doing? I've asked Catherine to go to the fountain controls to see if we can make the fountains go high with lots of mist. That may give us some time and cover. If it works, he would have to wait inside."

"Good, I need to talk to Catherine immediately."